Paul Scott's absorbing novel
and socially adrift. The centr
postwar Everyman', is a man
a shiftless pattern of life that

'An original, grave and distin
The Bookman

'This is true originality ... The characters ... move with the
quiet convincingness of people you see every day. An impressive book'
The Tablet

Paul Scott was born in London in 1920 and served in the army
from 1940 to 1946, mainly in India and Malaya. After demobilization he worked for a publishing company for four
years before joining a firm of literary agents. In 1960 he resigned
his directorship with the agency in order to concentrate on his
own writing. He wrote thirteen distinguished novels, including
the famous 'Raj Quartet', and also reviewed books for *The
Times*, the *Guardian*, the *Daily Telegraph* and *Country Life*. He
adapted several of his novels for radio and television.

In 1963 Paul Scott was elected a Fellow of the Royal Society
of Literature and in 1972 he was the winner of the *Yorkshire
Post* Fiction Award for the third volume of the 'Raj Quartet',
The Towers of Silence. In 1977 *Staying On* won the Booker
Prize for Fiction. Paul Scott died in 1978.

By the same author

Paul Scott

A Male Child

A PANTHER BOOK

GRANADA
London Toronto Sydney New York

Published by Granada Publishing Limited in 1974
Reprinted in 1981

ISBN 0 586 03874 4

First published in Great Britain by
Eyre & Spottiswoode 1956
Republished by William Heinemann Ltd 1968
Copyright © Paul Scott 1956

Granada Publishing Limited
Frogmore, St Albans, Herts AL2 2NF
and
36 Golden Square, London W1R 4AH
866 United Nations Plaza, New York, NY 10017, USA
117 York Street, Sydney, NSW 2000, Australia
100 Skyway Avenue, Rexdale, Ontario, M9W 3A6, Canada
61 Beach Road, Auckland, New Zealand

Set, printed and bound in Great Britain by
Cox & Wyman Ltd, Reading
Set in Intertype Plantin

Granada ®
Granada Publishing ®

For
my mother and father
Frances and Tom Scott
with love

Contents

Part One   Seed   9
Part Two   Gestation   91
Part Three   Parturition 179

SEED

CHAPTER ONE

IN nineteen forty-two, when I was twenty-six, I went to India as an officer-cadet on the troopship *Athlone Castle*, and although it would be untrue to say it was on the ship I first met Alan Hurst, that is how I look upon it. Being together in the same cadet draft, we had seen each other before, of course; exchanged smiles over piles of kit, or grimaces of exasperation over the interminable delays in going from point *a* to point *b*, but he had had his friends and I, mine. I knew him as Hurst; he knew me as Canning; each could have pointed out the other to an inquirer in a crowded canteen or mess-deck.

It was June, and in the Arabian Sea, a few days' slow sailing in convoy from Bombay, we steamed into the wet monsoon. I had never seen anything like it: sea and sky merged, and it was difficult to say whether the sea was being sucked upwards or the sky downwards in vertical rods of water. My nearest companion at the rail happened to be Alan. He pulled down the corners of his mouth and nodded his head in a quick movement of mock dismay which, unaccompanied by words, implied: *We'd better watch our step!* or so I came to interpret it. It was a habit of his for which he found frequent use during lectures and demonstrations, and after interviews with pompous staff officers.

At that time Alan was sporting a somewhat puffed and purpled eye, given to him by a smaller man in a recent bout on the sun-deck, where the officer commanding troops had done his best to combat the lethargy of weeks at sea by organizing a ship's boxing contest. A few had watched; fewer had entered the ring. Alan's eye was inevitably a topic of conversation, and so I asked him whether he had done much boxing before.

He smiled and said, 'No, but that other blighter had.'

It was much the sort of answer I had expected. There was just the right mixture in it of personal pride and self-depreciation and it neither closed the subject nor invited further discussion of it. But, unsurprising as the answer was from the sort of man I had always taken Alan to be (a man, that is, with no intellectual gifts, happy, extrovert, ideal 'officer-material'), there was such a good-natured friendliness about it, such an alert twinkle in his unswollen eye as he took what was, I imagine, his first real look at me (sizing up what sort of a chap this Canning was), that I found myself taking an interest in him in return, and liking him.

He was three or four years younger than I, but he had that particular cast of features which comes to maturity comparatively early on in life and this, with his height and breadth, made him look older than he was. His hair was dark, wavy, rather over-greased: his face was inclined to a fullness which in later years would become fleshy and heavy, but his nose and mouth were clear cut enough, and I seldom saw him when his expression was not one of pleasant anticipation of what life had to offer. I had not expected to find that he was married, for he appeared to me to be the sort of young man who had no intention whatsoever of doing what he would call 'settling down' until he was thirty and grown tired of the expense and the demands on his time of constant flirtations with women. It had been my habit to place people into categories and to observe any deviation in their expected behaviour not as an indication that I had put them in the *wrong* category but as a discovery of a new characteristic hitherto overlooked. The habit died hard. I had earlier adjudged Alan to be of what I called the Kingston-by-pass era, with its week-end cricket, open sports-cars and road-house crawls, and I should now have taken hasty war-time marriage at an early age to be a characteristic of his kind had I myself still been single.

It is said that every seven years of your life you undergo a change which reflects itself in your attitude to your circumstances and to other people, and I think this may be true. If it is, then the change begins towards the end of a seven-year span, at the point, perhaps, where dissatisfaction with what you are doing and with where you are going sets in, and at the time I met Alan this point had probably been reached. I certainly think it likely that had I met him in exactly similar circumstances, even one year before, I should have had no time for him beyond the few seconds it would have taken me to say: Hurst is this sort of man or that sort of man. His world is not mine.

My world had been, in comparison with his, scholarly, I believed liberal, and biased in the angle of its axis towards that part of an imagined universe where the stars of the common man shone brightly, the more brightly for being seen at distance – although this I did not recognize. But by nineteen forty-two I was inclined to be condemnatory of my pre-war world, prone to a feeling of having been betrayed by it, and by myself. Schooled in literature, fireside politics and arts more gentle than that of war, if the war in Spain were to be excepted (and my experience of it was only vicarious), I had once laid the foundations of what my life was to be; the foundations remained bare and bleak as those of a house on which work had been suspended. Meanwhile I enjoyed being a soldier.

I enjoyed the cessation of intellectual exercise, I enjoyed the monotony, the sleeping on bare earth sometimes, the rising at impossible hours and shaving in cold water; the gradual achievement of proficiency, the utter pettiness of administrative detail, the outward gloss, the inner corruption; the preoccupation with rights and privileges, the mass emotionalism, the private malice. I had found in myself an unexpectedly broad streak of the banal.

My discovery put me at a distance from my fellows and from myself: I say from myself, for I had the advantage, or disadvantage, of being able to stand away from Officer Cadet Canning to view him with detachment, some amusement and a certain despondency. These things which I enjoyed and to which I responded (without necessarily offering my admiration) were, of course, the very things about our situation against which my fellows spoke most strongly, and with possibly genuine concern. I call them fellows, meaning companions with whom I had fallen in, clannishly, exclusively. When Alan joined us, as he sometimes later did, he was like a fish out of water. He had no politics other than those which prodded the patriot in him, no gift for words or analytical thought, no apparent liking for the world of books and the men who wrote them (or, more pertinently in that once-present company, intended to write them) and he thought us collectively an odd bunch; smiled a little apprehensively when he caught me watching him while someone spoke at length, and held his tongue. I always expected him to say, 'Bit out of my depth there, old chap,' but far from brushing off something he didn't understand as beneath his notice he grew into the habit of asking me, when we were alone: What did so and so mean when he said such and such? I saw that he asked because he was interested, and not because he wanted to learn or become a convert to this or that line of thought in order to acquire a social grace. Explaining politics, contemporary art and literary movements to Alan made me feel a prig; it was like groping my way through the maze of my own disbelief; it was a catechism of the no longer faithful. Sometimes my insincerity must have shown, but he refrained from comment. He had the integrity of a man who accepts others at more than their face value.

We saw rather less of each other at the Officers' Training School to which the cadet draft was sent, but being commissioned into the same regiment of the Indian Army we spent our end of course leave together in Bombay. We had a good time. Afterwards we went to the Regimental Depot and joined our battalion in Central India. It was there I fell sick with the first attack of what I believed, and the doctors believed, to be malaria. When I came out of hospital Alan had been posted to another battalion, on active service on the Assam-Burma frontier. I did not see him again until, at the end of 1944, through the coincidence of war, I went to Magpyiu Island, as his administrative liaison officer: a divisional staff appointment. Alan, then Major Hurst, M.C., was in command of troops on this island which, a few miles off the West Burma coast, he had assaulted some weeks previously and taken against unexpectedly stiff resistance from pockets of stranded Japanese. Magpyiu, known inevitably as Magpie Island, had a jetty, a few godowns for stores, a fighter strip, and little else. Magpie Island was my first taste of anything which could remotely be called active service. For me it had a two-fold charm. It was a lovely spot, and a world away from the dusty cantonments, the depot routine, the technical courses and the ever-recurring idleness of hospital that had encompassed me hitherto. My arrival seemed to please Alan. He had not changed, except in superficial ways. After I had been with him for a month or two he resigned himself to seeing out the war on Magpie. 'And always you know, Ian,' he used to say, jabbing a finger at me over a glass of beer, 'there's the possibility of the Jap trying to push us out.' And down would go the corners of his mouth as he jerked his head briefly in the familiar way.

Between our parting at the depot and our meeting on Magpie, a matter of nearly two years, Alan had done some hard campaigning, and while it would be wrong to say he had enjoyed himself it was easy to see that, having come out of it well, he looked back on it with a certain pleasure and some nostalgia. Physically he was thinner, and he had lost the healthiness of complexion I remembered from earlier days. His skin had acquired the jungle soldier's patina of grime and jaundiced tan which, in certain lights, gave him a haggard look. He was very efficient and I felt he had little use for me from an official point of view, but he had developed no fixations about things or people – no tendencies towards what was called 'going round the bend'. He attended to routine with promptitude but no finickiness, looked after his men decently with no air of possessiveness, neither kept the island at an unnecessarily strained pitch of readiness to meet attack nor allowed it to fall into apathy. If ever there were an average man, I thought, he would be Alan. I told Alan so.

He said, 'Good Lord!' and looked genuinely surprised.

The illness returned.

The symptoms were similar to those of malaria. I have a recollection of Alan hovering by my bed, improvising hot water bottles from gin bottles filled and refilled with water which was brought into the tent in old ghi-tins. I experienced alternately a dreadful bone coldness and a swooning heat. I fought delirium, but the shadow of it was above me, descending slowly.

Afterwards, when I could sit up, weak and depressed, angry and bitter at what I looked upon as the rawest possible deal, Alan told me I was leaving Magpie. The M.O. stood in the opening of the tent. 'You're a sick man, Canning. I'm damn well not going to take the responsibility. With your hospital record you should never've been sent. I'm flying you out tomorrow.'

And so it was. But on the night before I left, Alan sat up in my tent and talked. As he made preparations to go he fell silent and I guessed he was trying to say something. Always uneasy about things I might call out in the midst of delirium I asked him what I had talked about, more to re-assure myself than to make it easier for him. He looked confused. 'Oh, lot of nonsense.'

'Nothing clear?'

'Something about a girl.'

'Helena?'

'That's right. Helena.'

I said, 'Helena's my wife.'

Instantly I regretted telling him; and so profound a look of astonishment and sympathy came over his face that I could not bear to ask him what I had said about her.

I left Magpyiu in March. Sometimes from hospital I sent Alan a brief letter which he answered in the fullness of time with as brief and as friendly an answer. He went to Rangoon and I, back to England.

I was losing weight. My temperature rose with monotonous regularity to a little over 100°. For three months in the autumn of nineteen forty-five I was under observation for I knew not what. It was not tuberculosis. It was not chronic malaria or any known fever. Specialists in tropical diseases took an interest in me. 'You've picked up some kind of bug, old chap. At least, we *think* so.' Then in the January of nineteen forty-six all signs of illness disappeared. I regained weight. My temperature stood firm and steady where it should. I acquired an appetite. We thought I was cured. At the end of February the symptoms returned. My despair communicated itself to the doctors, or theirs to me: I know not which. They sent me north to a hospital where there were cases not dissimilar to my own. These men were rather further advanced along the road to what seemed to me permanent disability. They wore their cheerfulness gloomily. Already they measured out their lives, not with coffee-spoons, like Prufrock in Eliot's poem, but with pill-bottles. Their resignation was infectious, part of the stupefying, acid smell of the ward which, in the beginning, was a circumscription of our joint existence and then, in the end, the definition of its safety: a safety shattered for me one day by the arrival of a letter from Helena. Reading it, I imagined her writing it, her back and shoulders curved like a bow over her desk, her face hidden by the long, honey-coloured hair which fell to her shoulders, as fine as silk. She formed her letters boldly, scrawled the words aslant across the blue paper as if impatient of moving her pen back to the left-hand margin, of artificial limitations of shape and space: of time, even. When I had read the letter I knew I had to get away.

In a week I was well enough to argue with the doctor. Without waiting to know to what extent I had impressed him, or otherwise, with my need for freedom, I sent a telegram to David Holmes, a friend to whom I had sub-let my flat in London before leaving for India, four years earlier. I wrote: *Want flat urgently wire.*

David telegraphed back: *What a blow but of course just arrive when ready.*

In the last week of March I left the hospital on indefinite sick-leave. 'It'll do you good to live a normal life, perhaps,' the medicos said. They were washing their hands of me. I was given instructions about reporting to this local specialist and that local military hospital. The wheels for my release from the army were set in motion. I carried forms for the India Office, forms for the Pensions people: prescriptions. I suddenly realized that the military career I embraced so eagerly as an escape from the past had ended before it had properly begun. I felt like an old man.

In the train to London I read Helena's letter again. She wrote:

DEAR IAN,
Your lawyer friend Thurlow has promised to forward this

letter to you and has confirmed what I'd gathered from various sources, that you're back in England and hospital ridden.

I'm writing to you because I thought you'd like to know Bobbie turned out to be the swine you always said he was, not that my reasons for thinking so are the same as yours were. More importantly, I've had another 'miscarriage', only this time it happened naturally. (Was all you cared about the child, Ian? If so, I wonder why? Boy or girl, it would have been melted to jelly by radiation in the next war.) This other child would have been Bobbie's and I imagine I couldn't give you *more* substantial grounds for divorcing me. So may we not get it over with once and for all? I don't want to continue in this Godforsaken existence.

Thurlow can attend to all the sordid details and documents, no doubt. Can I get alimony if I'm the guilty party? How ignorant one is when faced with essential practical matters. How they trick and trap you into holes and corners. The marriage allotments you made to me out of your army pay are intact, untouched. I'm surprised you continued with them when you transferred to Indian service and they became voluntary. Sending the money but no letters was meant, no doubt, to emphasize your detachment, your silence, your cloak of utter indifference. Odd to think I may need the money now. You are very clever. Dammit, *clever*.

Do you want me to come and see you? If so, I ought to warn you that four years have made a difference to me. But then I expect they have to you. That would make us quits, Ian. My book came out last month. You probably saw the stinking reviews it had.

Yours,
Helena

A trick of the wind caught the smoke from the engine and trapped it between the carriage and the steep bank of the cutting through which the train was passing. I looked out of the window and had an impression of travelling through air and cloud, back through the years, towards Helena. For an instant I pictured her, remembered the greyness of her eyes and the way the colour of them could deepen when she was moved, the way her mouth would tremble and her cheek be turned, her hand come up, to hide her face when the bitter weapons of mutual reproach had somehow turned blunt and left us unarmed and speechless. Often, then, I had taken her hand in silence, forcibly, twisting it round,

15

not only to hurt but to turn her to me and burn the pain away with the greater pain, the joy, of an act of love.

The cutting ended in a tunnel and when the train came out into the open again the ground was level, the smoke no longer trapped but thrust away by speed and wind across the country-side. Looking down at the letter I saw that my hand was clenched hard round it so that the knuckles showed white.

My flat was on the top floor of a house in Lowndes Street, in that bleak hinterland of mewses, hat shops and dry cleaners behind Sloane Street and Knightsbridge. Its one room was partitioned by double doors so that there were really both a large and a small room. The larger room, with the window on to the street, was a bed-sitting room, with two divans in opposite corners. The other room was a combined dining-room and study. There was a kitchen and a bathroom, and a lavatory with a coloured glass door on the first bend of the stairs. It had been my splendid beginning: now it smelled of stale scent and David's tobacco. It was loud with the echo of high-heeled slippers and the contented Sunday-morning chatter of a man and his mistress. No trouble had been taken to hide away the evidence which would tell me I was an intruder. I stood there in the late afternoon light of a March day, listening to the distant traffic in Sloane Street and the closer sounds of single cars reconnoitring towards Victoria, and recognized for the first time that all was past and present and nothing future. I was expectant of nothing in life but David's arrival, tweeded and piped from his Ministry.

When he came he told me I looked a bit dicky. The room was full of us, restless with us. We both felt it. It gave him the excuse he needed to take me to the club-round-the-corner. There amongst the mufti, the uniforms, the medal ribbons, the mous-taches, the women who had hung on and the women who had let go, I met David's girl. Her name was Peggy, and she sat expertly on a stool at the bar, standing her round, scrabbling with lac-quered fingernails in her bulging handbag for cigarettes, matches, her powder-compact, or loose change. A conversation between us died, she and David, as though compelled, drew closer together; and when I looked up from pocketing what little silver remained from a one-pound note – they had made me a member, a mere formality of signing a printed form and promising a cheque – I found them both staring at me as though I had been accused of a perfectly understandable but somehow surprising cruelty.

David took his pipe from his mouth and asked what my plans

were. Peggy looked away, and, turning to face the mirror behind the bar in which were reflected its otherwise hidden mysteries of rinsing water, dirty cloths and bill spikes, as familiar yet intriguing as the exposed mechanism of one's own wristwatch, my eyes met hers, and in the anonymity of the reflection neither felt it necessary to smile. She and I were enemies. I threatened her security. We had come like foreign powers to the conference table to settle the agenda for a meeting we were certain could never take place.

David repeated his question, framing it differently. 'Are you going back to the old job in London?'

'A modified form of it perhaps. The doctors haven't finished with me yet.' I answered his question, but as I turned my head I looked at Peggy and not at him. She nodded. She did not ask me what job it was. She knew all about me, or rather as much as David knew. With this knowledge she had armed herself against what she must have known to be my inevitable return, my stone flung selfishly against the walls of their glass house. I wondered how far the advance echo of it had spoiled for her the harmony of her affair with David in the borrowed flat, and which of them had been happier in holding on to the belief that possession of my flat was nine tenths of a law which would eventually allow them to send me about my business should I ever show signs of invoking the remaining tenth.

They fell to talking shop, inviting me, as it were, to an intimate glimpse of their lives under the same roof at the Ministry where David worked and where she, in a junior post, paced endless corridors, penetrated sanctums either closed to David or below his notice, collecting and disseminating gossip and rumour and fact; and always, it seemed, taking opportunities to tip him off, to warn him, to suggest a course of action likely to help him in his advancement. Woven into the pattern of their joint and several official lives was the *motif* of their private life in Lowndes Street. It was a shape, a colour, a sound, offered to me as a set of ingredients to mix so that I might myself be sensitive to its quality, its decency and fitness, and conjure a picture of the two of them at mind's and heart's ease in Lowndes Street at the end of the ministerial day. Surely, they were implying, you cannot disrupt this?

But their attack upon my conscience was mounted with military precision. David, the strategist, remained like a general in the background. Peggy was a clever tactician. She knew the worth of a dependable intelligence system. The object of David's campaign was to get me to 'come to some arrangement' or, at least, in the first instance, to get me to admit they had a problem, with living-accommodation so hard to come by. To achieve that, Peggy had to bring me into the open and soften me up. At her instigation the talk turned upon subjects she expected would interest me; the theatre, the war-time revival in popular culture, the lunch-time concerts in the National Gallery. The subject of books, adumbrated, was then closed. Helena's name lay unspoken on lips now hidden by three glasses raised in unison. It was a bold feint. I was supposed, now, to steer the conversation away from painful associations, and she had gambled upon my taking the line of least resistance and asking about her own affairs, or those of David or both. For a moment, in hopeful silence, David puffed his pipe and Peggy's eyes, chameleon-like, coloured themselves with the friendliness she thought I ought to feel for her.

After a while David said, 'How's the Commander?' referring to my godfather, who had somewhat awkwardly, but eagerly, fulfilled a parental role, less for my sake than for that of my dead parents whom he had admired; and once again Peggy showed no lack of comprehension, asked no question. She had traced my past history with care and attention. How recently? I imagined her kneeling, huddled by the gasfire as it popped blue and orange, cross-examining a David slippered and at ease in my own fireside chair. How old is Ian? What is he like? Did he and Helena live here? Would he like me? *Has he anywhere else to go?* Stemming from that last question would grow a tendril in David's mind, curling and twisting, striving through all its convolutions to point to that source of warmth which was at once my going and his staying.

'How's the Commander?' David had said.

'All right I think. We still correspond.'

David's eyes blinked. Is that all? No greater desire for intimacy than that?

I added, 'I may look him up one day.'

Peggy said, 'Is he nice? He sounds a pet. Being a Commander I mean? *He's buried away in the country isn't he?*'

Hope had been revived for them. It was like a flower out of season, paler, fainter in odour, but a focus for thoughts wandering towards the impasse of winter. I saw it myself, not as they did, but as a symbol of the Commander's care and nourishment of me at a time when the body harboured nothing malignant.

When I first saw the wild flowers growing in the exposed

basements of bombed City buildings, I was reminded of it. But here in Ludgate Hill, and elsewhere that I looked, there were no symbolic, out-of-season-flowers that, cut, would bloom miraculously on the brow of a statue. They sprang from new-sunned earth and rubble, were in it, of it, pointed no plan other than the haphazard one of nature; would bloom, seed, wither and die according to the rule of rain and heat, sap and growth, the chance sowing of birds in flight and the movements of gritty, seed-bearing winds.

That first day following my return to Lowndes Street I walked to the City, to St. Paul's, but I did not enter the Cathedral. It was a lovely day, with a hint of summer warmth, too fine to be indoors; but before midday I had walked to Gray's Inn and called on the lawyer, Thurlow. He sat in his dark room at the great desk I so well remembered, and I in the carved chair with the padded velvet seat in which my mother used to sit and nod her never-withheld approval of Thurlow's plans for her widowhood. Behind him on the wall was the painting in oils by Cooper; above him in the recess, the black deed boxes, with the names of Executors faintly discernible: such safety, such certainty. Now, as always, our talk began with the old joke, 'How is F. J. Wheeler, Deceased?'

And Thurlow, smiling at the window and then at me, replied, 'We don't expect to wind up for several years. When we do the Cooper picture goes.' He added, 'Remarkable, your remembering the Wheeler Estate.'

'Time stands still when I visit you.'

He looked down at his stumpy hands, ruefully. His hair was much greyer. I said, 'I thought we should talk about Helena.'

'I've had a letter from her, by the way.'

'So have I.'

Again he smiled at the window. I never resented his smiling in circumstances where other men would look professionally grave. His smile gave me confidence: it was not possible to think he ever kept anything back.

He said, 'What do you propose to do?'

'Ask for your advice.'

'My dear Ian. I hate divorces. They're so messy. If you must have a divorce I'll put you on to Rossiter who's by way of being an expert.' He paused. 'How's Commander Owen?'

'Fairly fit, I believe.'

'Does he still collect butterflies?'

'I think so.'

'Such an unlikely thing to collect. It's so obvious. I'm collecting paper weights.'

'For the Wheeler Estate documents?'

'No. No. We use a special size of pink tape for those. I've forgotten why you used to be so interested in the late Mr. Wheeler by the way.'

'I was interested in the painting.'

'Yes.' He paused, crinkling his eyes in anticipation of the second joke. 'They say it was *Cooper's best period*.'

I felt him watching me as I looked up at the picture in its wide gold frame. One day, when the Estate was wound up, the picture would go, leaving a rectangular, unfaded patch on the dull green wall: but by then Thurlow would surely have gone too. The bared wall would overlook his empty chair. When I looked at him he was still smiling, yet I felt he had known my thoughts. The smile was of acceptance, resignation, and there was a deeper look in the eyes like that of someone imprisoned for a long time.

I said, 'Have you enjoyed all this – being in the law?'

His expression did not change. 'When I was quite a boy I ran away to sea.'

'What happened?'

'I was sea sick.'

I questioned him further: what kind of a ship it had been, where had it sailed, for how long? He answered all my questions unfalteringly. His memory of it was still sharp, as though the experience had been but yesterday. When I rose to go Thurlow said, 'What are you going to do about Helena?'

I hesitated.

'I can't make up my mind,' I replied. 'Is that unfair on her?'

'*She'll* think so.'

'Then you'd better put me on to that chap you mentioned. Rossiter.'

'Are you sure?'

I shook my head. 'I don't think I have any feelings in the matter at this stage.'

He took my hand in farewell, gently forcing me towards the door in the manner I remembered as his habit. Some considered it rudeness in him: but, like his smile, it had never bothered me, for so abrupt was the ending of an interview that it seemed only to have been interrupted. Goodbye was never said, an invitation to return was never needed: and thus you were always present in his office, along with the deed boxes and the gently litigious ghosts who hid in the shadows watching Thurlow growing older.

The publisher Selby, on the other hand, had the ageless face of a somewhat startled baby.

He was saying over the house telephone, 'I say, guess who's in my office?' and fumbling with a packet of cigarettes which I knew he would forget to offer me. 'Well, you'd better come down and see, if you can't,' he went on. 'Oh, all right. It's Ian Canning. But come down and say Hello.'

He looked at me nervously. He wanted the moral support of Barnstaple who was now on what Selby called the 'financial side'. Before the war he had been sales manager.

'Ian, dear chap—' he began: then, 'We heard you were sick,' he continued but stopped before saying from whom he had heard. They had published Helena's book. Selby's cheeks were pink, he was nearly bald. He had a habit of smoothing his sparse hair, displaying the over-large jade and gold ring on his left hand.

We discussed my medical history. Then Barnstaple came in, thin, meticulous, his eyes darting, taking you in, taking Selby in, Selby's desk, Selby's papers. Barnstaple said, 'You look pretty thin. When are you coming back to us?'

Selby looked a little surprised. Half watching Barnstaple he leant back in his chair. 'Yes, Ian. When are you coming back?'

'I couldn't work full time.'

'No, of course.'

'Nor come in a great deal.'

'No.'

'You might chuck some of the reading at me.'

'That would be jolly good. Let's have lunch one day and we'll tell you the sort of books we're looking for these days.'

'Good. How's your father?'

'Pretty well considering.' Selby's face went rather blank. The old man had been the publisher Selby could never hope to be. Selby senior, the founder of the firm, had worn his black coat and striped trousers rather shabbily, his collar had been old-fashioned, high and winged, and when you spoke to him and he listened with his round head on one side, his eyes sometimes wandering to the glass-fronted bookcase where all the books he had published bore labels with a number on them written in ink, you had a vision of him as a boy of fourteen, entering the world of publishing through the doors of cold warehouses, climbing ladders, pushing trolleys, filling his expanding days with the duties of string and sealing wax, brown paper parcels, stamps, envelopes and glue, and all the exciting smells and sounds and senses of the physical world of trade below stairs. There, amongst the stock, he had seen books selling quickly or slowly or not at all: it had helped him, he used to say, to develop an eye for a book's commercial possibilities. 'My main difficulty now,' he told me, when I had first joined the house of John Selby, Publisher, 'is to see a manuscript in terms of an item in the stockroom. Once I can do that I know whether it's for me.' Selby Junior had been present at that talk, I had been Selby Junior's protégé, his bright young man. He had confided in me: 'The old fellow's a jolly good businessman, of course, but the list needs new blood, new ideas.' His freshly pink face had coloured with enthusiasm and embarrassment at his daring, as though the new blood were all in his own veins. He had been ashamed of John Selby's humble beginnings: but that I understood; I sympathized. I even thought the old man tended to make a virtue of what had been his necessity. Brian Selby and I had seen considerably eye to eye, in our brash youthful way.

Now I saw we no longer did so. He had put on weight with office. The reasons for his exemption from military service had always been obscure and it was difficult not to hold that against him. There was a softness about him, an air of unreliability which made discussion almost pointless. When he saw me preparing to go he was not so much remorseful that he might have made me feel unwelcome as regretful that he had not made a better personal impression.

He said, 'It's nearly five. Come out and have a drink at a place I know.' Barnstaple declined to accompany us. He said goodbye and returned to his own office with a laugh and a joke which carried a sting for Selby. 'Someone's got to do some work.'

'Barnstaple's all right really, Ian. But he's getting a bit finicky. Still – he's able.' Selby looked fatuous, but I warmed more to this new mood, this expansion of himself in his own mind into a man of business who bore the responsibilities of an employer. It was better than the depressing reality of an empty, a dry Selby.

In the taxi he talked of paper quotas, printing costs and the lack of talent amongst new writers. His overcoat had a velvet collar: the sort of coat which would make him sad at the advent of the warmer weather. I did not watch where we were going in the taxi. His shoes were so highly polished, his nails so well manicured, that I gave his person my whole attention, until I became conscious of my own feet thrust out in front of me on the bristly floor mat. My shoes were dull, with thick traceries of lines and cracks between the toe caps and the insteps. My pre-war trousers, with no knife-edge crease like Selby's, were beginning to fray at the turnups, and there was an old caked stain of mud on one leg. I looked up at my reflection in the glass which the driver's broad back turned into a dark mirror, and saw a long thin face which was my own, hatless, with a lick of pale colourless hair hanging over the forehead. The reflection brought fingers to its cheeks to explore the deep hollows which mapped the progress of illness and then, lowering my hand I saw its wasting, its ugly boniness, its uncared for nails. Selby's reception of me came into perspective.

The reflection of me seemed to ask, 'When did *you* come back?' And I replied: I have not yet returned.

The club we went to was the one to which David had taken me the previous night.

In my dazed mind Thurlow was there, and my guardian, Commander Owen, piercing the slender body of a Red Admiral which had been chased over a summer meadow and netted with a cry of 'Got him! Oh the beauty! The beauty!'

The gin had run out and Selby had taken to rum and orange. David and Peggy had arrived but had not seen us there in the alcove which overlooked a roofscape. They sat at the bar, and whenever I turned to watch them they were glumly silent, hunched over their glasses in a kind of loving misery, as though they had spent the day in the offices of mushroom estate agencies, shifting their weight from one leg to another, listening to one-sided telephone conversations. In the club there were wicker chairs and potted ferns and two unclaimed letters tucked into the crisscrossed metal strips of a green baize rack at the entrance to the club's one room. I imagined they would still be there when the lease ran out and the club changed hands. Below the rack, on a wall bracket, was a feint-ruled memorandum book and a stub of pencil hanging on a string, for the ritual of signing-in.

Selby said, 'Are you feeling all right?'

'Yes. I just have to be careful.' My last drink was untouched, but the room was still contracting and expanding as it had been when I first suspected the fever was returning and had stopped drinking. I glanced at Selby, and the movement of my head set loose vibrations which had been sealed up between my ears, behind my eyes, so that Selby's face created a mirage of itself a little to the left of his further shoulder.

I said, 'How's Helena's book going?'

In duplicate, Selby raised his glass. Two mouths opened: only one voice issued. 'Oh, pretty well. Have you read it?'

'No, not yet.'

'We've just about broken even on costs Barnstaple tells me.'

'Have you seen her recently?' I inquired.

'No, she never comes to town. She ought to. But then—' and Selby hesitated, so I looked away and then at him. The mirage had gone. Selby's single pair of eyes were now full of malicious inquiry. He said, 'She's been a bit under the weather I gather.'

'An abortion.'

He was shocked. 'Really an abortion?'

'It's the medical term isn't it? A miscarriage before three months is an abortion. I didn't imply its artificial inducement.'

Selby laughed. It was like Helena's laughter when she saw an action or remark of hers which had been designed to annoy had created no response other than a mild contempt.

'But I think—'

I asked Selby what he thought.

He said, 'She was a little over three months gone, as they say. At least, that's what she told me. She rang up a few days ago to ask how the book was going.'

He thought for a moment.

'Poor Helena,' he said. 'She *ought* to have a child.'

'Why?'

'She was awfully cut up about it. In tears actually.' I smiled at him and he didn't know quite how to take it.

'What amuses you?' he asked.

'The apparent change in Helena.'

'Change?'

'Yes, change.' I went on, 'She wasn't in tears the first time. She laughed in my face.'

Selby fidgeted with his jade ring. I felt that he wished Barnstaple were with us.

I spent most of April in a private nursing home in North London. My only visitor was David, although I also had contact with Selby through the manuscripts he occasionaly sent me for a reader's report. 'Is it a thriller?' the nurses used to say, showing their natural distrust of any unpublished book which was not. David usually came on a Wednesday evening and stayed for half-an-hour. The atmosphere of the sickroom and his own health and fitness gave him confidence. He was no longer reticent.

On his second visit he said, 'Peggy and I are planning to get married as soon as we've found a suitable place. Of course you know we've been living together on and off at Lowndes Street?'

'What does on and off mean?'

'Officially she shares a flat with a girl friend in Red Lion Street. We can't have gossip at the Ministry.'

He had no sense of humour.

'We used Lowndes Street at week-ends mostly, until Muriel started her own affair with a Polish chap.'

'In Red Lion Street?'

'That's it. Muriel's Peggy's friend. Frightfully sordid isn't it?'

'You mean Muriel and the Pole?'

'Well all of it. You know.'

'What happened when I came back?'

'Poor Pegs had to pig in in Muriel's spare.'

'And what are the current arrangements?'

'Well – we're together in Lowndes Street except Mondays when Muriel's mother comes up to town shopping and expects a meal with Peggy but not the Pole.'

'Why do you tell me all this David?'

'Because I've a proposition to put to you.'

The nurse came in. She wanted David to go. I said, 'Tell me next week.' He nodded, took his unlit pipe from between his teeth and said, 'I'll drop you a line so's you can think it over.'

The letter came on Saturday evening.

Dear Ian,

The proposition is, of course, that I take over the flat on a proper basis. Actually the Landlord's quite willing in view of the fact you really sub-let to me without his full approval (and I've proved a good tenant from his point of view). Actually he takes a view to which I could never whole-heartedly subscribe, but it does rather look as though he wouldn't renew your lease when it falls in. It would be the end if between now and then he found someone outside the two of us to favour, wouldn't it?

But the whole point old chap is that you really do look seedy and if you come back here you'll have no one to look after you. Pegs and I cannot too strongly recommend that you go to the Commander at least until you're really fit again. You can do your little bit of reading for the publishing johnnies just as well from Wendover as from here or where you are now. The air would do you good, too, and if you need to come to London, it's quite quick from Wendover to Finchley Road.

This is, I'm afraid, rather taking for granted that you and Helena are separated for good, though if you were to renew your life together I've always rather imagined you'd team up with her in her place like you did before (when you only used Lowndes Street during the week).

By the way, Pegs says there's a friend of hers who knows a fellow who's a wizard at tropical diseases. This chap seems to think you should go back to India and fight it on its own grounds so to speak. May be something in it.

See you Wednesday. Take care of yourself.

Yours,

D.

I lay back. I think I turned my face to the wall. The nurse, a pretty girl with no professional qualifications but a warm heart, said, after she had clattered the supper tray down and grasped my wrist, 'Oh Lord! You gave me quite a turn.'

The sky over Wendover was loud with fighter planes, but the Commander had grown used to them. 'We still feel in the midst of hostilities here, Ian. We regret the official end of the war.' The overhead lights on the landing and in the lavatory were masked by black-out shades.

'What do you mean regret?'

'The devil we know. The devil who's a stranger.'

The streets were full of men in Air Force uniform. 'They remind us of chivalry and John Pudney's poems,' he said. 'Sheet anchors for the mind you know, after Hiroshima.'

'You should have spent the war in Portsmouth. Been near sea and ships,' I said.

Sometimes we went out to the pubs. There were photographs of pilots on the walls, taken when the men's faces were still round with youth, their eyes self-conscious. Brassware gleamed amidst what the guides would call a wealth of old oak. A flying officer came in. The Commander touched my arm. 'There's Johnny-head-in-air.'

'My house used to be full of them,' he added. 'Open house. Always open house. They called it the Crows Nest and ribbed me about the Navy.' He looked at me. 'It's changed, hasn't it? The house, I mean. The new lot never come.'

It was May, nineteen forty-six: but on the Commander's desk was a calendar showing September the fifteenth, nineteen forty, and an Air Ministry photograph of a Spitfire flying over chequered fields. The portraits of my mother and father, painted by a man who had shown promise but not fulfilled it later, were still in position in the twin recesses on either side of the fireplace. On the grand piano, in a green velvet frame, was the photograph of myself, aged eleven, standing with my mother in the garden of the Commander's house. It was summer nineteen twenty-seven, and she wore a white cloche hat and a shapeless dress of flowered georgette. She had never worn mourning: 'Daddy *knows*, Ian dear. He *knows* how I'm feeling. It's between us. Not for other people.'

The following autumn, when she died, I had tried to resist the black arm band. But the Commander insisted on it. After the funeral I burnt it in the kitchen grate and then had been afraid as though, in a reckless moment, I had condemned my mother to hell. That strange, interrupted term at school I became religious. Holy Canning. Canon Canning. That was a winter of low clouds and warmth indoors. Spring which followed was no time for God.

'No. The house hasn't changed,' I told the Commander.

'I'm leaving it to you in my will.'

'Thank you.'

'I hoped you'd make it your headquarters from now on, Ian. But you say you haven't decided what you're going to do.'

'It's difficult to make plans.'

'What about the flat? London's so *depressing*.'

'David Holmes is probably taking it over officially.'

'Probably?'

'I said I'd let him know. He wants to.'

He passed wax-like fingers over his lined face. His look said: I'm worried about you. This old man's house with its knick-knacks, this old man's garden with its wall facing south trapping the sun, all this I would share with you.

But I felt he was too withdrawn into himself to be lonely without company and there was nothing in the house of an old man at Wendover which could return to me what was now lacking: the vital spark of reaction to people and surroundings. In July the limes flowered, and the Commander was out with his net, returning to the shaded house with jars within whose glass walls coloured wings beat.

One day the sun had been too much for him. We searched for aspirin. I found the bottle, but it was empty.

'I'll go to the chemist,' I said.

'Don't bother, Ian. It'll pass.'

But I went to the chemist. I bought two bottles, each containing one hundred tablets. One of these bottles I kept for myself. The idea had begun.

Half-way through August I returned to Lowndes Street. David and Peggy were on holiday in Cornwall. I called on Thurlow.

'Shouldn't I make a will?' I asked.

'There's never any harm.'

'Will you draw one up then?'

'Yes, if you'll give me your instructions.'

There was little to leave: personal possessions, with the exception of books, were worthless. But there were the investments inherited from my parents which produced a small private income.

I smiled. 'All that I do die possessed of. Isn't that the phrase?'

Thurlow was smiling, too. He spoke to the window.

'Who is to inherit?'

'My wife, Helena.'

'Are you sure?'

'There's nobody else. And the money might make a difference for her. She has talent as a writer. She could live abroad somewhere cheap.'

'Are the doctors bothering you?'

'No.'

Thurlow looked at me. He said, 'Are things improving?'

'There's a lull.'

'You're looking better.'

When I returned to the flat, the postman had been. There was a package from Selby. For a moment I thought he had sent me a copy of Helena's book, but when I opened it I saw it was an old novel, a file copy taken from the glass-fronted bookcase, bearing its label with a number on it. I looked at the title. 'Opal' by 'Isabella'.

Isabella.

Vague pre-war business memories stirred. The book smelled stale from its long imprisonment on the shelves. It was cheaply produced, printed on poor quality paper which had become brown round the edges. Turning the pages I found that Selby had published it in nineteen twenty-one. There was a note from Selby Junior.

DEAR IAN,

It's been suggested that there might be a public for reprints

28

of one or two of these Isabella books. They're comically old-fashioned, of course, but she was pretty popular in a middle-brow sort of way years ago and of course we're moving towards a period of nostalgia for the past, in publishing. The Twenties, etc.

Let me know what you think. She's dead, but the widower's rather keen (and a bit of a pest). Barnstaple says 'No'.

BRIAN SELBY

I glanced at the first few lines and then, from habit, I turned to the last page, to the last paragraph. What I read interested me. There was so wide a gulf in manner between its beginning and its end. I read it through that evening but, having done so, emptiness returned. I wrote my report in the form of a letter to Selby.

DEAR BRIAN,

You can't publish Isabella, I'm afraid. What is in your mind, I suppose, is that she might become a museum piece, she was a tragedienne, and old-fashioned tragediennes do often with time, become amusing. But she's just that much too near real tragedy to make you want to laugh. She knew – or guessed – too much about the conflict of minds and personalities ever to pour all her effects into the conflict of puppets.

She intrigues me as a woman though, particularly in this book which begins as one thing and ends as another, as though in the course of it her eyes were opened in a way they'd never before been open. Briefly the story is of two sisters, pre-nineteen fourteen war, who are poor but well bred. Lucy, the elder goes as companion to Mrs. Lorringer, a parvenu – whose only son, Tom, is sent down, and so arrives on the scene. The younger sister, Fern, is a hussy, but Lucy doesn't see it. There's a tremendous lot of plot and counter-plot involving Fern being rescued from this and that situation by Lucy, visits to watering places with the Lorringers, and Mrs. Lorringer's opal ring, which she gives to Lucy who loses it. Fern has stolen it, and Tom threatens her with exposure but becomes infatuated when she works her charms on him. Mrs. Lorringer is impressed with Lucy's family background – (your background, my money) – and sees her as an ideal wife for Tom. Tom and Lucy are married, but do not love each other. (Isabella has a strong realistic streak!) Fern, now possessing and possessed by the opal (evil) sets out to break up the marriage and – and this is where the change comes over the book – succeeds in doing so. Lucy, after bearing a child, tells Tom she is leaving him, and Tom feels the beginning of love for her and hatred for Fern, who is left high and dry. In fact, they're all left high and dry, because Isabella chooses to end her book with the scene in which Lucy sends Tom 'out of her life'. (Presumably she's satisfied to have her child.)

Until the last few chapters the writing is slick and pretty awful. Then there are some flashes of imagination and a feeling for visual effect which lift it a measure or so out of its mediocrity. But you can't launch Isabella again, as a bit of coy publishing. What happened to her? I mean in 1920 or 1921 when this book was written? I see there were some previous novels, and you may want to have a look at those.

I suspect she won't fill your bill anyway, though. I do now recall your father mentioning her as someone who'd once been a worthwhile property.

IAN CANNING.

I put the letter in an envelope, reopened it and added a post-script. 'P.S. Hold up on the reading for a bit. I'm finding it gives me rather a head and that means another specialist, I expect. I'll drop in and see you when I'm all right again.'

A day or so later I signed the will Thurlow had drawn up.

But now I began to lose confidence in the method I had chosen. I took to going to bed at night with a glass of water near to hand and the unopened bottle next to the glass of water. The bottle was of brown glass, so that the white aspirin looked like large yellow tablets of mepacrine. I had taken it for granted that a considerable number of aspirin would do the trick: but how many? Twelve? Twenty? Fifty? The whole hundred? Was there not, perhaps, a dose adequate for my purpose, to exceed which might only lead to violent sickness and a vomiting up of the precious, lethal substance?

It was a question I could ask of no one. Gas was obscene. Other methods required physical courage. I wished to sleep quietly, to be borne out on the ebbing tide of my own concern with life, as though surrendering to a force of nature. When my confidence in the aspirin was at its lowest, I thought of asking a doctor for sleeping pills; but the idea of doctors, more doctors, was not to be borne. I began to hope for a swift flaring up of the poison in my blood stream that would, I believed, in any case complete its business in due course. But I was tired of waiting, tired of the clinical minds which tried to analyse the cause creating the effect. I could only give the aspirin a fair chance.

On a Sunday evening, a week before David and Peggy were due to return, I walked to the deserted City. I hesitated half-way up the flight of steps leading to the entrance of the Cathedral, then I turned my back and went round into Cheapside, and back again, thinking for no reason, other than that of association of place and people, of Soames Forsyte, the man of property, who, according to Galsworthy, had walked here soberly, outwardly composed, inwardly as empty as the house he had built on Robin Hill.

I went down Ludgate Hill, through Fleet Street into the Strand, across Trafalgar Square, and down the Mall. The railings were gone from Green Park. The park was in darkness with the lights of Piccadilly shining through the trees: this had once been the world of pierrot and high summer carnival when Harlequin, his eyes aslant through a black domino, kicked coloured balloons into the air. One year our drawing-room had been papered black, the chairs upholstered in orange, and I had collected the theatre programmes brought home by my mother, eaten the chocolate saved for me in the red and yellow chequered boxes father always gave her.

It was an odd, unlikely memory, that of the black and orange room, in which at this distance the faces of those in it were almost featureless, like masks. Laughter was never far off. It had been a happy, comfortable time, warm with the promise of coming opulence which my father seemed to bring with him into any room he entered. Now it was, in my memory, all a scent, a series of still pictures, or pictures in which only hands or heads moved: touching, bending to listen, turning away with eyes coming to life at the sound of a calling, grown up voice.

At Hyde Park Corner, I crossed to my own territory. Here was neither scent nor voice, but stone and shape and remembered sunlight illuminating a man-made world in which imagination had first flown, testing its strength with all the provocative insolence of youth. And here, somewhere, I had met Helena who once came into the room of a friend where I lay on the floor, listening to music I had previously enjoyed but then found irritating. From here the light grew diffuse, the direction unsure as though, at some point, I had taken the wrong turning and approached the single-lamplit darkness of a one way street.

That was the pattern in the unfinished design, and

I approached Lowndes Street with the impatient footsteps of a stranger searching for the address of a friend, watching the numbers, crossing the road, eager now to be home and safe and done with it before I could succumb to the fascination of deliberate melancholy.

I was already searching in my pocket amongst the copper and silver coins for the ring holding the yale key when I saw a man coming away from the front door of the house. There was a lamp-post nearby. He went to the edge of the pavement and gazed up at the windows, then turned and began walking away. But he must have heard my footsteps, for he looked over his shoulder and then stopped, unsure of himself, or of me. Something about his uncovered head and set of shoulder was familiar. When I came to the house I, too, hesitated.

He took a few steps towards me.

'Is that you, Ian?' he said.

He came closer. The light from the lamp-post was on me, so that I could not see his face clearly. He put out a hand in greeting and I took it, not knowing whose hand I shook, but feeling it warm and firm and friendly in my cold one, knowing it different from the probing professional hands of doctors, the waxen hand of the old man in Wendover, the limp hand of Selby, the flabby hand of David, the clawlike hand of Peggy. It was a hand reaching out to hold me back from the darkness to which all these other hands had pointed so that I might see and enter it alone.

He said, 'Don't you recognize me?'

I did, then. I said, 'Yes, it's Alan Hurst, isn't it? How are you?'

'Fine, Ian. But what about you?'

'All right. How did you find my address?'

'I got it from those publishing people.'

'Selby?'

'Yes. My uncle has dealings with them.'

'Who's your uncle?'

'Chap called Rex Coles. He married my Aunt Isobel.'

'Aunt Isobel? Would I know her?'

'I think you read her book.'

'Isobel? Isobel Hurst?'

'Well, yes. But she called herself Isabella.'

I stared at him.

He said, smiling, 'Does that disqualify me?'

'Disqualify you from what?'

'From knocking back a pint with you?'

CHAPTER TWO

In the pub to which we went I saw Alan jerk his head almost imperceptibly in my direction as he leaned over the counter. The barmaid looked at me over his shoulder. I heard her say, 'I'll see, ducks.' She passed between green serge curtains; returned expressionless, with a small bottle which she placed behind bottles of light ale so that the label could not be seen. Spirits were in short supply. When Alan handed me a glass I held it to my nose. The glass contained brandy. I looked up at him, catching his eyes, his unspoken thought: Good Lord! The chap's done for!

Other customers were looking at the glass I held. I was oppressed by them and by the sliding looks of men raising their glasses of beer to their lips. There was nothing open or frank in the room, nothing of zest: only sharp elbows, sharp minds. But when I drank the brandy it burned through me, cleansing and comforting like the heat of the sun. Raising my head I saw Alan properly for the first time that evening, big, brimming over with life and vitality and sound common sense.

He raised his own glass, which held beer, and said, 'The best.' He smiled. The warm spring of his good nature had not failed. He said, 'Remember the rot-gut we had in Bombay that time?'

'Bombay?'

'On leave, when we were through at O.T.S.'

'Yes, of course.' Memory filtered through, like sun through tumbling clouds. 'It was better than the stuff that man of yours brewed up on Magpie.'

Alan laughed. 'Sardar Singh's firewater! God, yes, you used to say he ought to've been shot. Do you know he nearly was in Penang? He made eyes at a Chinese girl—'

'You went to Malaya then?'

'Yes.'

I was watching him carefully. I said, 'How long have you been back, Alan?'

'Nearly three months. I got back the first week in June.'

'You're still on release leave, then?'

He nodded, drank; then said, 'It's good to see you again, Ian.' It was difficult to believe he did not mean it. I searched his face for signs of mere politeness and, as I did so, I remembered Magpyiu Island, and Alan's face in front of me, jerking downwards, the lips depressed at their corners. *We'd better watch our step.* There it was, the island itself, in his eyes, behind his eyes; through him I lived it again. I felt on my skin its odd, clammy yet sea-exhilarated air; screwed my eyes up against the glare of sea and sky, was alive again to its fecundity and sense of growing, its secret look of being something to be reckoned with. There your body relaxed, your mind took in, remained alert through all the idleness of bone and muscle. There was the sunwracked beach, the wooden jetty, the smell of oil and salt, the ridiculously pompous chugging of an outboard motor, the sheen of unruffled harbour water. From the beach the track led past store godowns which cast their dark blue shadows over the pinkish sand, up to the huts with their corrugated roofs, and still farther up where the cluster of green palms hid bamboo bashas; and beyond was the hill where once, in Alan's day, the stranded Japanese held out for forty-eight hours: twelve men and a mortar; and, on the north shore, the airstrip, innocent of fighter planes, its empty control tower nothing but a decayed hut on wooden posts but oddly moving with the continuing challenge of courage once expended there.

Alan said, 'Have another of those.'

'I'm sorry. I have to be careful.'

'About drinking?'

'Yes.'

'What's wrong exactly?'

I shrugged. 'Nobody seems to know. I've just run down like a clock somebody's forgotten to wind.'

'You need oiling.'

'Or taking to pieces and putting together again.'

Alan smiled; then asked seriously, 'What do the doctors call it?'

'They don't.'

'You've foxed 'em?'

'Yes.'

'A chaser won't do any harm will it?'

Not wanting him to go, not wanting to be alone or return alone to Lowndes Street, I said, 'I don't suppose it will, but it's my round.'

I asked for two bitters. The barmaid avoided looking at me directly. I said to Alan, 'Someone I know thinks I should go back to India and fight it on its own ground.'

'There may be something in it.'

'That's what David said.'

'Who's David?'

I told him. I told him about Peggy and David and the flat, about Thurlow and the old man in his sad house at Wendover. When we had finished our beer I said, 'Come back to the flat. I'll make coffee.'

We climbed the stairs and I flooded the landings with light as I went. I opened the door of the sitting-room and stood back to allow Alan to enter. He went in, encountering without seeing it the pale distraught ghost of Helena lying in the torment of a childbirth she had never experienced.

'My God,' he said, 'but this is a jolly nice flat.'

'And books,' he went on, 'what a lot of books you've got. Don't tell me you've read all this lot.'

'There are more at Wendover.'

I switched on a table lamp, Peggy's handiwork: chi-chi, back-street Kensington. 'I lived there as a child.' I went on, 'In Wendover there's Henty, Stevenson, Marryat and Rider Haggard.'

'The King Solomon's Mine chap.'

I laughed. King Solomon's Mines! Trapped within the four walls of the flat the wings of adventure lay folded forever. 'Tell me, Alan,' I said. 'There's something I don't understand.'

'What?' He was fumbling with pipe and tobacco, at ease, companionable.

'How you got hold of my address.'

He paused. 'But I told you. From Brian Selby.'

'I didn't know you knew him.'

'Uncle Rex does. Aunt Isobel's husband. Isabella to you.'

I said, 'Was Isabella really your aunt?'

'I'm afraid so.'

'Why afraid?'

'Well, she wasn't up to much was she?'

'As an aunt or as a writer?'

He laughed. 'I meant as a writer. How d'you tell an aunt who's not up to much from one who's up to a lot?'

'From the colour of her hair, I should think,' I replied. Helena's ghost had gone.

'Aunt Isobel's hair was mouse.'

'She wrote a lot of books didn't she?' I asked.

Alan put his pipe between his teeth, folded his pouch, his head raised a little against the weight of the pipe. 'Good lord, yes. There's a whole shelf full of them at home.'

'Where's home?'

'I mean at my mother's home. She's in Pelham Green.'

'In Surrey?'

'Yes.'

Where else, I wondered, would Alan's mother live but in Surrey? Thoughtlessly I quoted lines from a poem by Betjeman. ' *"Take me Lieutenant, to that Surrey homestead ..."* '

He smiled, but did not see the point.

'Where are you living now?' I asked.

He hesitated. 'Stella got hold of a place at Belsize Park during the war.'

'Stella's your wife isn't she?'

He was looking at me squarely. He said, 'Yes.'

'A flat?'

'Calls itself that but it's really only a bed-sitter.'

'A far-cry from Pelham Green.'

He grinned. 'A bit.'

'Did Isabella live in Pelham Green?'

'Yes. I say, Uncle Rex is wasting his time isn't he? Pestering Selby to do a re-hash of the books?'

I recalled Selby's letter: *'The widower's keen, and a bit of a pest.'* I said, 'Rex is the widower – Isabella's husband you said?'

He nodded.

'Yes,' I said. 'I'm afraid he's wasting his time.'

I went to the little kitchen to make coffee. Later Alan found me there. He said, 'What's up?'

I did not understand what he meant.

He explained, 'You're just gazing into space.'

'I'm waiting for the coffee.'

He edged me out of the way. 'Where d'you keep it?'

I showed him the tin. I returned to the room, trying to remember what it was I had forgotten to ask him. I hadn't yet adjusted myself to him. The connection with Selby was confusing. I lay back on my bed. Alan stood over me, holding in his hands two cups of coffee, as once he had stood over me tending my fever on Magpyiu; then I remembered.

I said, 'You say our uncle got my address from Selby. How? Why?'

'No. I got the address. But Uncle Rex had seen a letter you wrote.'

'A letter?'

'Didn't you advise Selby about Isabella's books?'

'But my letter was confidential. A reader's supposed to be anonymous.'

'Well Rex said he'd seen a letter in Selby's office.'

He sat on the end of the bed. 'Rex has been bothering Selby for quite a time about these damn books. When I saw him a couple of days ago he was in one hell of a temper because Selby had given him a final No. I thought he said Selby had shown him a letter from what Rex called a literary adviser—'

'Selby's pompous expression,' I said.

'Well, whatever you call it Rex was bloody mad. He mentioned your name, or anyway the name of a chap called Ian Canning. I remembered you'd been in publishing and I thought it must be the same chap. I didn't say anything to Uncle Rex but I rang Selby.'

'Why didn't you say anything to Rex?'

'He'd probably have tried to turn it to his advantage.'

'How?'

'He's stretched tight for cash and could do with the money Aunt Isobel's books might bring in. If he'd known I knew you he'd expect me to work on you.'

I said, 'Yes, I see. What happened when you rang Selby?'

Alan looked at me uncomfortably. 'Well, I let the cat out of the bag properly for poor Rex. He must have sneaked a look at your letter when Selby wasn't watching because Selby denied showing it to him and was a bit put out. I went round to see him to try and straighten it out, and he put me through the hoops before he'd give me your address.'

'What do you mean, put you through the hoops?'

'Well, I had to establish my credentials. You know. Prove you were the person I thought you were.' He paused. 'He was quite pally eventually. He told me you'd been pretty sick. I thought I ought to look you up.'

I said, because it had just struck me, 'You knew years ago that I was with Selby. Why didn't you tell me about Isabella then?'

'You may've told me you were with Selby, but in any case I didn't remember the name of Aunt Isobel's publisher. I never mentioned Isabella to you because I thought she was the sort of writer you'd not have heard about.'

'It's absurd.'

'I've never really been sure what a publisher does.'

'But you must have seen the imprint on her books.'

'Imprint?'

'Selby's name.'

'I suppose I must. It didn't register.'

'Don't tell me you've never read them.'

Alan said. 'I tried once.'

'Poor Aunt Isabella.'

'Not at all. The rest of the family thought she was a genius.'

'How long has she been dead?'

'Quite a time now. She died before the war, round about nineteen thirty-five.'

'And she lived at Pelham Green, you said?'

'Yes, we all lived there together.'

'You mean your parents, Isabella and Rex?'

Alan grinned. 'And Aunt Louisa.'

'Who's Louisa?'

'Isobel's sister. But she's dead too. There's only my mother and Uncle Rex left.'

'In Pelham Green.'

'Yes, but not at Aylward. Only Mother's at Aylward.'

I asked, 'Is that the name of the house, Aylward?'

'It's let into flats now.'

'Were Louisa and Isabella your mother's sisters?'

'No. Father's.'

'Did anyone else in the family write?'

'Oh, no. My brother Edward might have come to something, though, but he was killed in the war.'

'You never told me that either. What was he?'

'A tail-end Charlie.'

'No, I meant as a writer.'

'Well, nothing, but he did some poetry.'

I said, 'A poet too! What about Rex?'

'He lived off Isabella.'

'She must have been very industrious.'

Alan smiled. 'I rather think she had to be. Everyone else in the family did what was called living on Capital.'

I said, 'Why haven't I heard about this extraordinary family of yours before Alan? We've known each other long enough.'

'You never asked.' He looked at me rather slyly, as if amused. 'I never thought of the family as extraordinary. Besides,' he added, 'most of 'em are dead.'

'What about you?'

'Well, I'm not dead yet.'

'I meant what are you going to do?'

'Get a job, I suppose.'

'What sort of job?'

He said, 'The old one perhaps.' He waited. 'I expect you've forgotten what it was.'

I had.

He said, 'I was training to be an accountant.'

'Yes, I remember now. Well, they say it's a safe occupation.'

'Oh, yes. Safe enough.'

He rose, took his pipe from his pocket and knocked it out on an ashtray.

'Or,' I suggested, 'you could do something like planting tea.'

He jerked his head round, and I saw that he did not know whether I was laughing at him or not. I had been quite serious.

'Why tea?' he asked.

'Just a thought. The pipe. The end of the day. The sun-downer.'

'Actually I'd thought of it.'

And then the walls of the room fell away and the wings of adventure shook with a tremor of excitement. Refilling his pipe he said, 'Tim Allen's in Assam. He stayed out there.'

'I don't know Tim Allen.'

'No, of course. He was after your time at the depot. Remember John Steele?'

'Vaguely. The name's familiar.'

'He's doing experimental farming at a place called Ooni, in India.'

'You should have stayed on too.'

He said, 'I nearly did.' I understood his regret.

'If you'd stayed on and got a job out there you could have got your wife out quite easily. Taking her out's more difficult.'

He did not reply.

I said, 'Do you really think there's anything in that idea I mentioned about fighting this bug on its own ground?'

'Couldn't say, Ian. Sounds a bit far-fetched when you come to think of it.'

'Kill or cure.'

'That sort of thing, yes, if you believe in it.'

I said, 'What would you do in my shoes?'

'Well,' he began.

'Well what?'

'Well without going so far as trotting back to India I think I'd want to break new ground.' He looked round the flat. 'These places get on your nerves when you're more or less stuck in them, don't they?'

'But David and Peggy are stuck here. It isn't mine any longer to be stuck in.'

'To hell with David and Peggy. If I wanted the place I'd tell 'em to clear off.' He spoke almost angrily.

'*Do* you want it?'

'Seriously?'

'Landlord willing, seriously.'

He looked at the room with new interest. I was surprised when he eventually said, 'No, not really.' I was grateful too. He would be content to go empty handed.

'Why not ask Stella? She might think otherwise.'

He said, 'I don't think so. Anyway where would *you* go?'

'You said break new ground. What do you suggest?'

He said, 'Purely for a brief change of scenery, why not come and stay a bit at Aylward?'

'Change one flat for another?'

He looked at me unsurely. He replied, 'It's a maisonette really. The rest is flats.'

'But why Aylward? You said you were at Belsize Park?'

'Well, I'm at Aylward for a bit. Stella's staying with her brother for a few weeks.'

'You're a grass widower then?'

He nodded. 'I'd be glad of the company.'

I got up from the bed, found and lit myself a cigarette. His offer moved me because it was undemanding. I found it difficult to accept. I said, turning to look at him, 'Mightn't Rex try to turn it to his advantage, my staying with you, I mean?' It was the wrong loophole to have offered him and I regretted it almost immediately.

He said, 'I hadn't thought of that. He wouldn't though. I wouldn't let him. Anyway – think about it.'

He was being careful not to press me. We began to talk of other things, of other days; I was conscious of time passing. It was important that he shouldn't go, imperative that he should go on talking. I could concentrate only on the need to talk and found it difficult to keep track of what was said. He thought I was tired, I suppose. Eventually he stood up. 'I ought to be off.'

'Yes, of course.'

'I'll be in Belsize Park for a day or two, Ian. Give me a ring.'

'Yes, I'll do that.' I wrote the number on a pad. Then there was nothing else to say except goodnight.

As he rounded the bend of the stairs, going past the coloured glass door of the lavatory, he looked up at me, raised a hand in farewell, and continued going down. I stood where I was, counting his footsteps as I might count my own. My imagination sped in front of him, foreseeing his opening of the front door, its closing, the bang with which the everlasting silence would begin; my turning on of all the lights in the flat, lights with which the eternity of darkness would enter.

He re-appeared at the bend of the stairs and looked up to where I stood.

'Look, are you all right, Ian?'

'Yes, of course I am.'

Patient, puzzled, he climbed the last lap to the landing where I stood.

'Go back in,' he said. 'I'll make some more coffee.'

After he returned I found that I could talk: about the fever, about Helena, the whole of the circumstances which formed the background to the decision I had made. He made me tell him exactly the steps I had proposed taking. He thought the aspirin 'a poor bet'. He said, 'You'd be browned off before you'd taken enough. Browned off or scared off.' He held out his hand, nevertheless, and added, 'But you'd better give 'em to me.' I did so, and as I watched him put the bottle away in his pocket I caught his eye and saw there no accusation, no contempt. He insisted on staying the night.

It was much later that, having feigned sleep to induce sleep in him, I lay awake in the darkness listening to his snores from the divan on the opposite side of the room.

I moved restlessly, leaned up on my elbow and reached for a cigarette, and was at once aware of his waking and cautious listening. We lay there at opposite ends of the room, each waiting for some sign from the other to resume conversation. I said lightly, 'Damn you, Alan. I'm all right now.'

'Damn you too,' he said, 'I was asleep.'

'Then go back again. I need no watchdog.'

But he sat up, groping for cigarettes. For a while he said nothing further. I watched the red spark of the cigarette swelling and dying like the light of a firefly.

He said, at last, 'Have you thought any more about coming to Aylward for a spell?'

No, I had not thought about it, but now I did, I tried to imagine the house, but failed, for it belonged to the world from which Alan had sprung and to which I was a stranger. I thought, then, of what the medicos had said. It might do you good to live

41

a normal life. By that I supposed they had meant a life such as Alan must have led: a life which had left him confident, unscarred.

I said, 'If it's still all right, I'd be glad to come.'

'Really?'

'Yes.'

'That's settled, then. We can't go tomorrow because I've got some things to do in Belsize Park. We'll go on Tuesday. I'll ring my mother tomorrow and tell her.'

I stubbed out my cigarette and lay back. A minute or so later he crushed out his own. I think he remained awake until I fell asleep.

CHAPTER THREE

IT was dark when we arrived at Aylward, dark and bitter with the smell of autumn leaves and the blue smoke of burning wood held, since dusk, in the mist. It had been dark, too, when we got off the Southern Electric train, thirty-five minutes from Victoria, and negotiated the High Road. A quick glance discovered for me a picture palace, a 'bus depot, lines of shops and traffic lights.

But now we had left the urban district and had walked across Pelham Common, a lonely hummocky place of thin winds and wartime shelters, and thus had reached the house, which stood at the end of Pelham Avenue, a narrow road in the older, select part of the town, with the trees of the common on one side and on the other, high brick walls which hid the houses and their gardens. The streetlamps were placed far apart, but one of these stood opposite Aylward and lighted the way into the drive, past the unhinged wooden gates which were thrust back, on either side, as though from bomb-blast, into the shrubs of a wild garden where the war's desolation had swept unchecked.

It was an ugly house, and as I approached it down the drive, half a pace behind Alan, I knew a shock of disappointment, not only because of its ugliness, its tall, rectangular nastiness, but because I could not entertain the illusion of having visited Aylward before. Twin bay windows jutted out on both sides of the main entrance, the doorway of which, lighted dimly from inside, I saw to be paned with strips of crimson and dark blue glass round squares of yellow, frosted glass. I was about to mount the five steps leading up to it when Alan spoke to me.

'We go round the side. This way.'

I followed him into a courtyard, darker and dank smelling.

'Up here,' he said.

We climbed an iron stairway, the perforated treads of which were somewhat narrow for the foot. Ahead of us, above Alan's left shoulder, was a lighted window. Reaching the platform I stood uncomfortably behind him, holding my case, while he set down a canvas grip and fumbled in his pocket for a latch-key. The trees with whose tops we were almost level whispered around

us, and through their branches I saw lights from the neighbour-
ing house.

The door opened upon a dark passage. When he switched on
the light I saw that the black-out shade was still in use, as those
in Wendover had been. Alan said, 'Come in, Ian,' and stood
aside as I passed through the doorway into the badly lit passage;
then, as one does in a strange house after a quick glance at one's
surroundings, I turned to him with a half-smile as though to
say, 'Well! What next?' He said, 'Leave your stuff here. Mother's
in the drawing-room I expect.'

Obediently I took off the light raincoat I was wearing and hung
it on one of a row of hooks. I pushed my suitcase against the
wall. Already he was opening the door on the left of the passage.
He turned to me. 'She's not here, but come in. There's a coal
fire.'

The room I entered was smaller than I had expected. Afterwards I realized it was only one third of its original size, one part
of a large bedroom which had been divided into three. Its one
window overlooked the side of the house up which we had
climbed by the iron stairway. The fireplace, being a bedroom fireplace, gave the game of conversion away. Later on, I noticed
that the room was used both as a sitting and a dining-room. In
one corner there was a Welsh dresser on which Willow Pattern
plates were displayed and, ranged along one wall, straight backed
dining-room chairs with Jacobean legs. A gate-legged table, being
folded, disguised its own main purpose and the room's dual role.
But, on my first introduction, what mainly took my eye was the
great sofa, dressed in a loose cover of oatmeal coloured material,
and the two wing chairs, similarly clothed.

'Sit down while I go and see what mother's up to.'

I did not sit but went over to the fireplace and stared up at
the framed portrait in oils which hung on the wall above. The
light caught the unglazed varnished surface so that I could not
make out, with any clarity, the features of the man represented.
There was a high, white collar, a large area of black and deep
brown paint, and – when I stood back – a face to which the artist
had failed to grant life. It was almost Alan's face, but older,
unsmiling, unseeing, unthinking: a bad portrait on which I
soon turned my back. I crossed over to the bookcase.

It held Thackeray, Dickens, Walter Scott, 'Peeps at Many
Lands', obscure books on Natural History, bound copies of
Punch, three or four novels by Elinor Glyn and, on the middle
shelf, a row of books by Isabella. I removed the last in the row,

44

its title 'Star', and found that Selby had published it in 1932. The next in the row was published in 1930. Quickly, I went through them. They were placed in order of publication. 'Star' was her last novel. She had given nearly all of them titles of one word, mostly the names of jewels, 'Pearl' 'Ruby' 'Opal.' I took 'Opal' down again, and glanced through the familiar pages. I checked the year of publication, 1921, remembering I had asked Brian Selby a question he had never answered. 'What happened to her?' I had written, 'I mean in 1920 or 1921 when this book was written?'

I still held the book when Alan came back into the room. He said, 'I say, I'm awfully sorry, but mother's a bit under the weather.'

'Oh, I'm sorry.'

'I'm afraid your room's not ready, either. But let's see how far it's got.'

He went over to a door in the wall opposite the window. He found it locked. 'We can get to it through my room,' he said, and I followed him out into the passage.

At the end of the passage was a green-baize door. He pushed it open: it was one of those which swing shut automatically: a pantry door. On the other side, lit dimly, was a wide landing. At one time, I could see, it had been the main landing on to which the bedrooms had opened. A short flight of stairs led down to a half-landing from which a similar flight led up again in the opposite direction: but only to a blank wall. From the half-landing, leading downwards into the dark, central well of the house, was a broad carpeted staircase. I could just make out the abrupt door at the bottom which made the flat self-contained. I wondered why we had come up the iron stairs.

Alan had passed round a corner and opened the door into his bedroom – the third part of the partitioned room. Sandwiched between this and the drawing-room was another room with no direct access on to the landing, but doors communicating with the drawing-room and Alan's room. Both doors were locked.

'Oh, blast,' he said. 'Just a sec. I'll ask mother for the key.'

When he came back he said, 'Look, Mother hasn't quite cottoned on about your room, so I'll fix my camp bed in here, and you have my bed.'

I stood in the middle of Alan's room, aware that in some other room, on the other side of the passage or landing, my arrival had been discussed, the arrangements for my welcome criticized, my presence become the cause of friction.

I said, 'The camp bed'll do me. Or the sofa.'

45

'No fear. I like the camp bed. Anyway let's have a drink first and then I'll scare up some grub.'

I hesitated. I said, indicating the locked room, 'What an odd idea to have a bedroom only leading into other rooms.'

Alan laughed. 'I know. The chap who did the conversion didn't have a clue. All done on the cheap I think.'

'It must have been quite a job, though.'

'I suppose so.'

'What did you all do when it was under way?'

'We weren't here. Aylward was sold in nineteen thirty-five to the chap who converted it.'

'The year Isabella died?'

'That's right.'

'Then you took one of the flats?'

'Not until much later. The family split up afterwards. Actually mother only came back here when Edward and I went into the forces.'

'Edward. Your brother who was killed?'

'Yes.' He pointed at the locked door with his thumb. 'That was his room. Come on. I've got a bottle of gin in my bag.'

I followed him back to the passage. Zipping open the top of his canvas bag he thrust a hand beneath a towel and straightened up, smiling, proudly holding up a bottle of gin for my approval.

'Go in by the fire,' he said, 'I'll get the necessary.'

I went in by the fire. He returned with glasses, water and a bottle of lemon squash.

'I'm warming some baked beans,' he said, 'don't move.'

I remembered being fascinated by his domesticity: and yet, considered, it was not domesticity but a general ability to deal efficiently with unexpected duties. Into the room at Aylward (which now, on second sight, revealed its shabbiness with a shy friendliness) there came an echo of Alan's tent on Magpyiu, our friendly banter, his voice saying, 'We'd better watch our step.' But no, he had never said those words, only implied them and, through them, the wry humour of a situation.

When he came back, carrying two plates of baked beans (on which there were also squares of bread), knives and forks tucked in his breast pocket, I said, 'I was thinking of Magpie.'

He laughed, his eyes bright from the fire he was stirring into life with his foot. He said, 'Were you? Come on, let's tuck in.'

We drank gin and ate baked beans.

He said, 'You know what you said about planting tea?'

'Yes, are you going to?'

46

'I'm thinking hard about it. I saw a man in the city today to find out the ropes.'

I said, 'I envy you.'

He leaned back on the sofa, I in one of the winged chairs. He said, 'Why don't you come too?'

'Don't be an ass, Alan.'

'Why an ass?' he asked.

'Because I'm not fit enough.'

He clasped his hands behind his head and looked at me.

He said, 'Well, when did you last have a go of fever?'

'April, it must have been.'

'It's September now.'

I said, 'But I've been caught like that before, thinking it was over and then getting a slap in the face. Still, it may've gone.'

He nodded.

Alan's bedroom was spartan, cold as we undressed. Together we had rigged up his camp bed. He shrugged off my protestations that he had insufficient blankets to keep warm. Now he stood over the wash basin, brushing his teeth, his long, muscular back bent beneath the glowing light hanging above. His waist was thickening, and the earlier, clear-cut development of arms and shoulders which I had noticed in India was rounding off a little with the beginnings of later fattening; but his strength was still imposing, more imposing perhaps, with the greater bulk he carried; and you could see how utterly unconscious he was of cutting a good figure.

I had opened my suitcase, emptied it of those things for which I had immediate need, and now picked up pyjamas, towel, soap, toothbrush and toothpaste. I said I wanted to go to the bathroom and he came to the door, opened it, and pointed the direction. Leaving him, entering the bathroom where an unshaded bulb cast a harsh light, I knew I had been ashamed to undress and display my wasted body in all its feebleness and gaunt falling away of the flesh. I washed in cold water (there being no warm), brushed my teeth and put on my pyjamas. With my outer clothes encumbering my arms I slid the latch open quietly, turned off the light in the bathroom, and came out on to the landing.

At first I did not understand that it was Alan's mother there on the landing outside the bathroom: she seemed so unreal, dressed in an oldfashioned silken robe trimmed with the sort of white fur that may be rippled and parted with a touch of your breath. She stood in an attitude of weary sleeplessness, one hand clutching the fur collar over her breast, the other groping for support on the wall. Her body was bent forward so that she looked even shorter than she was. I could not see her face clearly, for the stronger light came from the bedroom behind her, her room, towards whose open door she was trying to retreat; but I could not help noticing the strange, glowing redness of her dyed hair, and the dark shadows which were almost all I could see of her eyes. I had an impression of paint and powder, there was a smell of perfume, and as her hand released her collar and pressed with extended fingers over one cheek, clawing up into her hair, I saw the dark tips of lacquer on her blunt, old woman's finger nails.

Neither of us spoke. Alan opened his door and came quickly across the landing.

He said, roughly I thought, 'Good lord, you ought to be in bed, mother,' and went up to her so purposefully that I felt sorry for her, crushed with her by her son's authority.

He forced her back into her room, but now that he had his hands on her I saw how gentle he was with her: gentle but firm, holding in his impatience. They seemed to pass into the room in one sliding, lurching movement, and as the light in the room caught her she turned her head, looking back at me round his arm.

'You ought to be in bed,' he repeated.

'I know, I know, but I thought he was Edward. He looks so like Edward,' she said. Immediately she had spoken I realized that she was drunk.

CHAPTER FOUR

Mrs. Hurst kept to her room on the first day of my visit, the Wednesday. A Mrs. Burrowes came in to tidy the flat, but it was Alan who prepared the meals, taking his mother's food to her room on a tray. Beyond saying, 'Sorry about that,' on returning to the bedroom the previous night he had seemed deliberately to steer our conversation away from what I presumed to be an embarrassing subject. I did not attempt to discuss it although I was interested in what his mother had said – 'He looks so like Edward.'

We spent most of our time together lazily exchanging reminiscences of India. We went to a pub for a drink before lunch and for a brisk walk on the common in the afternoon. I felt better already.

In the evening we heard someone climbing the iron staircase. There was a knock at the door. Alan looked at me.

'Blast,' he said. 'It can only be Uncle Rex.'

'Does he know I'm here?'

Alan grimaced. 'I'm afraid so. Mother spilled the beans, apparently. D'you want to make yourself scarce?'

'No. I want to meet him.'

Alan hesitated. 'There'll be lots of opportunities for that. We can't keep him away these days. So if you'd rather disappear—'

'No. Let's get it over.'

When he went out to the passage to let Rex in he left the door of the drawing-room open and I rose to my feet. I could hear what they were saying.

'Hello, Alan old chap.'

'Hello, Uncle. You didn't say you were coming round.'

'I know, old man. But I thought I ought to come and see your mother.'

The front door was shut.

'I think she's asleep,' Alan said.

'Well, I'll just peep in and see, old man. Don't you bother.'

'No. I'll go. Let's have your coat, Uncle.'

'No, I shan't stay if Marion's asleep. I don't want to crash in on you.'

'Nonsense, let's have your coat. Come on. You can meet Ian Canning.'

'No, really old chap. Don't let me bother you. I'll just put my head into Marion's room.'

There was a pause. Alan said, 'I'll go and see if it's all right. Ian Canning's in the sitting room. Why not say Hello?'

I did not hear Rex's reply: perhaps he made none: but I heard the baize door swing open, and because I knew Alan knew I could hear what had been said, and forgot that Uncle Rex was less aware of my proximity than I was of his, I acted spontaneously upon, as it were, Alan's invitation to the two of us to meet and walked out into the passage.

He was a short man, dressed in a big tweed overcoat. The dull light overhead shone directly on to his head. The hair was silver, sparse on top, but growing thickly above the ears where it was lovingly curled and puffed with deft twitches of the comb to stand out like little folded wings. All this I noticed, for his head was bent, but it was not the man and his physical appearance that struck me so much as what he was doing.

In his chubby little hands he held a bottle. It was wrapped in paper, but was quite unmistakably a bottle. The paper was that soft tissue-like paper in which wine merchants wrap their wares. It hugged the shape of the bottle and was twisted with a little flourish above the stopper. It looked like half-a-bottle of a proprietary brand of gin: of all this I was quite sure. I was also sure, from the general position of his body and arms, that he had just taken the package from the right hand pocket of his coat. He carried it now, head still bent, and thrust it deep into an inside pocket at breast level where it made less bulk.

I took in the man and his action (which was carried out swiftly and secretively) without pausing as I walked through the open doorway of the sitting room, and when he looked up he would have seen me only in the act of entering the passage. He could not have been sure whether I had noticed what he was doing.

I gave him good evening and added, unnecessarily, 'I'm Ian Canning.'

'Hello,' he said in a friendly way, 'my name's Rex Coles. I'm Alan's uncle.'

We shook hands and took stock of each other. His face was pink and shiny and this, with the silver wings of hair, gave him a curiously innocent look which, I doubted not, had stood him in good stead from time to time: almost, a dog-collar was lacking. This air of goodness was somewhat dissipated, though, by a looseness, a soft pudginess of the flesh of his cheeks which hung down, dragging away with their weight some of the skin from the lower lids of his eyes, exposing the yellowing whites and the inner blood-shot rims. His nose was his best feature, a neat small-boned structure on which the flesh was stretched tight, so that the line of yellow bone down the centre of it stood out, a ridge of sensitivity. He smelt quite strongly of whisky.

I said, 'Yes, Alan has told me of you. I'm the chap who read "Opal" for Brian Selby.'

'I know old man. Quite a coincidence Alan knowing you.'

'Can I help you off with your coat?'

'Thanks old man, but I've only popped in to see Mrs. Hurst.'

The green-baize door opened. Rex looked over his shoulder, his head tilted up in inquiry.

Alan said, 'You've met then? Mother says would you go in, Uncle?'

'Thanks old man. Don't bother about me, I'll let myself out afterwards.'

Alan was holding the baize door open. As he passed through it Rex paused and looked back at me.

'Let's meet for a drink one day. Get Alan to bring you to The George.' He poked Alan in the ribs. 'We could have a spot of lunch old chap and talk about things. Adela was asking the other day when she was going to see you again. Don't stand in the cold.'

He passed through the doorway. I followed Alan back into the drawing-room.

'Who's Adela?' I asked, over-inquisitively.

'Rex's daughter.'

'Isabella's too, by the same token?'

'No, by his first marriage. Isobel was his second wife.'

'Has he ever married again?'

'Not conventionally.' Alan smiled, jerked his head sideways as one does to express reluctant admiration. 'He's a bit of an old devil.'

'Did Adela live at Aylward too?'

'No. She lived with the first Mrs. Coles until she was old enough to set up for herself in London. She rather went the pace.'

'What an old-fashioned expression.'

Alan laughed. 'It's what the family always said I suppose.'

'Is the first Mrs. Coles still alive?'

'No. She died, I'm fairly sure. Yes, a year or two after Adela left her.'

'When did Rex marry Isabella?'

'Oh lord.' He frowned. 'Yes, I know. The year I was born. Nineteen twenty.

'Are you only twenty-six now?'

'Yes.'

I looked at him: and then something clicked into place. The thing which had happened to Isabella while she was writing 'Opal' was her marriage to Rex Coles. 'How interesting,' I said aloud.

'That I'm only twenty-six?'

'No. Something else entirely.' I thought for a moment. 'Was Isabella the reason for Rex and his wife being divorced?'

'Good lord no. At least—' and he paused, unsure of his reasons for refuting the suggestion. 'At least,' he went on, 'I always understood the first Mrs. Coles was the guilty party. Some army officer, the story went. She didn't marry him though.'

'But she got custody of the child.'

'The child?'

'Adela.'

He smiled, and said, 'I never think of Adela as the child.'

'How old is she?'

'Getting on,' he said.

'Is she married?'

He shook his head.

'What does she do for a living?'

He looked at me. 'Lives on her wits, I think.' He grinned. 'The same as her father.'

I hesitated. 'Did Rex give Isabella hell?'

'Why d'you ask that?'

'He looks as if he might've.'

He laughed. 'I don't know about Isabella, but many's the tanning *I* got to please the blighter.'

'Sins of omission or commission?'

'Commission mostly. Trespassing on their side of the house.' He pulled out his pipe. 'It wasn't a bad sort of place to muck about in on a wet day. Decent lot of stairs and passages and dark attics, but all the best ones were on Aunt Isobel's and Louisa's side.'

'Which side was that?'

'This side. This' – he flicked his hand round – 'used to be

52

Louisa's bedroom – absolutely sacrosanct – she was a bit of a tartar – all this room and mine and Edward's. Used to be all one. Where mother is was Isobel's and Rex's drawing-room, and next to it was their bedroom. But that's part of another flat now.'

'You had separate drawing-rooms?'

'More or less. But we ate communally. The old dining-room's underneath us.'

'Where were your family?'

'On the other side of the house.'

I thought for a moment, considering the layout of the maisonette. 'Up the other set of half-stairs that now lead to a brick wall?'

'Well, yes, but we used a side staircase. The main stairs were Louisa's and Isabella's and Rex's. You know the two branches at the top?'

'Yes.'

'Those coming this way were Louisa's and those going left Isabella's. We used to call 'em Louisa's stairs and Isobel's stairs, and if Edward and I were caught up there an official complaint was lodged with father.'

'Were you often caught?'

'Well, I was. But I was a clumsy sort of beggar, and made a lot of noise. Edward could creep around as quiet as a cat.'

'Was he older than you?'

'Yes, a couple of years.'

There was a knock at the drawing-room door. It opened. Rex put his head round. 'Good-bye old chap. Sorry to've butted in.'

Alan went to the door and I followed.

'Won't you have a drink, Uncle?'

'No thanks old man.'

We went out to the passage. Rex opened the front door himself and the light from the passage caught the drizzle which was falling. He stood on the platform, turning his coat collar up; the thin rain looked like slow falling sparks.

'What a filthy night,' he said. 'I'll break my neck on these steps one day, Alan. You oughtn't to allow your mother to be silly about the main staircase.' He paused. Our glances met. Alan was standing pressed against the wall of the passage, holding the door wide open.

Rex cleared his throat. 'Sorry you didn't think much of poor Isobel's books, old chap.' He huddled himself deeper into his overcoat. He made me feel we were turning him out into the night against his will. With a nod he disappeared down the steps into the darkness.

Thinking about it later, I realized that his capacity for making you feel a bit of a rotter was his most effective weapon.

Edward's room had remained locked, and for the second night in succession I slept in Alan's bed while he 'shook down' (as he put it) on the camp bed. As we prepared for bed I noticed for the first time, consciously, that there was a school photograph on the wall over the fireplace.

'Are you here?' I asked. Beneath the photograph was the inscription 'Pelham House School. School House Athletics Team July 1935.' That was the year the house was sold.

'What's that, Ian?' He wasn't looking.

'Are you in this picture?'

'Oh, that. Yes.'

'Let me see if I can pick you out.'

I soon did so. He was in the front row, seated, a few chairs to the left of the man I took to be either the Head or the Housemaster. He sat like the others, arms folded across his chest and legs crossed; a sturdy, good-looking boy, grinning from ear to ear.

He came to my side. 'Have you spotted me yet?'

'Yes, easily. This one.'

'That's right. Laughing like a drain.'

'Had you won something?'

'I think so. Yes, I had.'

'What?'

'The odd race or so, but chiefly the high jump.'

'Was that your speciality?'

He said nothing for a moment; then, 'In a way. It certainly was that particular summer.'

I sensed an anecdote. 'Why?' I asked.

He put a finger on the glass. 'See that dark, sallow-looking joker there?'

'Yes.'

'That was a fellow called Lacy. He'd turned up in the Easter term from a school on the south coast, the sort of poor blighter whose parents dashed around from one end of the world to the other moving him from school to school. The result was he was only interested in sports and came with a hell of a reputation for the high jump.'

We both looked at the photograph silently for a moment.

Alan went on, 'He was rather a loud mouth and people tailed him around, getting in on the ground floor in the hopes of basking in his glory.'

'Did you have a reputation for the high jump too?'

'Well, cricket was my main interest. Anyway, I trained like billio all through the Easter Holiday and the summer term.'

'And beat him.'

'By the skin of my pants.'

I looked sideways at him. He was smiling. I turned my attention to the photograph again.

'He looks damned miserable,' I said.

'He wasn't a very good loser. He left at the end of the term and hiked off to France or Italy. I've forgotten which.'

Alan turned his back and continued undressing. My journey to and from the bathroom was unadventurous this time, but there was a light under Mrs. Hurst's door. When I got back to Alan's room he was already in bed, smoking a cigarette, his knees making a hill of the blankets.

'I've got to go to town tomorrow on business,' he said. 'Do you want to come?'

I thought about this.

'Not unless you want me to,' I said.

'Well, we could do the rounds, couldn't we, when I've finished the business?'

'No – I think I'll stay here – if that's all right.'

'Mrs. Burrowes'll be in to do the lunch,' he said, then added, 'What will you do on your own?'

I said the first thing that came into my head. 'Read. Read one of Isabella's books.'

'Good lord.' He smiled. 'Not "Opal" again?'

'One of the others I expect.'

'Well, you'll find 'em all in the bookcase in the drawing-room.'

I said, 'Yes, I know.' I hesitated. I said, 'Rex is a funny chap isn't he?'

'He's all right, really.'

'Does he always carry bottles of gin round in his overcoat pocket?'

'What?'

'I said – does he always carry bottles of gin round in his overcoat pocket?'

Alan, having heard and understood, turned his face away from me and gazed up at the ceiling, drawing on his cigarette.

'I don't know,' he said, 'Why? Was he doing so tonight?'

'Yes. He was fiddling with it when I went out to say hello.'

'Fiddling with it?'

'Taking it from one pocket to another.'

After a while Alan said, 'He drinks his quota I should say.' He paused. 'Let's get some kip, Ian,' he said. 'You deal with the light.'

I reached out and put up the switch. I wanted, now, to explain to Alan why I had told him about Rex and the gin bottle: a friendly warning to him of what I suspected: that Rex, for some reason best known to himself, kept Mrs. Hurst secretly supplied. But that was not possible, for he obviously did not want to talk about his mother's drinking.

I woke, in the darkness. I heard Alan move, and I knew that he was out of bed, listening. Perhaps it was his getting out of bed that had woken me. For a long while, it seemed, he waited silently.

Then, from Edward's room, I heard the rise and fall of a voice, a strange, half-singing complaining cry, the tread of a foot on a loose floorboard. A dark shape passed by my bed, then the door on to the landing opened, and I knew it was only Alan leaving the bedroom. He shut the door behind him and I sat up, surprised at the intensity of light which lay beyond the windows, the brightness of a star-stricken sky when streetlamps are turned out and the damp autumn night is brushed clear by a chill, drying wind. I shivered.

It was then that I heard Alan's voice, low, but distinct. He must have entered Edward's bedroom from the doorway in the drawing-room. I caught the note of patience in it, the unmistakable bite of firmness, and knew because of it that it was his mother to whom he spoke. But then his voice became more urgent, and sibilant as it dropped to a hurried whisper. Suddenly, cutting across it, a woman's voice cried, 'Edward!' There was another sound, a rustle, the click of a heel on the floorboards and then a broken cry, 'No—' and something unintelligible, muffled. A door shut – the other door of Edward's room – but not before I had detected the bitterness of weeping.

By the hushed shutting of a door, the opening (a whisper more than anything) of another, the renewed silence, I knew that it was over and that she had suffered him to lead her back to her own bedroom. I lay back, feigning sleep. The door opened and I felt Alan standing near me, assessing the naturalness of my

56

behaviour, retiring satisfied to lower himself carefully on to the camp bed, so as not to disturb me.

I did not sleep again that night, and towards dawn Alan, in a waking dream, spoke his wife's name and then cried out, once, twice, three times.

CHAPTER FIVE

ALAN left the house, just after ten in the morning, to catch the ten-thirty train to Victoria. Mrs. Burrowes, he explained, would arrive at eleven, clean the flat, prepare lunch, wash-up and be gone by two-thirty. He expected to be back for tea. His mother, he added, had decided to stay in bed for another day. About to say something further, he seemed to think better of it. He was gone with a cheery wave.

At ten-thirty Mrs. Burrowes telephoned.

'Is that Mr. Hurst?' she asked.

'No, it's Mr. Canning.'

'Is Mr. Hurst there a moment?'

'No, he's gone to London.'

'Well I just rang to say I can't get along. I hope it won't put you to any inconvenience.'

'Oh. It's going to be very awkward actually. Mrs. Hurst is still in bed.'

'Oh yes?'

'So you see it's difficult about lunch,' I went on.

'I'm most upset to put you to inconvenience, I'm sure, but it's quite impossible for me to get round.'

'Mr. Hurst said you'd be here from eleven to two-thirty. Could you just come in to see to lunch for Mrs. Hurst? I could get my own.'

'Oh no. I have to go to a relative in Maidstone you see.'

'Oh, do you?'

'I couldn't come to Pelham Avenue to do lunch and go to Maidstone all at a time, Mr. Canning, but as I've said I'm sorry to put you to inconvenience. Will you be sure to tell Mr. Hurst I phoned?'

'Naturally.'

'Well, good-bye. Sorry I couldn't oblige you.'

She rang off.

I went into the drawing-room, sat down, and smoked a cigarette, the better to consider what should be done. Afterwards, I went into the kitchen to inspect the stores in the larder. There was sausage meat, and plenty of potatoes, and this solved the immediate problem of lunch for myself and Alan's mother. Methodically I set out upon the table the things I should require when the time came to prepare the meal. When I left the kitchen I did not return across the passage to the drawing-room, but pushed my way through the green-baize door and stood on the main landing.

Louisa's stairs, Isobel's stairs.

I turned left, in an exploratory mood, towards Alan's bedroom at the side of which was another flight of stairs leading upward. The stairs were narrow attic stairs covered with dark green linoleum. They twisted round, facing and then turning their back upon the front of the house. I came upon a square landing with a single door opening on to it. I opened the door and entered a large room. It was empty except for a few odd pieces of old-fashioned furniture (a circular walnut table, a leather armchair, an unhung mirror) all pushed into one corner, gathering dust. There was also a dismantled bedstead and spring leaning against one wall. The big room was dark, lit by one window only, and this was grimed and smeared. It hadn't been washed for months: perhaps years. I crossed to it, rubbed on one of the panes, and looked out on to the back garden. There was a wide, overgrown lawn, shrubs, and a line of tall elms at the end of it. Part of the lawn had been dug for vegetables. A middle-aged woman was tending a neat plot which was flanked on two sides by runner-bean poles. She was making a bonfire. Thin blue smoke rose from its peak. As I watched her she straightened up slowly and turned towards the house to look up (I could have sworn) at the window. She had a foreign look about her. I moved away, and inspected the room. There was a faint smell in the air which I found familiar, but could not name for the moment. Then I saw a chest of drawers that had escaped my notice when I entered, for it was in a recess behind the door.

I went to it and opened the drawers, which I found empty: but in one of them the smell was so strong that I recognized it immediately. It was the smell of oil paints and turpentine. It is a smell that clings for a very long time.

I returned to the floor below. On my return journey I realized how dark the stairs leading to the attic were. One could stand (I felt) on the lower steps and watch all that passed on the main landing, the openings and shuttings of doors, the arrivals and departures down Isobel's stairs and Louisa's stairs, and not be seen: or be seen only by someone actually looking straight at you and making out the shape of you against the darkness.

'Edward,' Alan had said, 'could creep around as quiet as a cat.'

I turned the corner and went into Alan's bedroom. I looked at the school photograph, not at Alan but at Lacy, the boy whom Alan had beaten and whose sad, defeated face stared out at me over Alan's shoulder. A warm current of sadness for time past, time lost, was flowing here and beyond, through all the rooms of Aylward, stirring the grey garments of ghosts who paused, turned down the pages of books, plumped up cushions and wandered, putting things temporarily to rights to leave approaching visitors, strangers, with a good impression. I listened. The silence in the house was filled with the small sounds of their patient waiting. I walked over to the window, looking at my watch, like someone in a house that lacks now only the expected guest. I stared down on to the tangled wilderness of the front garden.

The woman whom I had last seen tending her bonfire had come now to the front and was standing on the drive, fork in hand, staring up deliberately: not at the window of Alan's room, where I was, but at a point level with the window to my left: to what must be the window of Edward's locked room. As I watched her she looked down and began to walk away into the courtyard, but she had only gone a few paces when she looked up again, over her shoulder, and this time she must have seen me. She stopped abruptly and her plump hand rested for a moment at the neck of her blouse. She was dressed in an old grey coat and skirt, of an unfashionable, somehow un-English cut. On her feet were thick gardening shoes which she wore over woollen stockings and ankle socks.

I came away from the window and stopped in my tracks, as abruptly as the woman in the garden had done. I had left the door of Alan's bedroom open. In the doorway, watching me, stood Mrs. Hurst.

'Ian Canning? I'm Alan's mother. May I come in?'

It was an old woman's voice, but rich, vibrant (sober now), and confident with the wisdom gained from a lifetime of dealing with people; that it should issue from so small, so wasted a body was a cause for wonder, almost excitement. It was to the voice, never to the sunken eye-sockets and cheeks, that the thickly applied paint and powder, the dyed, flamboyant red hair paid tribute.

She was dressed in black. A jade pendant hung round her scrawny throat and rested on the little pad of flesh high on her breast which was exposed by the V-shaped neck of her dress. The

60

hand which she extended to me was bony and mottled with the yellow and blue stigmata of age. Arranging her toilet she had forgotten her finger nails, and the dark red lacquer which had been applied on some earlier occasion was chipped and lustreless. Now that she was close to me I saw her deep, dark brown eyes shining out at me appraisingly, inquisitively. There was no sign of drunkenness. I said, 'How do you do?' Her hand reposed in mine long enough for me to be aware of its frailty.

'You must forgive me for not receiving you before. Alan will have explained that I was unwell.' There was no mention of our previous meeting. I wondered whether, once sober, she had forgotten. I believed she had not. She looked round the room. 'I hope you haven't been too uncomfortable,' she said. 'I'm afraid you'll have found Alan a rough and ready host.'

I mentioned that all had been most pleasant.

'He has told me a lot about you,' she said, not looking at me but searching the room for, as it were, signs of laxity on Alan's part to his guest. 'And now he has gone to London and left you with no occupation?'

'Not at all. As a matter of fact, I was about to prepare lunch for us.'

Her surprise, if feigned, was well enacted. 'Oh, but that is for Mrs. Burrowes to do.'

I explained what had happened. She said something to the effect that it was quite dreadful and most unmannerly of Mrs. Burrowes, and ended, 'Thank goodness I'm better and can look after you.'

We went together to the kitchen where I showed her the preparations I had made.

She told me to go and sit quietly in the drawing-room ('for Alan tells me you've been in the wars yourself') whilst she made mid-morning coffee and finished the arrangements I had begun to make for the meal. I obeyed her and, having met and talked to her, found a different atmosphere in the room where, on my first evening, Alan and I had eaten baked beans and drunk gin. The furniture, the pictures, the knick-knacks: all had acquired an air of being possessed. I appreciated what had so far escaped my conscious thought: that in this one room were collected most of what remained of more spacious days. When she entered the room she gathered them round her. She protected them, and they, her.

As she poured coffee she said, 'Alan told me you are with John Selby.'

I confirmed that I was, explained that John Selby himself was no longer active, and that I was engaged on no more than occasional outside reading.

'But the firm trusts your judgment.'

I said that I believed this was so but that it was of little significance.

'Tell me,' she said, 'is Brian Selby anything like his father?'

It was stupid of me to be surprised that Mrs. Hurst had even known old John Selby. What, as Isabella's sister-in-law, living with her under the same roof, could have been more natural? But I was surprised, as one is, I think, whenever the tenuous thread of one's life suddenly connects, as friends, people one would have thought strangers.

I said, 'If you knew John Selby you'd be quite struck by the physical resemblance between father and son.'

'But there the similarity ends?' she suggested.

'That is so.'

'I rather gathered. A new broom always sweeps clean, even when it's wielded by one's own son.'

We drank coffee.

We talked for a while of old Selby. I gained a picture of her own memories of him. They had been brief but lasting, apparently. It was inevitable, too, that through the picture of Selby I should also see Isabella; but there was only a glimpse, a tantalizing flicker of light without shape.

'I remember Mr. Selby quite clearly,' she said, 'although I only saw him twice, I think. Once in town when I went shopping with Isobel – she whom you know as Isabella of course – and we called at his office. Let me think. That would be in nineteen twenty-seven, in the summer holiday, because Edward was nine in the August, and was going to Pelham House for the first time. His father and he were buying football boots and Isobel wanted to buy something he would *like*. We talked about it to Mr. Selby and when he knew how interested Edward was in books we drew up a list of suitable ones which he hadn't got.'

'Upon which did you finally decide?'

'Well.' She smiled. 'Dear Isobel always had her own ideas. She bought him Shelley's poems. Mr. Selby said he was too young, but Isobel pooh-poohed it. One of her sayings was that Mr. Selby had never been young, regretted it, and hated to think of other boys having to leave boyish things behind.' She held out her hand, asking me whether I wanted more coffee. As she poured my second cup she said, 'Perhaps his own son found that restricting.'

62

'Was Edward pleased with Shelley's poems?'

'Yes. He was very pleased.'

'Did Isabella – I'm sorry, that's how I think of her – Isobel – did she buy a book for Alan when he went to Pelham House?'

She handed me the cup. 'I don't think so. Alan went to Pelham House when he was a year younger than Edward had been. He was perfectly happy buying football boots, I expect.'

I asked, 'What was the second occasion you saw John Selby?'

'He came to dine at Aylward.' Again she smiled. 'Poor Isobel was in quite a dither about it. I remember her making us all dress ages before it was time so that we sat about looking at the clock, waiting.'

I said, 'I find that odd. I imagine her as having been a very self-possessed woman.'

'Oh, yes, in her work, and outside amongst people.'

'But not at home, in this house?'

Mrs. Hurst looked at me. 'Why do you say that?' she asked.

'I think I imagined you implied it.'

'Perhaps I did.'

I ventured, 'I find the family background to Aylward fascinating.'

'Oh? In what way?'

'Alan's told me how you all lived here together.'

She nodded. 'It was a plan that had its disadvantages, but the advantages outweighed them. One lived pleasantly enough and learned a great deal about give and take, more I believe than a normal family does. The boys' grandfather built Aylward. He's there over the fireplace.' She paused as I looked up at the bad portrait. 'It was his leaving it to his three children jointly that led to their living here together. My husband was the eldest, then came Isobel and Louisa in that order. I suppose that to be honest I have to say I found it a little intimidating in the early days to be mistress of only one third of a house – and not the best third – but I was never foolish enough to believe I should have been better off being mistress of the whole of a house one third of its size. I've never believed in living like pigs in a poke merely for the sake of calling the poke your own. Of course, I used to visualize Isobel and Louisa marrying themselves off elsewhere, but when it came to it Louisa died a hypochondriacal old maid and poor Isobel married Rex Coles.'

I waited.

She added, 'A disastrous alliance.'

'Disastrous?'

63

'He had no money, he'd been divorced, he established himself at Aylward as lord of the manor, drove us nearly to distraction with his schemes and his women, and destroyed Isobel's life, her genius and everything.' She fidgeted with her pendant. 'Poor Rex,' she said, 'he's a perfect misery to himself and to others.'

I laughed, but quietly. 'You sound as though you've forgiven him.'

'Oh no,' she said, 'I could never do that. I can't get it out of my mind that but for Rex and the things he's done my poor Edward would be alive today.'

'Tell me,' I said, knowing that she wished to do so.

'Well, you see, Mr. Canning' (and the formality with which she suddenly addressed me put me neatly into my place: that of a stranger outside the family circle whose curiosity would, for the moment, have to be satisfied with less than the whole of the truth) 'it was really due to Rex and his affairs that Aylward had to be sold. It was sold to a horrid little parvenue who converted it into horrid little flats and let them to horrid little people. I think if ever Aylward was understood by and belonged to anyone, spiritually, it was to my elder son, Edward. He had never been a strong boy, in the way Alan was. We moved to a rather unpleasant flat on the Finchley Road in North London, and although we managed to keep the boys at Pelham House, Edward knew it was a dreadful struggle and also knew all sorts of degrading things such as his father having to arrange special terms for their boarding. They'd only been day boarders before, of course. Edward was very sensitive and it was from that year – nineteen thirty-five – that he began seriously to outgrow his strength and conjure up in his mind the sort of fears and inhibitions a young boy should be a stranger to.'

I nodded, but did not otherwise interrupt.

'Sometimes I'd look at Edward and then at Alan, and wonder how two boys could be so different. Temperamentally Alan is his grandfather, while Edward was his poor father, but even so I found it difficult to reconcile them as brothers. I used to long to take Alan and draw off some of his strength and energy and pour it into Edward.' She laughed, but without humour. 'When the war came it was an awful shock to find Edward was actually *accepted* by the Air Force. He didn't go in for a commission, but he volunteered for aircrew duties and became a rear-gunner.'

'What Alan calls a tail-end Charlie,' I said thoughtlessly.

64

She went on, 'When I had the opportunity of moving back here – my husband died before the war as Alan may have told you – I did it because I thought it would please Edward. I thought it would be nice for him to come back here on leave, and – well, I'm sure you know what I mean.'

I agreed.

She clasped her hands on her lap. 'He came only twice, though. The first time a few weeks after I'd moved. Then he seemed to have a long period when he didn't get leave. The second and last time he came it was for ten days. He'd been posted to a new squadron of bombers. He was killed on the first mission after his leave. I had a letter from his Commanding Officer,' and again she laughed; 'it was funny because I didn't think they really *did* that. I thought it was only in films or an old-fashioned idea from the Crimea or something. The Commanding Officer was very kind and said how popular Edward had been in the short time they had known him and that he'd died well. I found it quite nauseating. You see I knew Edward was afraid and had been killed being afraid. I tore the letter up.'

She paused. She looked at me. 'We've got a long way from Aylward, Mr. Canning I apologize.'

'Not at all. We're much closer to it.'

Again her hand sought her pendant.

We looked at each other for quite a long time. I said in explanation, 'I mean, to know something about the people who live there gives the house itself another dimension.'

She said, 'I find it odd that you should be Alan's friend.'

On that rather disturbing note our first talk ended, for she rose to take out the coffee tray.

She had invited me to pour myself a drink before lunch from the bottle Alan had left for me, but had resolutely refused to join me. I fancied that she kept her head too much averted, her tongue too much occupied with idle chatter as I came to the fireplace to drink, solitarily, and so my main pre-occupation was to appear at ease, as if for all the world the glass in my hand was but a glass and not a discomforting tongue of fire issuing from swollen fingers. even when I turned, woodenly, and placed the glass on a little mahogany table, I was not rid of it, and I determined never again to drink alone in her presence, if I could help it. Quite unreasonably, but very really, I found myself seeing something warm, companionable and understanding in Uncle Rex's sly bringing in of bottles of gin (for I had made up my mind that this was his frequent habit) to one whose need was controlled only with the greatest difficulty. I began to wonder whether she had put herself in Rex's hands. Break me of it, Rex, she may have said, but – as you pity me – slowly, gradually; and I visualized a carefully planned reduction in the supply, a plan of Rex's, acquiesced in by her. But as we sat down to lunch I asked myself why she had fallen into the habit.

She supplied the answer herself, without knowing that she did so (unless she had read my thoughts, which wouldn't have been beyond her powers, I believed) when next she spoke.

'Edward's death,' she said – and there was my answer – 'was like the end of the world to me, you know. It was the real end of Aylward.'

'Did you wonder,' she went on, 'why we never use the main staircase now?'

'Yes, I did wonder about that.'

'I'll tell you.'

I held the dish containing the mashed potato while she helped herself from it. We sat close together at one end of the gate-legged table. With a few deft touches she had laid the table in such a way that the paucity of the food was no matter.

'When I first came back here and took this flat, I kept myself very much to myself, as one does if one is old and doesn't much care for the people round about. Aylward's been turned into four flats, or rather two flats and two maisonettes. As you know there's an attic above.' She looked at me. I nodded. She had heard me moving about upstairs. Had she also heard me in the kitchen? Answering the phone to Mrs. Burrowes? Had she, I wondered, deliberately awaited the opportunity to meet me on her own terms? She was saying. 'I know nothing at all about the families living in the flats on the other side of the house, except that they made a great deal of money during the war and have been away now for several months spending it. In the last war we would have called them profiteers. In the recent war I suppose they were classified as engaged on work essential to the war effort.'

I said, 'Quite.'

'The woman below, however, is a German. A Mrs. Vorem-berg. You may have noticed her. She's a great gardener. Her husband died I don't know when. She was one of those who left when Hitler came to power, which means they had money, and her husband principles, perhaps. I don't know whether you've found the same, but people like that always strike me as being over eager to interest themselves in things which are no concern of theirs. I suppose they have an inflated sense of their own importance – why else, after all, should they consider themselves too good to stay in their own country?'

It was a line of thought I had never previously pursued. I suspected I should not find it rewarding, but limited in application to the character of Mrs. Voremberg I was prepared to accept it. That, I imagine, was all Mrs. Hurst asked of me.

She continued, 'Mrs. Voremberg showed a great interest in me right from the beginning, and of course it soon leaked out in Pelham Green that I'd returned to Aylward. She got to know who I was and gave me little peace.'

This arrogation of the position of a woman of importance touched me. She made it seem unthinkable that her return should have been unremarked or made nothing of. Would she not (her tone implied) have shed about her a glow, a warm reminder of longer happier days when the family at Aylward had significance?

'Oh, she meant to be kind,' she was saying, 'at least, I gave her that credit then. I thought of her as a poor depressed creature anticipating unkindness in others because she was German. It brought back to me memories of people throwing stones at dachshunds in the Great War.' We smiled, politely at each other. 'She was already a widow, as I think I have said, and I was too. I think she believed that this misfortune created an affinity between us. And you know – no matter how *rude* I was – and it had to come to that I'm afraid – she wouldn't be put off.'

I murmured something about people like that being difficult to deal with. She was eating sparingly, but with that great gift of appearing to keep her guest company. Considered, her movements at the table were ritualistic, executed for their own sake and the sake of the spirit of hospitality: last of all for her own.

'Yes, they force bad manners upon oneself, and that in itself is unforgivable,' she said. 'But this is only half the story.' She paused. 'When Edward died, her real persecution of me began.'

'Persecution?'

'Yes. Persecution. You see, Mr. Canning, she conjured him from the dead.'

'Conjured him from the dead?'

'Yes.' She paused. Her hand touched the pendant. 'She forced her way in one day and said that he'd come back. At first I didn't believe her. I thought she was just trying to frighten me. But next day when I came up the stairs Edward was waiting for me at the top.'

CHAPTER SIX

WHAT stuck in my mind was that 'waiting for me'. It had a conscience-stricken ring about it, almost a ring of guilt; better, it seemed, she might have said, 'lay in wait'.

We had cleared the dining table and washed the dishes. Now, we sat before the fire I had helped her to lay. 'We get so little coal that it seems an extravagance to have a fire before it is properly winter,' she said. 'This grate has done considerable service in its day. Louisa was so often laid up.' She paused. 'I never thought to make so free of Louisa's bedroom.' She turned to me and smiled. Hers was an odd smile, with little softness in it.

She said, 'Have I disturbed you by telling you about Edward?' 'Not at all.'

'You'll understand why I could never bring myself to use the main staircase since that day?'

We sat for a while in uncomfortable silence. She broke it by saying, 'Tell me, Mr. Canning, what was your opinion of Isobel's work?'

I hedged. 'I've only read "Opal",' I said.

'But, in its way, that was her best, you know. We were all agreed on that. All of us except Rex, I should have said. And even he liked it once.'

'What made him change his mind?'

She had one leg crossed over the other; she began to swing it up and down. She said, 'Edward made him change his mind.' She hesitated. 'Perhaps I ought not to tell you this.'

I smiled. 'But you must now.'

She went on: ' "Opal" was the book she was writing before Rex got her to marry him. I suppose she was about half-way through, and let's face it, it was going to be just another light romance, the sort the public expected of Isabella and the sort Mr. Selby told her she should go on writing.

'Rex had been hanging around for some time. He'd become rather a family joke. We called him Isobel's gentleman caller, never knowing that the poor woman found something genuinely attractive in him. Men had played no part in her life whatsoever, and I suppose if she'd been younger we'd have taken it more seriously and taken earlier steps to discourage it. At least, we'd have been prepared for the announcement she suddenly made about her forthcoming marriage to him.

'Louisa told her not to be a fool and said that anyone with half an eye could see what sort of man Rex was. George – my husband – on the other hand, asked her to make it a long engagement so that she could be quite sure. But they couldn't move her. She was quite determined. I took no part in persuading her one way or the other. I was expecting Alan to be born in a month, and Edward wasn't a robust baby. He needed all my attention.'

Mrs. Hurst paused. When she was not speaking the swinging of her leg became more pronounced. It was as though either speech or movement was essential to her.

She said, 'I used to catch Isobel watching me, you know. Alan was a big baby and I suffered a great deal of discomfort. I used to feel that she was – I can only call it envious.

'I'm sorry,' she went on. 'I'm wandering from the point. Isobel had a tremendous row with us and said some unforgivable things. She said that we all depended on her for our money, for the up-keep of Aylward, in short for everything.'

'And that wasn't true?'

For some time she considered this. 'Not wholly true,' she said at last, 'but at the time I thought it was a most dreadful thing to say. Later, when she died, I discovered that there had been some truth in it. My husband had been ashamed to admit that Isobel bore by far the greatest burden of expenses, and apart from that there had been loans to him. It gave me some insight into her dislike for me, or what seemed to be dislike. But for the fact that I had children and she had not, and that indirectly she shared the upkeep of my household, we should have got on. I think we liked each other fundamentally you see. I was ready to give her my friendship and she was ready to accept it. I never did understand fully, until she died, what had stood in the way of it. I put it all down to my status as a married woman and to Louisa's lies about me. I'm sure if Louisa had ever guessed to what extent we depended on Isobel she'd never have rested until we were in no doubt about it and went round on our knees thanking her every day of our lives.'

I nodded, but she wasn't looking. I said, 'And after the row she married Rex.'

'Yes, soon after. She said we ought to be pleased because, depending on her as we did, we should welcome her opportunity of broadening her experience of life and becoming by virtue of that a better and more successful writer. I kept out of things as far as possible, and later she apologized to me, and said I wasn't to take any notice of what she'd claimed, that it wasn't true about the money and that she hoped I'd understand that a single woman didn't lightly give up a proposal of marriage, even at her age.

'I felt rather sorry for her because she was getting on for fifty, but I suppose I was also rather shocked that such a seemingly gentle old maid should be – so bent upon marriage.' She broke off. I waited, but she said no more, so I asked, 'And what was happening to "Opal" during all this?'

'Oh, we knew she'd begun it, but she didn't work on it at all for several months and during that time the marriage took place. One of these hole in the corner Registry Office affairs. At first, there was talk of their going somewhere else to live and Isobel would have liked that, I know. But Rex was set on lording it at Aylward. I think she was only happy with him for a month and then the money business began. I only heard of it indirectly. He had debts everywhere and drove her like a slave, drove her to finish "Opal" and get the advance from Mr. Selby, drove her on to the next and the next, and once to an abortive attempt to write crime stories under a pseudonym.'

'And "Opal"?'

'Well – you've read it, Mr. Canning. In the process of finishing it Isobel's eyes were opened in a way they'd never been opened before.'

Mrs. Hurst looked at me again. 'It's so odd, Mr. Canning. I'm quoting what Edward said years later, but I'm also quoting from your letter to Mr. Selby junior, if my information is correct.'

I had been annoyed to discover that Rex had had access to my letter; that it had become common property was exasperating. I blamed Selby. I put it down as another example of his weakness and lack of principle. My annoyance must have shown.

'Please don't be put out. I know what you're thinking, but we have to remember Rex puts little value upon the privacy of opinions privately expressed. He made out that Selby had shown him your letter, but I'm more inclined to believe he managed to read it without Mr. Selby's knowledge.'

'It doesn't matter,' I replied. 'There's no real harm in it and it's my own fault for writing a letter and signing it instead of writing a report in the usual way.'

'The usual way?'

'Reports are anonymous usually, in case it's considered wise to show them to an author.'

She said, 'That bears out what I feel – that Rex wasn't shown the letter.'

'Actually, showing it is the sort of thing Brian Selby would do. I expect, when Alan called, Selby realized he'd started up a hare and pretended Rex had seen the letter without his knowing.'

She turned to look at me, uncomprehendingly.

She said, 'When Alan called on Selby?'

'Yes. Didn't you know?'

She turned her face away. 'I did not.'

'But he wanted my address.'

'I always took it he knew your address because he was a friend of yours.' She looked at me again, smiling her bitter smile. 'What an odd, secretive boy he is. The first I knew of his knowing you was when he rang on Monday and said he was bringing you down to stay. When I asked your name and he told me, I said, "But surely that's the name of the man Rex was so angry with?" All he said was that it was, that he'd looked you up and was bringing you down.'

'Well, he told me he'd called on Selby to get my address.'

Her lips were tightly pressed together. Then she burst out, 'Oh – it would make us look so – so importunate. I'm surprised at Mr. Selby for giving it to him.'

'Brian Selby has little strength of character. I imagine Alan found it easy to persuade him.'

She stood up, without real purpose. Standing, to give herself occupation, she poked the fire into a brighter flame. She turned round to me, 'Mr. Selby will think we're beggars – leaving no stone unturned to get him to reprint poor Isobel's work. He's sure to think we're all trying to get you to reverse your decision—'

'But—'

'I'm extremely angry with Alan. He's the most tactless, interfering boy.'

'I should have said he showed great tact.'

She was standing in front of me. She said, 'How?'

'In managing not to give away to Rex that he knew me.'

'I know all that,' she replied. 'I was pleased with him when I thought of that. I should have been less pleased if I'd known he'd gone begging favours of young Mr. Selby.' She came and sat down again, but not at ease: she sat on the edge of the sofa, her elbows resting on her knees, her hands clasped in front of her, so that her body was crouched forward as though desperate

71

for the warmth of the fire. Her back was very thin, with the shoulder blades, protruding, making an ugly shape beneath the stretched material of her dress. 'Alan has the most infuriating habit of not taking you into his confidence,' she said. 'He was here the day Rex was speaking so crossly about Selby and the report. He said nothing to me then about knowing you, and when he rang and told me about you he said nothing about not letting Rex know you were coming. When he found out I'd told Rex, he was quite unreasonable about it.' She paused. 'I shall never understand Alan. He's always been the same. Edward used to say he was *of* us but not *with* us.'

She unclasped her hands and leaned back, staring at me. Her face looked like a skull. She said, 'You remind me a great deal of Edward, Mr. Canning. You have the same build and the same shaped face, and I don't think you're unalike in temperament. That is why I said this morning that I find it odd you should be Alan's friend. He and Edward had so little in common, and it was a great sorrow to Edward. He was a very loving boy. So much a dreamer, though, that Alan had no time for him. Alan could always beat him in a fight and prowess of that sort was all Alan ever considered worth while in his sex.'

She hesitated, as though unsure of my reaction to something she had decided to say. But she said it. 'Alan was a very cruel boy – oh – I don't mean sadistically cruel, but cruel in the way only boys can be. He used to dare Edward to join him in pranks which could only end in punishment, but when I saw his main concern was to see Edward punished and in tears and that he didn't care a fig himself for being caned I – I put a stop to it.'

She began to twist the rings on her fingers. I watched them, fascinated by their sparkling, geometrical patterns of light, reminded for a moment of the old-fashioned Kaleidoscopic tubes I have gazed through in childhood.

She said, 'But we learn from mistakes too late, don't we? Long afterwards, I discovered that giving them different punishments had only worsened matters. Alan had jeered at his brother for being let off canings. So you see, Mr. Canning, he was a very cruel boy.'

The skull turned to me again.

She said, 'Will you forgive me, Mr. Canning? I know he is your friend, but I think his bringing you here was meant as an act of cruelty. No – no – please don't misunderstand me. I think he sees your likeness to Edward and expects me to be hurt by it. Oh, subconsciously perhaps. But the cruelty is there. That

I am not pained is no matter. I am most—' she broke off. Then she ended, 'I am most happy for you to be here.'

'It's not for long,' I replied, but she put her hand out and placed it on mine. It was dry and warm. 'I want you to understand you are most welcome here,' she said. 'You have *always* been welcome.'

I raised my eyebrows, but she ignored my unspoken question. She looked deliberately away as though bidding me consider for myself the full import of what she had said. But she gave me no time, then, to do so. She said almost at once, 'I was telling you about "Opal" and I said something I don't think has yet registered with you. I explained that years after "Opal" was published Edward said of it that in the process of writing it Isobel's eyes had been opened in a way they'd never been opened before. But that's also what *you* said in your letter to Mr. Selby. Rex didn't know what Edward had once said to me, but he remembered that line in your letter and was very puzzled by it. He asked me what on earth I thought you meant. Without quite seeing to what extent, he had a feeling it reflected upon him, which of course it did. He had opened her eyes to actual evil as distinct from the sort of evil she understood from books. Poor Isobel. She had her illusions shattered too late in life to see clearly what lay behind them, and "Opal" was neither fish nor fowl. She believed it was a great book and that her next would be greater and the one after that greater still. But that wasn't to be, you know. One real life tragedy doesn't make a tragedienne, and her tragedy was only a rather sordid minor one. Her tragedy was Rex and his everlasting affairs with barmaids, and his never-ending demands for money. All that and the fact that she could never have a child, as her heroine in "Opal" had, to make up for things. One book followed another and each sold less than the last. That was why she gave the dinner party for Mr. Selby, or so we found out later. Rex put it into her mind that Selby would lose interest in her if he wasn't entertained from time to time; but all the same, when she died she did so in the full flush of failure. Aylward was mortgaged to the hilt and there were debts in many directions, even debts owing to old Mr. Selby. Rex had got him to anticipate the advances on two books which he never got, but he was a very kindly man. He waived his claim on the estate, but it made little difference. Rex introduced a man who was willing to buy Aylward. No doubt he got some sort of commission. Anyway, we sold up, and the family went their separate ways. It killed my husband, finally, and much to our surprise it killed Louisa too. Who

73

would have thought she had tender feelings for the past or could have her heart broken?'

I took out my cigarettes. She did not see my invitation to her to have one and did not even look up when I lighted one for myself. I had the impression she had become unconscious of her surroundings and was watching the past flick by like a series of moving pictures, silent, uncaptioned; a gate here, a fence there; doors opening upon rooms sometimes empty, sometimes crowded; and stairs, endless, endless stairs down which one was afraid to go for the terror that awaited one's return.

'It was truly the end,' she said. 'After we left Aylward we seemed only to come together for funerals. I remember interminable journeys in red omnibuses and their contrast with the black paint-work of funeral cars – a sort of momentary return to the opulence of balloon tyres and a driver wearing chauffeur's uniform. Then there'd be the long journey back to Finchley Road, counting pennies. It was Edward who felt the melancholy of those times most of all. I was so concerned with depressing, practical things like the state of my clothes and keeping house. But Edward saw it all as a remembrance of things past and the inevitability of age and change. The poor boy had wanted so desperately to go to University, but at eighteen he had to go into an office, shipping at first, then petrol and then insurance. He had no aptitude for commerce at all, whereas Alan had. Alan left Pelham House when he was seventeen, although he tried very hard to get his father to let him stay another year—'

'For any particular reason?'

'Oh – he'd have been Captain of School and Captain of cricket or something. But Edward had had to forgo reading English literature, and it seemed only fair Alan should give up the things he wanted.'

'He went into accountancy didn't he?'

'Alan? Yes. We couldn't article him, of course, but we got him with a good man with a city practice.'

'Things were easier then, I suppose.'

She nodded and said, 'Yes, they were, and it was odd, because once both the boys were out to work their father had a change in fortune. He'd hung on to a particular block of shares, much against Rex's advice I might add, and they suddenly skyrocketed. He sold up and bought some other shares. He'd never dabbled in such things before, he'd always played safe except when he followed a tip of Rex's and lost money, but all this latent flair for it developed quite inexplicably, and rather sadly when you come

74

to think of it. He might have made our fortune so many years before.' She glanced at me. 'There wasn't any question of making a fortune now, you'll understand, just a matter of easing an almost hopeless situation, but for a time it looked as though we might be able to send Edward up to study for a degree.'

Again she crouched forward. She looked very frail.

She said, 'That's when Rex came on to the scene again. He was in some sort of horrid trouble and talked about going to prison if something wasn't done for him. He'd got to his weepy stage by then, tears always coming into his eyes when he talked about poor dear Isobel, as he called her, and what a saint she'd been. It played on George's family feeling, and in spite of all my protests Rex got the money, or some of it. In a way I can only be thankful my husband was killed before Rex had time to drag the last penny out of him and leave me completely destitute.'

'Killed? You mean, in the war, in an air raid?'

She looked at me. 'Didn't you know?' she asked. 'He was knocked down by a bus.'

'No. I didn't know.'

'I keep forgetting how short a time you've known us.'

'When did this happen?'

'In nineteen thirty-eight at the time of Munich. He had become frightfully patriotic, and because that was Alan's disposition as well they took to being companionable for the first time in their lives. Alan had always despised his father, I think, because he was quiet and gentle and showed no interest in Alan's athletic successes. But then, at the last, they had this thing in common and saw qualities in each other they'd missed before, I suppose. George's patriotism was that of a tired old man, but Alan's was part and parcel of him. That didn't matter, though. They took to going to pubs together, drinking beer.' She paused before saying with an emphasis I was meant to notice, 'Alan was with him when he was killed.'

I asked, 'How do you mean, with him?'

'They were crossing the road together. It's something I try not to think about. After it was all over Rex came to see us. He wanted to join up with us again and get himself looked after, have me acting as a housekeeper for him, you see. That would have appealed to him. It was then that Edward lost his temper for the first time in his life. There were the three of us, Rex, myself and Edward, all sitting round a dreary little table in the Finchley Road flat. Alan was away playing cricket, which in itself was hardly decent, but when I saw there was going to be trouble, I

75

suddenly felt it supremely unfair that he should avoid it when physically he was so much more suitable for the occasion than poor Edward. It seemed quite grotesque to me that all those years he'd spent playing games and being extrovert and masculine should merely end with his being away hitting a ball about when he should have been with us throwing Rex out on his ear.'

'Is that what Edward did?'

She shook her head. After a while she went on, 'Rex is a frightful coward and Edward's going for him deflated him like a pricked balloon. Edward said some terrible things to him, but some wonderful things too, things I would never have been able to bring myself to say, but all of them true, things about Rex and his women and his dreadful dissipation. It was all rather terrible to have it brought home just how much Edward had been affected by the past, and how things which shouldn't have been seen or heard by, or known by, a young boy *had* been known, and brooded over. Rex just broke down and wept, and cried out something about his poor dear Isobel, and it was then that Edward said this thing about "Opal". He said, "If you want to know what Aunt Isobel thought of you read 'Opal' again, and all the books she wrote after it."

'It was an awful shock to realize that a young boy had understood "Opal" in the way *we'd* understand it. Edward left us then, and I found myself feeling sorry for Rex. That was one of his greatest tricks, that ability to make you feel sorry for him. He hadn't come from a bad family, you know, and one recognized it was difficult between the wars for a man with no business training, and no money either—

'Somehow the air had been cleared a little. From that moment I understood him, understood him because he hadn't the slightest idea what Edward meant about "Opal". I know he read it again because he told me he'd done so, and asked me what I thought Edward had been suggesting. He just couldn't see it, and because of that I realized he had never seen and never would see that the awful things he did hurt anyone but himself. He always knows when he's failed, and is sorry for himself. What he can't see is that other people get involved in his failure. He didn't recognize himself in "Opal" because the man in "Opal" did things which *affected* other people and involved them in suffering. All the same, he took a dislike to the book, feeling as he did that other people saw it as an indictment of himself. He was terribly upset when he found young Mr. Selby had deliberately chosen "Opal" as the book to consider reprinting.'

'Deliberately chosen—?'

'Yes. Rex had made a point of telling Selby he didn't like that one.'

'Then Selby's choice would be automatic.'

'I know,' she said, 'and that's also why he was so angry with you. What you said set him thinking again of what Edward said.'

'That Isabella's eyes had been opened in a way they'd never been opened before?'

'No, you forget. Edward only told Rex to read "Opal" again if he wanted to know what Isobel thought of him. It was to me Edward said what he did about her eyes being opened. After the row I asked him what he had meant, and that was his reply. When I heard about your letter I couldn't but be struck by the identical reactions of yourself and Edward.'

I stubbed out my cigarette. I said, 'It didn't require a great deal of thought you know. "Opal" would strike almost anybody in that way because of the difference in mood between the beginning and the end. Anybody, that is, who has to do with books and their authors.'

There was a pause.

'Yes,' she admitted. 'But the particular expression, the image of the opening of Isobel's eyes, is shared only by yourself and Edward.'

It had become impossible any longer to disregard her wish that I should feel myself and Edward one. I grew restless, uncertain, a little angry at the idea I should be imposed upon in this way, or used to further some cause of hers, some scheme she had on hand. And yet, I felt a strange excitement too, one I believed I should experience if confronted in the mirror with a face not wholly familiar as my own.

She said, 'You may be wondering why I've told you all this. You've been very patient and you're entitled to an explanation. Mr. Canning, have you literary ambitions of your own?'

'I don't quite follow. You mean, have I plans to write books?'

'Yes, that's what I mean. Have you?'

I took out another cigarette. She had touched me on a spot I had thought long since healed. Without looking at her I said, 'I used to have such ambitions, but not any longer.'

'Oh?' I felt her regarding me. 'You have the look of a man of letters.'

'Like Edward?' I asked.

'Yes, like Edward,' she agreed. 'I should be surprised if you hadn't some talent. Did you never write?'

'I have dabbled in my time.'

'Dabbled?'

Bluntly, salting my own wound, I said. 'I had no staying power, Mrs. Hurst. Not for the things I wanted to do, at any rate. I imagined much, started little, finished nothing and published not at all.'

After a brief pause she spoke again.

'Tell me, Mr. Canning, that is if you don't mind. Unfulfilled writers have prejudices against it, I believe. But I should like to know. Was it poetry?'

'No more than is usual. No, I had pretensions as a novelist.'

'I think you are too easily discouraged.'

'Why?'

'You are still very young.'

'Old enough to have recognized my limitations.'

'Which in your opinion are—?'

I said, 'I had no original creative talent. In the field of what might be called literary research I had a sort of painstaking, plodding conscientiousness which simply meant I was well on my way to becoming a hack of sound judgment.'

'*Were* on your way?'

'Yes. Was on my way. I have since arrived.'

'Might it not be,' she suggested, 'that you have given in too easily?'

I shrugged. 'It isn't a case of giving in as if, you know, it would be something or someone you have to overcome to get there. Giving in doesn't enter into it at all. Ambition doesn't exist without inner conviction, does it? And so long as the conviction remains, a man could go on turning out fatuous tripe until the cows come home, without necessarily knowing it.'

'So you lost your conviction?'

'I suppose so.'

'And who was responsible for that?'

I stared at her blankly. 'Who?' I repeated at last.

'Yes, who? Who was responsible for your losing your faith in yourself?'

I shook my head. 'I'm sorry. You misunderstand me. That's not what happened at all.' But I knew that I stored her suggestion away in my mind and was beholden to her for it, as though she had given me comfort, an excuse for failure.

'Are your parents living?' she asked.

I told her they were not.

'Did you lose them recently – or some long time ago?'

I told her my circumstances. I told her about the Commander in Wendover, about my flat in Lowndes Street. I did not tell her about Helena. All the time that I spoke I maintained an expression of detachment so that she should be sure I saw through her, so that she should be certain her ruse to make me grateful to her for her interest, accept the sympathy that went with it and the obligations which accompanied the acceptance, had failed; but when I finished I felt that my smile had turned inwards upon itself. Our relationship had become imperfectly definable. The walls of the room were drawing nearer, the light becoming subtler, our conversation moving towards that intimate silence through which members of a family speak one to the other.

'I can see,' she said, 'That circumstances haven't helped you in your ambitions.'

I made an impatient gesture, which she caught with the corners of her eyes.

She went on, 'And while time alone will tell whether you ever feel yourself back in full possession of those ambitions I wonder whether you haven't considered using the talents you still believe are yours in their logical direction?'

'And what is that?'

'Well—' and she settled back in the sofa again, crossed her legs and began swinging her foot, up and down, gently, rhythmically. 'You talked about research and taking pains, being a plodder. By that I visualize the collection and sorting of facts, the drawing of conclusions, the arrangement of the whole into some orderly form?'

I nodded.

'Surely then,' she said, 'the logical thing for you to do is engage upon biography?'

'You'd only do that if you were particularly interested in a subject.'

'Of course. Interest comes first. I've read some fascinating biographies which I expected to find dull because the subjects were dull or obscure. But they've been fascinating because the author was genuinely interested in the person he was writing about. I think you'll agree that the subject of a biography need not be a well-known figure?'

Again I nodded.

Encouraged, she continued, 'Sometimes it's a background or a period which has been the main spring of the biographer's interest, and then suddenly he finds a subject, someone who lived against that background or in the period, who seems a perfect vehicle for all the biographer feels about it.'

I said that undoubtedly that was so.

The foot stopped. I had been watching it. Now I looked up at her. I caught an expression on her face of uncertainty, timidity, which left her mouth slightly open. Aware that I had caught it, she appeared to tauten the muscles of her face to dispel it. The skull-like look was heightened.

'I wondered, you know, whether you mightn't be intersted in writing a biography of Isobel.'

I did not know what to say. It had, of course, never occurred to me: considered now, it seemed so unlikely a thing that I would have brushed it off there and then with some well meant excuse.

She said, 'It was Edward's intention to do so.'

Edward's intention? Was his intention to become my duty?

Mrs. Hurst had risen, begging me to excuse her for a moment or two. I was left alone. Having risen myself, I stood now before the fireplace. It was a dark afternoon, with a hint of rain outside, an air of welcome within. When she came back she carried under her arm a black, cloth-bound book of large proportions. She did not immediately refer to it, but placed it on her lap as she resumed her seat on the sofa. I sat on a different chair. Now, when I looked beyond her shoulder, I could see the door of Edward's room.

I said, 'I've been thinking of what you told me, that it was Edward's intention to write a biography of Isabella.'

'Yes?'

'Well – forgive my saying so – but wasn't it rather an odd idea, an unusual one? I mean, to write about comparatively recent family affairs?'

'It was to have been in the form of fiction, Mr. Canning.'

'Oh, I see. A novel.'

'Yes. A first novel. They say most first novels are autobiographical.'

I smiled. 'So Edward's book would have been more about himself than about Isabella?'

I could tell from her reaction that she had not seen Edward's plan in that light until now. She said, 'He told me it was to be a book about his Aunt Isobel, but that it would have to be in the form of fiction, so that everyone could have different names, in order to get over libel difficulties.'

'It wouldn't necessarily follow,' I replied. 'But wouldn't the same difficulties arise now, libel difficulties?'

'You're thinking of Rex, of course,' she said.

'Yes, I'm thinking of Rex Coles.'

She smoothed the binding of the book on her lap with one hand, thoughtfully. 'Rex has never been a man to put obstacles between himself and the acquiring of money.' She looked at me with the same expression of uncertainty. In its way it was disarming. She gave me the idea that she was seeking my advice. 'Forgive me for mentioning such things, and tell me if I'm wrong, but isn't this the situation? You, or anybody else who cared to, could write a biography of Isobel, but if it were necessary to have the co-operation of the family, the family could exact a consideration for their co-operation?'

'Roughly speaking, yes. There's seldom any point in trying to write a biography without the family's consent and help.'

'The family couldn't stop you from doing so, though?'

'No, but they'd almost certainly bring a case for libel if there were the slightest grounds in your book for their doing so.'

She nodded. 'In other words, the consent of the family and a share in royalties is a sort of insurance for the author against their taking troublesome steps?'

'Well – that's one way of putting it.'

She placed a hand on her pendant. 'By the family, you'll understand I mean Rex, won't you?'

'Yes, of course.'

'You would find him only too eager to co-operate, I assure you. Naturally I should raise no difficulties on my side.'

I said, 'Is it Rex's idea that someone should do this biography?'

'Most decidedly not. I doubt that such a thing could ever occur to him, concerned as he is almost entirely with himself. No, no.'

'Couldn't it have occurred to him from the financial aspect?'

'If it has he's never come to me about it.'

'Is that what you'd expect him to do?'

'What? Come to me? Oh yes. He needs a great deal of moral support, you know, a great deal of bolstering up. If he ever has an idea, he's round at once to discuss it. Of course, it it goes wrong afterwards, he makes out you're responsible. Rex has never really grown up. He's still a small boy.' She broke off. Again she smoothed the book on her lap. She was seldom still or composed, and this had the effect of emphasizing the lifelessness of inanimate things, their stubborn intractability to the desires of the human heart. Suddenly she took her hand away from the book and touched her pendant with it, so that the pendant, now, was twisted in the fingers of both her hands.

'Would you be interested, do you think, in doing this book, Mr. Canning?'

'I scarcely know,' I told her.

'I had in mind that it would be at once a pleasure for us and a practical form of convalescence for you.'

'Convalescence?'

'Why, yes. Alan told me you've been ill. There was some disagreement amongst the doctors as to the cause, wasn't there?'

'Not really. They all agreed I had some sort of fever, but couldn't give a name to it.'

'You had specialist opinion?'

'I had every kind of opinion.'

'I'm glad to see you haven't let it get you down.' And down came both hands upon the book on her lap, where they moved, tracing the edges of the binding. 'Most people who are, or have been, invalids become so wrapped up in themselves. I'm thinking of Louisa. She was an excellent example. At times one felt depressed merely to be in her company. She was all limbs and joints and organs on the one hand, and bottles, prescriptions and pills on the other. A great sufferer as they say. Whereas one would never guess you had had a day's serious illness, Mr. Canning.' She paused. 'Unless one looks closely. Then one sees it hasn't been easy, and that—'

'And what?' I prompted.

'That you hesitate to make any sort of plans because you don't quite know where you stand.'

I smiled. 'You have a remarkable intuition.' I told her.

'It isn't only intuition. Men commonly over-estimate that quality in women, you know.' She returned my smile. 'Forgive me for saying so, I know you will, but in general men are very thoughtless creatures. Single-minded rather. That is what life demands they should be, I think. You only have to take the example of primitive man as hunter and breadwinner. Life demands that he should be singleminded, and nature compensates him by giving him a supreme self-confidence in his ability as a hunter. All his thought is directed towards that end, and at the end is food for himself and his family, and protection for them all. His wife, on the other hand, depends on him for food and protection, but can't actually share his self-confidence from the inside where it matters. Oh – she can believe in him through the sort of

82

vicarious self-confidence something like love can bring, but nature demands that she keeps alert for any slightest sign of failure in the man, because she depends on him for life and livelihood.'

We were hovering on the brink of good-natured laughter.

'And so, Mr. Canning, your so-called intuitive woman takes to watching and interpreting every shadow of expression on her man's face. If he's losing confidence, her training in observation detects it as surely as a wart on the end of his nose, and so she bolsters him up, praises him, *pushes* him, you see, into regaining confidence – and all for the most selfish reasons as you see – and off he goes with his chest out thinking what a fine fellow he is. He might even pause to consider how understanding his wife was, and no doubt he'd then shake his head in mystification and tell his neighbour that woman's instinct was a thing to marvel at.'

She laughed. I joined in with her.

She said, 'Of course, civilization has played havoc with what was a simple basic pattern, but I think we've all retained a semblance of the primitive virtues, or perhaps I ought to call them necessities. Man, his single-mindedness, and woman, her talent for what we know as instinct. I've lived my life surrounded by people, Mr. Canning. Sometimes I've grown dizzy in the exercise of my talent, and I can't claim to have exercised it with success. If anything it has only been a source of anxiety to me, but then—'

For a moment she kept silent, and our laughter had come to an end.

Now she said, 'But then the talent itself has its roots in anxiety, hasn't it? Just as a man's single-mindedness has its roots in hunger.' She glanced up at me. 'We've come a long way from my intuition about your hesitating to make plans for the future haven't we? I was right of course?'

'I suppose so. I don't know.'

'At least that is better than my first intuition. When I first saw you, I thought you had decided against having plans of any kind.'

Without thinking, I said, 'When you saw me this morning, you mean?'

And then our eyes met and we could neither of us look away. She said, 'No, we met first on the landing and I mistook you for Edward. You hadn't forgotten?'

Dumbly I shook my head.

'I mistook you for Edward, but when I saw my mistake I thought this other thing about you, that you have decided to have no future. You had Edward's look of that last leave when he went away and I knew he knew he was going to die.'

I asked, gently, 'Has Alan been talking about me?'

She replied, as softly, 'No. Has he to you about me?'

I told her he had not.

'He tells us nothing, does he? Perhaps for once, each of us has cause to be thankful.'

I looked down at her hands, prompted to do so by a movement of her shoulders. The book was clasped tightly. Her knuckles showed white. She said, 'Nothing outside Alan's immediate prospect has the power to cause him sorrow or a moment's anxiety. He is self-confident, self-sufficient, and single-minded to the point of absurdity. He plods along on one undeviating course to goodness knows what end, other than his own self-satisfaction. At the time when Isobel died and we knew we had to go, and all of us, including Edward, were suffering this terrible anxiety, all Alan could think of were his own affairs at school. You will think me horrid to speak of my own son so.'

'Not at all, Mrs. Hurst. I put no value upon the sentiment of family ties.'

'That is because you've had no family ties, Mr. Canning.' She almost snapped the words at me. Momentarily I was taken aback.

She laughed. 'I know. I'm being inconsistent, but that's my privilege as a woman. I *have* sentiment for family ties. You cannot conceive the distress my feelings towards Alan cause me. I find them unnatural and unmotherly, and am often bitterly ashamed.'

I was still off-balance, unnerved by the sudden change in her behaviour I said, 'Mightn't Alan's what? Reserve? Mightn't it be because he's unsure of himself, in fact *lacks* confidence?'

'Please, Mr. Canning, that is surely the first explanation you might expect me to seek. Don't think I haven't often tried to make myself believe it. But can you honestly, knowing Alan, tell yourself he lacks confidence? You've only known him a very short time, but I doubt if you could ever persuade yourself for long that he's timid or reticent or unsure of himself, anything, indeed, but unspoken and devoid of all *shades* of feeling. Alan sees everything in blacks and whites and what is neither black nor white he's blind to. I can see you don't really believe me.'

She leaned forward. 'You've been in his company now for several days, haven't you?'

'Yes. More or less since last Sunday.'

'And how would you describe his behaviour?'

I was beginning to find the conversation distasteful. My instinct was to defend him, as a friend. I could not follow her subtleties. I said, 'Why, he's been as I've always found him. Friendly and accommodating.'

'And in good spirits?'

'Why yes. Isn't that his great asset? He's done me a lot of good.'

'He's shown no signs of distress?'

I became suspicious. I guessed already that I had said the wrong thing, something that would damn him in her eyes.

She said, 'You wouldn't have suspected that he's lately undergone an experience that would make a man of normal feeling morose and deeply unhappy?'

My surprise overcame my suspicion. The expression on my face answered her. She smiled. She said, 'No, I can see you haven't suspected that. No one could suspect it. The answer is that he has felt no remorse, no anger, no regret, in fact nothing whatsoever. As far as he is concerned it's over and done with and he can carry on as if nothing has happened.'

'But what has happened?'

'Frankly, it's a wonder he didn't tell you. He's quite undisturbed by it. He told me without a qualm, much as he might tell me it rained yesterday.' She paused. 'The fact is, Mr. Canning, that his wife Stella left him a little over a week ago and he's come back here to live.'

She made it sound so cold-blooded that automatically the word 'callous' passed through my mind. And yet, in the back of my mind, there was a certainty that I had cause to know her view of his reaction false.

It was only as she apologized for her heat, and invited me to join her on the sofa to look at the book she had been resting on her lap, that I remembered my wakefulness of the night before and, toward the end of it as dawn came, that urgent cry of Alan's, 'Stella! Stella!' and the defeated silence into which he awoke from the ugly, unreturned passion of his dream.

But this I could not offer in his defence.

The book that she had nursed was an album of photographs. I only remember it now, clearly, in one particular respect: the photograph of Alan. It was what I believe is known as cabinet size, by which one supposed it suitable for framing. I remember it because of what happened later in connection with it.

He cannot have been more than eighteen years of age when it was taken, but that early maturity, of which I have spoken before, was already apparent. There was no gawkiness about him. Except for a pair of swimming trunks he was naked, reclining against a stone wall which, from the background of trees and a partly revealed roof, I took to be in the corner of a garden: an ensemble pleasant enough with its dappling effect of filtered sunshine, its implication of lazy enjoyment.

He was smiling in the direction of the photographer, and so easy and natural was this two-dimensional representation of the boy, in whom I recognized the man, that I anticipated that quick depression of the corners of his mouth, that mock, unspoken warning: *We'd better watch our step!* By his side, supporting her weight with a stiffened left arm, was a woman.

She was looking, not at the camera, but at Alan and there was something in her expression which vaguely shocked me. Perhaps it was that her face, being turned towards him, pointedly drew attention to an awareness between them that he was unclothed whilst she was not. It created in him a sexuality which would otherwise have been absent, and because of this it was impossible to overlook the fact that she must have been considerably older than he.

There was, in her features, a certain familiarity, particularly about the nose which was small-boned, at odds with the rather puffy face in which there were signs of petulance and self-indulgence; a strange, masculine face and head, with short-cropped hair, uncomplementary to the soft, rounded arms and well developed breasts. She wore a short-sleeved jumper and a tweed skirt.

Until we came to this page in the album, Mrs. Hurst had needed no prompting from me to explain the photographs and tell me the names of the people shown in them, but now she fell silent, made no move to turn to the next page; became, indeed, quite still, so that I could not help being aware that the picture of Alan was one about which she had something special either to say or to withhold.

I said, 'And who is this?'

'But Alan, of course. Don't you recognize him?'

'I meant the woman.'

'That's Adela Coles. Rex's daughter by his first wife.'

'Oh, yes. Alan has mentioned her name.'

She smoothed the picture with her hand. 'This was taken a few months before the war. You must meet Adela. She's in your line of business.'

'In publishing?'

'She moves in that sort of circle, but I've never quite been able to sort it out. A very clever girl. She admired Edward's poetry tremendously and gave him lots of help.' Mrs. Hurst hesitated. 'She and Alan were great friends, too. I think if it hadn't been for the difference in their ages they might have been married.'

Still she did not turn the page.

I said, 'Is there a picture of Alan's wife here?' I looked at her as I spoke and saw the angry little pursing of her lips.

'No,' she answered. 'We have no picture of Stella.'

That, as I said, is all I now remember clearly of the photographs I saw in the album. An accurate mind picture of Isabella has long since gone. There were many pictures of her, old sepia prints which merge one into the other as I recollect them, and harsher black and white snaps of the ungenerous, later years. There was in all of them, though, a faded, almost wearied air about the woman they represented which enabled me, even then, in my Aylward days, to think of her ever as climbing stairs, sometimes looking back in some small gesture of inquiry or absent-mindedness, or standing, perhaps, in the middle distance, shading her eyes against a too-hot sun so that her features never made a real impression on me. No subject, I believed, for a biography. Louisa, her sister, I recall as a fierce, dark woman, short, self-absorbed, Alan gone wrong, a physical embodiment of a temper he himself kept well under control. George Hurst, the boys' father I never could distinguish from the aloof men he so much resembled and in whose company and shade he sat or stood, whenever someone intent upon snapping them grouped them uncomfortably facing the sun on the lawn.

Mrs. Hurst, I knew, and Alan, and Rex Coles. Only one face is missing, was missing then. It was after Mrs. Hurst had left me, taking the album with her, that I remembered I had seen no picture of Edward.

When she returned she carried folded bed sheets under her arm. She put the pile of white linen on the gate-legged table. Dangling from the middle finger of her left hand was a key-ring bearing a single key. With this key she opened the door of Edward's room.

I did not follow her inside, but I guessed I was to be allowed to sleep there after all. I felt that I had passed a test and, in that, found pleasure; but my pleasure was not unmixed with apprehension. There was a clatter as she unlocked and lowered a sash window. It was difficult not to imagine that the window was opened less to allow fresh air to come in as to let something out.

Returning to collect the sheets and pillow-cases she said, 'I shan't be long. I'm just making up your bed.'

'May I help?'

'If you'd like to.'

The room, like Alan's, was long and narrow, lighted by one window. The bed was placed lengthwise beneath the window, an odd arrangement the only virtue of which was in the greater space for movement it provided. At the other end of the room there was an electric fire, an easy chair, a desk, bookshelves: the beginning of a library. The pictures on the walls were reproductions of Gauguin, Matisse, Sickert and Beardsley, familiar subjects which I took in at a glance.

We made up the bed in silence. When we had finished, Mrs. Hurst unlocked the door which communicated with Alan's room, but left it closed.

She said, 'The bed's quite well aired, but I'll put a hot water bottle in it.'

'Please don't bother.'

'It's no bother.'

For a moment she stood surveying the room. Her glance finally rested on me. She said, 'You don't mind sleeping in his room, do you Mr. Canning?'

'Of course not. But I feel it's put you to a great deal of trouble.'

'Do you like it?'

I looked round it. 'Yes, indeed. It looks most comfortable. Is it—' I broke off, but she understood.

'Just as he left it? Oh, no. That is a morbid idea. I change it around a great deal. He was always restless in that way himself.' She paused. 'Shall I help you to bring in your things from next door?'

'No. Please. I can manage perfectly.'

'Then – I'll leave you to get comfortable.'

I went to the door which led into the drawing-room, and held it open for her. She went past me with a nod, moving her lips in an inaudible 'thank you'. The scent she used came to me very strongly. As I closed the door I caught a glimpse of her sudden movement: her hand thrown out towards the arm of a chair as though, for an instant, she had been unsure of her ability to get there unaided. I hesitated, then shut the door and went over to the bed. I sat there for a minute or so.

I felt out of sorts and looked about me, wondering whether it would turn out to be the sort of room in which one would feel trapped. My glance fell on one of the framed reproductions: the Sickert: *L'Ennui.*

It was a picture I myself had had, surely. I rose and crossed the room to stare at it. In the foreground is the figure of a man, seated, content. One feels the narrow confines within which he finds it possible to experience pleasure. Behind him, half turned away from us, is a woman lost in the contemplation of what? An old love? Her lost youth? A day in the country away from urban squalor? Or is her mind atrophied, no longer impressionable by reason of a long succession of days and hours the man has selfishly absorbed, leaving nothing of them for her?

Where had I once had this picture? I asked myself. At Lowndes Street? At Helena's place? In Wendover?

I went into Alan's room and collected my few things together, bringing them back to my new quarters. For so long had I lived in suitcases that the putting away of possessions into drawers seemed but to rob me of them. I went again to look at *L'Ennui.*

I remembered.

It had not been my picture, but Helena's. Beyond that it had no special meaning. I did not recall ever having discussed it with her, did not recollect its ever having played a part in our lives. Perhaps I had looked at it whilst waiting for her to come down, dressed, ready for a party. Perhaps my attention had wandered to it, taking it and its meaning and message in, subconsciously, whilst Helena spoke, or shouted or cried or fell into my arms.

I returned to the bed. My heart was beginning to pound as it did whenever I was about to fall into the fever. I anticipated the feeling of my skin becoming hot and dry, the always recurring fear that it would be bad this time, worse, far worse than ever before. Then, in a while, the muscles of my face and neck would begin to contract with anger and that particular despair I never could help but feel.

I drew up my legs so that I was kneeling on the bed, facing the closed, lower portion of the window which had, behind it, the other pane of glass, the lowered upper half. I reached out and began to struggle with them. For a bit they defeated me, and as I struggled to raise first one and then the other I found myself wondering, too, whether I had been foolish not to have ended it, as I had intended; whether the time would ever come when raising a window would be the first step of a leap into darkness. The windows gave: gave on to air and freshness and the buoyancy of space.

And it was at that instant that I knew, without any doubt whatsoever, that Edward was there. There was nothing unpleasant or frightening about it. I did not see him, but unmistakably he was there, quite close to me, the whole of him making itself known in a resigned exhalation of breath which I heard, and felt upon my cheek; and there was something so melancholy about it that I was filled with an overwhelming sense of loss.

I knelt on the bed for a few more moments, but the manifestation had taken its course. It was over. I leaned forward and pulled the window down again, and turned my back on it. Gradually I could feel the warnings of fever abating. I was retreating from them, retreating from the fever itself as from the edge of a deep chasm; withdrawing myself from it, withdrawing myself from death and from Edward.

I understood, then, that the sense of loss had been a sense I shared, briefly, with him. For that moment we had come together and I had been touched by it; his loss, his sadness; moved, too, by his grief that, whilst I might join him, no power of mine or his could ever help him to return to that state of grace which was my ignorance of the world in which he moved, that gulf which separated us and now grew wider and wider until, with a quieter mind, I rose, and took possession of my room at Aylward.

Part Two

GESTATION

CHAPTER ONE

WHEN the post came to Lowndes Street it used to be piled on a table in the common entrance hall, and there remained until claimed by the tenants. Before coming to Aylward I had left a forwarding address with the woman who occupied the ground floor flat, and in this way, on the Saturday at the end of my first week's stay with Alan, I received a letter from David Holmes.

DEAR IAN [he wrote],

The weather here isn't too bad and on the whole we're enjoying ourselves, especially as it's the first holiday either of us has had for years and years. But this letter isn't just to tell you about what we're doing so much as about what's happened and what we've got to do in the circumstances. The long and short of it is that poor Pegs is in the pudden club and so we're going to get married right away and no more nonsense. I must say women have the rough side of things don't they? Well Ian, what are you going to do about the flat? That's blunt enough old boy, but when you're in this sort of a spot there's no time for by your leave and what not. If Pegs and I could take over Lowndes Street officially we'd bless you eternally dear old man. (Sorry! but Pegs and I've been celebrating, and anyway you are a dear old man.) We love you dearly, both of us, but we want a place to hang the hats and the nappies. Lord, what a thought. I hope it's a boy of course, though Pegs hankers after a girl I think. Will you be godfather? Do let us hear from you soon. Lord isn't it comic! All these years taking every possible care and suddenly there's one up the spout. Just off to re-join Pegs in the Cabin.

Ever yours—

The Cabin? I pictured it as a low-ceilinged, panelled room, the bar as confined, as rosily-lit as a Punch and Judy: I came to a decision and wrote back:

DEAR DAVID AND PEGGY,

Yes, have the flat. The books are mine. The desk is mine, too, and three of the pictures. I'll arrange to have these removed. No doubt you're in touch with the landlord and can do whatever is necessary to do in that direction. On second thoughts perhaps in the circumstances you could cope with the transfer of my possessions to Wendover? Be careful with the books. Don't go to the Cabin too frequently, or if you do get Pegs to drink tomato juice. And tell her to be careful about the stairs in Lowndes Street. I hope nobody at the Ministry is a good mathematician!

Yours IAN.

P.S. The above is my temporary address.

Having disposed of David and Pegs I wrote to the old man at Wendover to tell him where I was. I also wrote to Thurlow and to Selby.

When I told Alan what I had done he seemed pleased. He said, 'You'll come out to Assam yet.'

'Are you really going?'

In reply he nodded, pipe in mouth, capable fingers probing the tobacco in his pouch. Neither of us had mentioned Stella.

'When do you expect to go?' I asked him.

'In about a month.' He had spent most of the last two days in town making the arrangements.

'Is it a secret?'

He hesitated, taking the pipe out of his mouth, thrusting it into the pouch to fill it. He said, 'I shan't tell mother until it's definite.'

'When will you know?'

'I've got to see this chap on Monday.'

I watched him. You might have thought he was contained within a shell; certain, assured, glowing with the pleasure of anticipation. But there was no shell, I decided, no measure of self-protection. One word expressing an interest in his plans gave you the right to enter.

In the evening, Rex Coles came. It was his third visit since my arrival. Whilst he was with Marion, Alan stayed with me. I pretended to read a page of the book I had on my lap – one of Isabella's. After a time the door opened and Rex looked in. He still wore his overcoat. 'Thanks, old chap,' he said to Alan.

'Come in and have a drink.'

We were all standing. Rex was ignoring me.

'I don't know, old man. I ought to get back.'

'Tell Trixie I kept you,' Alan suggested.

'Well just a quick one.'

He came to the middle of the room.

'Hello,' I said.

Without looking at me he said, 'Evening, old man,' then to Alan, 'Have you seen Adela yet?'

'No, Uncle. Haven't had a moment.'

Alan gave him a drink and asked me what I wanted.

While we spoke I felt Rex take a quick look at me, then raise his glass. His left hand was deep in the overcoat pocket.

He spoke to Alan, when he had finished, and returned his glass. 'Thanks, old man. Excuse me if I toddle. You might try and look in on Adela soon. She's still at the same place.'

'Righto, I'll try.'

'By the way, old man. D'you want me to have a word with Lester about cricket?'

'Who's Lester?'

'The new Secretary. They've a place for you next season if you want to play, I think.'

'I don't think so, thanks Uncle.'

'Why not old boy?'

'Too old.'

'You ought to keep it up. A build like yours goes to fat if you're not careful.' For the first time Rex looked at me directly. 'We used to hope Alan would play for the County.'

'Did you? Who was we?'

'All of us. The family. We were very proud of young Alan, weren't we, old boy?' Rex's eyes were watering. He huddled himself in the overcoat, looking lost. Then he said to me, 'Marion tells me you have a notion of doing a book on poor Isobel.' He glanced at the book I had left on the arm of my chair. 'It'd be better than nothing. She ought not to be forgotten.'

I mumbled something non-committal. As Alan saw him to the door, he turned. 'We'll have to have a talk about it,' he said.

When Alan came back I asked him, 'Who's Trixie?'

He grinned. 'His housekeeper.'

We sat opposite one another in silence for a while.

'What about coming to town with me on Monday?' he said.

'But aren't you seeing the man about the Assam job?'

'Yes, in the morning. You could come up with me, then we could have a minor beat-up.'

'As a celebration?'

'Yes.' He smiled.

'You must be pretty sure you'll get the job.'

'I suppose so. If I don't we could still celebrate.'

'Celebrate what?'

'Not getting the job.'

There was no ruffling his calm. He relapsed again into silence. Suddenly I knew he was waiting for me to say something about what Rex had called my notion to do a book about poor Isobel. I knew, too, that he would not mention it unless I did so myself. For a moment I tried to put myself in his shoes: formulated the questions I would want to ask of Ian Canning, had I been Alan Hurst. What happened on Wednesday? What did mother talk to you about? Has she told you about Stella? About father? About Edward? What has she told you? What is all this about writing a book on Isobel?

And more questions. What are you going to do now that you've given up Lowndes Street? How long do you want to stay here? Do you like it? Are you comfortable in Edward's room? What were the circumstances under which mother put you into the room? Did she tell you about the time she thought she saw Edward's ghost? Did you believe it? Do you believe it now? Has she said anything about me, and how and why I wanted you here? And Rex? In spite of your warning the other day I haven't stopped him coming, have I?

But Alan asked me none of these questions. I could not help thinking of what his mother had said. Nothing outside his immediate prospect has the power to cause him a moment's anxiety.

Was all his thought then, upon his own plans, upon Assam, his own future, his own happiness? I did not believe it because I did not want to believe it. He had shown me nothing but generosity. He had respected my own silence; the least I could do was to respect his. That was the first lesson.

I came to believe he trusted me not to think badly of him, in spite of what I might hear.

Thurlow said, 'I'm glad you looked in.' I sat in the padded velvet chair. It was Monday. I had come to town with Alan. I was filling time until three o'clock when Alan expected to be free, having lunched, he hoped, with the 'Assam chap'.

Thurlow went on, 'I had your letter this morning.' It was on the desk in front of him. By his right hand was a large, red file. Written neatly in ink was the title 'F. J. Wheeler, Decd.' 'Correspondence from 1st January, 1946.' Each year's letters required a complete file. In the old days – the heyday as it were – of the Estate there had been two, even three, files every year. I felt there was something sad in the tapering off of Thurlow's duties as Executor; it implied a diminution of himself, and of the use to which the world put him.

'How long do you expect to be at this place—' he glanced at the letter, 'Aylward?'

'It depends on my host. He's likely to go to Assam.'

'Fortunate young man.'

I cleared my throat. 'He's suggested I might go too.'

Thurlow looked out of the window.

'What would you do?' he asked. 'Plant tea?'

'I imagine there's nothing else to do in Assam.'

He said, 'I was never a great tea drinker.' He smiled at me. He had expressed as much disapproval as he would ever allow himself. He went on, 'Is there anything particular on your mind?'

'No. I just looked in.'

'I like people to come and see me for no reason.'

'What about this chap Rossiter you mentioned?'

Thurlow frowned, thoughtfully. 'The divorce expert?'

'Yes.'

'He has pneumonia. But don't bother. He's as strong as an ox. You have to be for domestic litigation.'

As I rose I said to him, 'Have you heard from Helena, at all?'

He had my hand. I felt the pressure from his shoulder, his hint that I was not to prolong my leave-taking.

'No,' he said; but not abruptly. To one who did not know him it would have seemed as if his mind were already on other matters, but I could leave him believing that his tongue would still feel the 'No' upon it when next we met, and that we could continue our conversation, or not, as it suited us. It was, perhaps, the greatest gift he had to offer his profession.

Selby's chubby hands were made all for receiving. I had intended not to see him, but the call was too strong. I could not pass the street without pausing, nor the doorway without entering. When I faced Selby across his desk, I regretted it.

'I've had the oddest letter, Ian,' he began. 'I was going to call you about it.'

'Do you mean *my* letter?'

'Yours?'

'I wrote you on Saturday to let you know where I was,' I explained.

'I haven't seen it yet.'

'It must be in that pile.'

He began searching. 'Perhaps. Aren't you still in Lowndes Street?'

'Not any longer.'

'No, It's not here. Second post I expect.'

'I'm in Pelham Green.'

'Pelham Green?'

He took a cigarette. Closing the box, he remembered his manners and offered me one. 'Do you mean where Rex Coles lives?'

'I'm staying with Alan Hurst.'

'Lord, yes. The chap who called here.'

'That's right. You gave him my Lowndes Street address.'

'You didn't mind?' Selby began to fidget. 'The fact is I was damned worried about you when we last met. And this chap Hurst seemed an old friend of yours. I thought he might—'

'Cheer me up.'

'Yes.'

'He did.' I drew in smoke deeply. I weighed the next words. It amused me to say them. 'Actually he stopped me committing suicide, so you saved my life, so to speak.'

'I say. But good lord. Oh lord, Ian.' He looked at me in a new way. There was something perverted about Selby. I had become interesting to him physically: a construction of skin, bone, blood and muscle which might by now have been decomposing, instead of sitting in front of him, in his visitor's chair, smoking his cigarette, reacting to him as a living being. He made me feel I had cheated him: rather, that he had cheated himself.

'You were saying you'd had the oddest letter,' I reminded him. He looked about him, thoroughly put off his stroke. He found the letter 'It's from Rex Coles. You know who he is, of course.'

I nodded.

'You'd better read it,' he said, and handed it to me.

DEAR MR. SELBY,

During her lifetime my wife Isobel must have written many letters to your house, by way of business and – I think – letters of a more personal nature to your father. I understand that these could not be published without my consent as heir to her literary estate although of course the letters, in themselves, belong to those to whom they were addressed.

I wonder, however, whether you would be agreeable to my borrowing them? You may know that Mr. Ian Canning contemplates writing a biographical work concerning Isobel and her family and letters are likely to be of interest. If I could see them I could help Mr. Canning – e.g. filling in, so far as my memory serves, the particular circumstances in which some of them were written.

May I hear from you?

Yours sincerely,

REX COLES.

I gave it back to Selby and waited for him to speak. After a few moments he said petulantly, 'Rex Coles is really a bit too much of a good thing.'

'What are you going to reply?'

His eyes flickered, trying to hold steady in my direction. 'I'll have a word with father, I think.'

'About the letters of a more personal nature?'

'Well, yes. I can't think what they'd be.'

'About money I should think.'

'I expect so.' He looked away in order to ask the question he had intended. 'Are you really going to write about Isabella?'

'I'm not sure.' I paused. Selby invited you to dig at him slyly. 'Would the firm commission me, do you think?'

Selby blinked. 'Honestly, I hadn't thought. We'd have to talk about it.' Suddenly he grinned and I caught a glimpse of the Selby I had once liked. 'Whatever we do we'd have to do it and tell Barnstaple afterwards. Come and have a drink, it's nearly mid-day.'

The search for a taxi, the journey to the club (the same letters were still on the rack unclaimed), the ordering of drinks, the settling into a corner, all gave Selby time to think. He said, after his first sip, 'I don't *see* Isabella as a book, somehow.'

But I was as good at this as he.

'I agree.'

He looked at me, suspiciously.

I went on, 'Isabella isn't the point though.'

'Well, what is?'

'The background, the family, the times. Isabella linked the

Edwardian era to the twenties.' Selby nodded. 'Both good subjects,' he said.

'And her roots were late Victorian.'

'Yes.' Selby looked at me. 'I see what you're getting at.'

'I think you'll agree that our fathers and grandfathers aren't so funny now as they were in the thirties. They add up to something.'

'I agree. What you have in mind is a sort of essay in nostalgia.'

I frowned. Now was the time to give him the reins.

'To be honest, I'm not sure what I have in mind.'

'Well,' he said, 'it would be a portrait of a family with Isabella as the centre-piece. Her – her books reflecting the sort of background they all came from and – well yes – as much behind the times as the family was itself? Behind the times, but in them, of them. A sort of polite tragedy behind a façade of respectability.'

I said, 'Or polite respectability behind a façade of tragedy.'

'Well, yes.'

I added, 'But it's all pretty nebulous at the moment.'

'If you could unearth something adventurous that would be good. Isabella had no exotic lovers, I suppose?'

'Only Rex.'

Selby laughed. 'It's not a bad idea, Ian. Why not go into it more? If we could see more clearly what sort of a book it would make I think we could enter into some sort of arrangement.' He paused. 'What should I tell Rex Coles about the letters?'

'Well that's up to you.'

'I could say we'd make them available to you. You could go through them in the office.

'That would be better.'

Selby finished his drink. 'Coles is the most awful bore to have around.' He looked at me, covertly. 'He happened to see that letter you wrote about "Opal".'

Just before we parted – he had a lunch appointment – he said, 'Is everything all right now?'

'Yes, fine.'

'Shall I send you some more reading?'

'Yes, would you?'

He seemed inordinately pleased. I had helped him to do a good deed; but I never had another manuscript from him.

I went to a pub for a beer and a sandwich. I had enjoyed playing the literary game with Selby. Only now did I see how far I had allowed the idea to grow in peoples' minds that I seriously considered writing a book on Isabella. The book had begun to have a life of its own. It would only die if I lifted pen to paper.

I left the pub, angrily, out of patience with myself. I muttered under my breath, 'What bloody nonsense. Why should it only die because I lift pen to paper?'

The Selby influence was still strong. The ghosts here in London were those of personal failure. In these streets, where I had walked with Helena, such ghosts were hard to lay. I found myself nearing St. Paul's. I turned my back on it. Why should it only die, I asked myself again, because I lift pen to paper? It isn't a matter of dying. Something that hasn't lived can't die. The book hasn't lived. Only Isobel has lived, and Rex; Alan and Stella and Edward. The time, too, has been with us; now it is gone. Consider that. Consider them. Pass through the mirror of themselves that they show you as their portraits. Analyse them, know them, for all the world as though what they were and what they are is worthy of capturing, pinning to a page. The book won't die because you lift pen to paper. Neither will it live. Face that. Face it. Face too that what *you* were and, for the moment, are, is at an end; that you have come to the end of yourself; that there's no going back to come a different way to a new conclusion.

The new way could only start from now. The conclusion could not be seen.

Alan said, grinning, 'I've got the job, Ian.' It hadn't been necessary for him to say it in so many words. His face had told me, the moment I met him, as arranged, at Leicester Square Tube Station. Already, for so short a time committed as he was, he looked out of place in this underground cavern of artificial light, this metropolitan clearing house.

'Good for you, Alan.'

We went up to the street.

'I've got to get kitted up,' he said.

'Well, let's do that.'

We began walking up Charing Cross Road. 'I don't know,' he said suddenly, 'I can do that any time.' We stood for a moment undecided. He was smiling. I felt that nothing could diminish his sense of freedom. It reached me so strongly it might almost have been irresponsiblity.

'You're bit bad,' I joked.

'Bit bad?'

'When you've 'eard the East a-calling you won't never 'eed naught else.'

He nodded.

'Anyway,' he said, 'it'll sweat the weight off me.' But already he looked fined down; younger, his eyes clear and eager like those of a boy just slipping into a pre-destined, wholly desirable way of life.

'I tell you what,' he went on, 'we could call on Adela Coles.' He began walking towards Tottenham Court Road and I followed, unable to formulate in words the resistance I felt towards his plan. It *was* a plan. There was no hint of suggestion about it. Calling on Adela Coles was something he had decided to do. We went through Percy Street and Charlotte Street. Autumn, and sunlight filtering through the London atmosphere, had softened and flattened the perspective. It was a magic with which I was familiar but which would always touch me with its solid unreality, would always dissipate the urgency of the present, fire the clay of the distant past to a bright and burnished immortality.

He stopped on the pavement. 'Is this all right with you, Ian?'

'Of course.' It wasn't really. The flat would be like all the other flats in which, in past years, I had drunk and talked and fostered illusions: watched them grow stale. It seemed unlikely, too, that Alan should ever enter a flat in the London I knew so well and had come to dislike.

We were there. He rang the topmost of a perpendicular file of bellpushes, then, leaving me at the door, went down to the street and gazed up at the house as he had that night he came to see me in Lowndes Street. I heard a window open.

Alan raised a hand. 'Hello,' he called.

She said something in reply which I could not distinguish. 'Is it all right?' he called back. 'I've brought a friend along.'

I felt it was my cue and joined him on the pavement. At an open window was Adela. She disappeared for a moment before coming back to thrust an arm through the window. 'Catch,' she said, and threw down a key which Alan caught with one hand.

Opening the door we entered a bare hall and climbed uncarpeted stairs to the top floor. The door to Adela's flat was ajar. Alan put his head through

'Hello,' he called.

She answered from another room, 'Just coming.' We entered. It was a fair-sized room, used as a living-room; the walls creamwashed, hung with gilt-framed mirrors; the windows tall, curtained gracefully. The furniture was the expected jumble. There were some Kensington period pieces, a studio couch, two club arm-chairs with ripped leather; books all over the place. There was only one picture. This was above the fireplace. It was an original oil painting of Adela wearing a black evening dress with the wide shoulder straps of the mid-twenties. Round her neck was a long row of pearls reaching to her waist. Her hair was cropped. Behind her, the artist had sketched in a Japanese screen. The representation of the face was flat, unmoulded; a flatness repeated on the bosom. The arms were shown as skinny, quite unlike my memory of the photograph. It was only the eyes that seemed to have caught the imagination of the painter. They were deep and dark; a clever stroke of the brush gave them a fire. Having observed this it was possible to believe the rest of the picture had been flattened to heighten this effect. When you saw the woman herself you were confirmed in that belief, even although, in middle age, she had put on weight. She had witch's eyes.

She came in from what I presumed and later knew to be the bedroom. She stared at Alan. 'Good God! You look positively old.' They didn't kiss or even shake hands. She wore a blouse and skirt; sexless, businesslike attire. Her hair was fluffier than in the photograph, but it emphasized the masculinity of her face. It had been combed upward and outward and on closer inspection I saw that it was thinning. In colour it was fair, but streaked with grey. I guessed her to be in the middle forties. Her likeness to her father was marked.

'I bet I know who this is,' she said, looking at me. Her look was not friendly. Neither was it unfriendly. She had the sort of vitality which is only expressed in extremes of passion. For the normal purposes of living she must have moved amongst people as a casual spectator of their follies: never involved unless the spring she skilfully concealed were touched.

'You're Ian Canning,' she said.

'How did you know?' The familiar conversational gambits lay before me.

'Father told me you were at Aylward.'

Alan laughed. 'That's no reason why this should be Ian.'

She looked at him. 'Have you come to cadge a drink or will tea be enough?'

Alan jerked his head at her. 'Don't mind Adela,' he said. 'She only pretends she's tough.'

That appeared to appeal to her sense of humour. She grinned

at him and then at me. It seemed more likely, though, that she grinned at a thought of her own and not at Alan's humour.

'Sit down,' she said. 'But not on that chair. It's mine.'

The chair to which she claimed a proprietary right was the more badly ripped of the club-chairs.

'What do you think of my *pied-à-terre*?'

The question was asked of myself. Once, I would have thought of something clever to say in return but I said, only, 'Very nice.'

She hesitated, turned and looked at Alan. 'Is he really going to write a book about Isabella?'

I watched Alan closely. He caught my eye. He raised his head slightly in a glance of good-natured inquiry. That was all. Adela looked from him to me.

I asked, 'Where did you hear that?'

'From father of course. Is it true?'

'Do you think it'd be a good idea?' I countered.

'I think it's the bloodiest silliest thing I've ever heard in my life.' She held out a hand. 'Someone give me a cigarette.' Later, blowing out smoke, she said, 'Now I'll get some tea. You can have a drink afterwards.'

She brought tea on a tray, but we had to help ourselves: she did not join us.

'Why did you look like a cat with two tails when you arrived, Alan?'

'I'd just landed a job.'

'What sort of a job?'

'In Assam, planting tea.' He looked at her, for approbation I thought.

'Very suitable,' she said. 'But God, how dreary. Shall you wear shorts and a toupee?'

'Topee. I'm not ready for a toupee.'

'Hairy boys like you go bald early.'

She turned to me at once. 'What on earth do you see in Alan?'

'See in him?'

'You're the first friend of his I've met who looks remotely civilized.'

'Actually I suspect I'm less civilized than any of them. Besides—,' I added, 'you can't have seen any of Alan's friends for years.'

She nodded. 'That's true. But a leopard never changes his spots.'

'That makes people sound static. As if there isn't any hope for them.'

'But there isn't and they are. Static. Stagnant. Look at me.'

She lit a new cigarette from the stub of the previous one. She had plenty of cigarettes in a silver box, but she did not offer them, a close-fistedness inherited from her father, I imagined.

'Are you married?' she asked me.

'Not for some time now.'

'What does that mean?'

'We're separated.'

She leaned back in the leather chair, narrowing her eyes at me. 'Then you and Alan have more in common than I thought.' There was a silence, made uncomfortable for me because Alan did not break it, and I knew he guessed I had heard about Stella. 'When are you going to Assam?' she asked him.

'Next month,' he said.

'You'll miss Christmas.'

'Christmas at home, yes.'

'Your mother won't like that.'

'No.'

'What self-centred creatures men are,' she said.

'Coming from you, that's a joke, Adela,' he said. In her company he was almost a different man.

A bell rang, in the passage outside.

'See who it is, Alan, there's a good boy.'

'How? By poking my head out of your bedroom window?'

'How else?' She was enjoying a situation all the ramifications of which were hidden from me. When Alan came back he said, 'It's a fair-haired chap.'

'What name?'

'He wouldn't say. He glared though.'

'Throw him the key. It's on the dressing table.'

Alan went to do as he was bidden. When the visitor knocked at the door Adela shouted, 'Come in, Terry,' and Terry entered. 'This is Terry. Alan and Ian. Alan says you glared at him.'

A subtle change had come over her, its outward sign a distraction of hands and head in which, before, there had been assurance. Terry looked a decent young man; but very young, in his late teens. He was very ill at ease, and yet alert in a peculiarly aggressive way, his shoulders hunched, his arms held a little away from his body.

Adela made no attempt to explain him. He joined us, sitting down suddenly, ungraciously. He gave me no more than a casual look, keeping his eyes mostly on Adela, but looking sometimes and then more and more frequently at Alan, as if wondering where he had seen him before, until the movement became automatic; the slight turn of the head in Alan's direction whenever he thought he was not observed; its quick jerk away the moment Alan glanced across at him. I felt a bit sorry for him, he was obviously having a miserable time.

He had refused a cup of tea. He kept wiping the palms of his hands on his trouser legs, and although it was not warm in the room there were tiny points of sweat on his forehead. Adela kept up a flood of talk. I offered Terry a cigarette. I had expected his hand to be trembling, but it was not. It was a very capable hand. I tried to guess his occupation from it. Adela said to me, 'You shouldn't encourage him to smoke. He's in training.'

'Oh? What for?'

She said, 'He boxes. He's a frightful barbarian.'

I looked at him. He was scarlet with embarrassment.

'Box professionally?' I asked.

She replied for him, 'Good lord, no.'

I spoke directly to him. 'What do you do professionally?'

There was a pause. He was looking at Adela as if expecting her to answer in his stead. When she did not he took a swift look at me and said, 'Nothing. I'm waiting my call-up.'

'He wants to get into the Army and stay there.'

'As a career?' I asked.

'That's right,' he said, 'as a career.'

Again there was silence. At last Adela said, 'It's a dead end, Terry. A bloody dead end.' That drew a smile from him. 'That's right,' he said, 'a bloody dead end.' For the first time Alan spoke to him. He said, 'You sound in favour of a dead end.'

'Why not?' The answer came back sharply. It was startling in its way, coming from so young a man. Adela laughed. 'My dear Alan, you're a fine one to preach about a dead end. What else is Assam?' She looked at Terry. 'He's going out to Assam to plant tea.' Terry grinned.

'Christ,' he said.

The call at Adela's had been a failure. I think Alan half-expected her to send Terry away, but when it became clear she had no such intention Alan rose.

'Well, Adela?'

'Well, Alan?'

'We ought to be off.'

She got to her feet. 'Come again soon, both of you.'

She accompanied us to the door. She put a hand on my arm. 'If you're serious about this Isabella business, let me know.'

'Why?'

'I could help. Ring me anytime.'

I thanked her. She and Terry stood in the doorway watching us go down the stairs. When we arrived in the street Alan laughed.

'What's amused you?'

He said, 'That chap Terry.'

We walked towards Oxford Street. 'It's bloody mad, isn't it? You spend six years messing about in a war and come back to that.'

'To what?' I asked.

'To chaps like Terry. It sums the whole bloody thing up.'

'Because he saw a dead end as his *raison-d'être?*'

'Yes.'

Later he added, 'No, I'm being unfair. If we had another war tomorrow he'd make himself useful. It's mad, isn't it?' The pubs were open. We entered one; drank beer; talked of Magpyin.

'This is what's mad,' I said. 'That you and I can only talk about Magpyin. You'd think nothing else had happened.'

He looked away, restlessly.

'What's wrong, Alan?'

'Every bloody thing. Don't mind me.'

He had his eye on a woman who sat alone, with an evening paper. She took no notice of him.

'We're supposed to be celebrating.'

He smiled. 'Yes. I'd forgotten. Drink up.'

He went to the bar. Having given his order he swung round and stared at the woman openly. She looked up from her paper.

'Would you like a drink?' he asked her.

She did not reply, but turned slightly away, dismissing him. He caught my eye. He nodded his head, pulled down the corners of his mouth.

I took him to the club. There was nothing to drink except rum, but that reminded us of our Indian days. There was no escaping them.

I said, before I could think better of it, 'Tell me about Stella.'

'Stella?' he echoed. He did not dissemble. He said, 'I think I made a mess of the physical side of things.'

Nothing could have surprised me more. I said so. He frowned, not looking at me, now, but at his hand clutched round the glass. 'It's damned odd,' he said. 'She suddenly didn't want me near her.'

'Didn't she say why?'

'No.'

'Didn't you ask her to explain?'

'Oh – I think I said, "What's wrong?" You know. But beyond that there isn't anything to say, is there?' He looked at me straight, honestly.

'When did this happen?'

'Things were all right for the first six weeks or so, after I got home I mean. Then I found they weren't. That lasted about two weeks. Then she just said she was going and went.'

'Where?'

'To her brother. She doesn't answer letters, but she doesn't send 'em back, so I know she sees them. Anyway, I saw it was no use, so I packed up the flat.'

'Does she know you packed up the flat?'

'Yes.'

I paused. 'How long had you had the flat?'

'Stella took it while I was abroad.'

'And before then?'

'She was at Aylward. She had the upper floor as a sort of bedsitting room. She used it as a studio too.'

'Yes,' I said. 'You can still smell the paint.'

He nodded.

'Was she any good?' I asked.

'As an artist?'

'Yes.'

'She wasn't a professional. She did some quite decent pictures though.'

'Landscapes?'

'Portraits mostly. She could get a good likeness sometimes.'

It had been meant as a compliment, but it was damning. I said, 'Isn't there a chance she'd join you in Assam?'

'Why should she?' He drained his glass. I went to the bar and bought new drinks. When I came back he said, 'What about you, Ian?'

'What about me?'

'What are you going to do?'

'When you go to Assam?'

'Yes.'

'I hadn't really thought,' I replied. I waited, but his questions, What about you? What are you going to do? were as far as he would go. There was no direct invitation to join him in Assam, no invitation to continue my stay at Aylward; no order to go; and still no reference to the Isabella project. I saw that this reti-

cence, this undemanding self-control might, in certain circumstances, inflict a wound. I pictured the scene with Stella;
imagined her body taut, withheld from him in the darkness, each
of them divided from the other by a silence each longed to break,
until he said, diffidently, 'What's wrong? What's wrong, Stella?'
and I compared this picture with the scenes between Helena and
myself; those angry, impassioned exchanges when we stripped
the feelings from each other in the way dead stalks can be stripped
of seeds.

I pushed button A and said into the mouthpiece, 'Adela Coles?'
'Yes.'
'It's Ian Canning.'
'Hello to you. Are you still in town?'
'Yes. I wondered whether you'd like to meet me for a drink.'
'Meet *you*? Isn't Alan with you?'
'No.'
'Well, I'm alone too. Come up here.'
'Thank you. I'd like to.'
When I arrived at the flat she said, 'What's Alan doing?'
'He had business. I'm meeting him at Victoria at eleven.'
She grinned. 'Last trains go so damned early. Come and sit
down.'
We looked at each other, testing the edge of the other's per-
sonality. I meant to say, Tell me about Aylward. Tell me about
Alan, but – 'I wanted to talk about this Isabella business,' I said.
The strongest light was behind her head, although the other parts
of the room were studded with table lamps and wallbrackets. I
went on, 'You said it was the silliest notion you'd ever heard.'
'It is.' She could be extremely abrupt.
'I wondered why you thought so.'
'My dear man—'
'Ian.'
'My dear Ian. What in heaven's name did Isabella ever do to
deserve a biography? I've never heard such a ludicrous sugges-
tion in my whole life. She was the worst possible sort of literary
hack. She was colourless from the day she was born until the
day she died.'
'No hidden mysteries?'
'What would a woman like that have to hide?'
'Did you know her well?'
'There was nothing to know. Anyway, you're not serious about
it so why pretend.'

I said. 'This afternoon when we were going you said I should let you know if I were serious, and said if I were you'd help. I took that as an invitation to discuss her.'

'Oh, it was an invitation all right. I wanted to see you again. I want to hear all about Alan.'

'But – in regard to what?'

'How long you've known him. What sort of a soldier he was.'

'He got an M.C.'

'I know. I'd have been surprised if he hadn't.'

'You like him, don't you?' I said.

'Yes. Father told me his wife had left him.'

'So I gather.'

'But no one seems to know why.' She paused. 'Do you?'

'I've no idea.'

'Is there another man in her life?'

'I don't know. There may be.'

'Or did Alan go after another woman?'

'Not to my knowledge.'

She said, 'That's what he's up to now, isn't it? He's gone after a woman.'

'So I gathered.'

'And will meet you at Victoria at eleven?'

I nodded.

She laughed, then said, 'I wonder why Stella has left him?' She helped herself to a cigarette. I crossed to give her a light; I remained standing in front of the fireplace as she puffed smoke up into the air. She felt her lower lip and scratched at it with her finger nail to remove a shred of tobacco. 'When I knew Stella I thought her a very sexy little piece.'

'So?'

'Well. Alan's a sexy man, so it couldn't be that he couldn't cope.' She looked straight at me, then, and said, 'I know all about him. I was the first woman he ever had. He was eighteen and I was – well – older. I'm only interested in very young men. What did you think of Terry?'

I said, 'I was rather sorry for him.'

'Yes, He's a bit out of place isn't he? He dislikes me so much, but can't keep away. Alan never disliked me for seducing him. He thought it a hell of a lark, thoroughly enjoyed himself and didn't regret it for a moment. Not like some of the others.' She rose. 'I'll get us some coffee.'

When she came back she said, 'You read for Selby's don't you? No chance of getting me in there, I suppose.'

I said I doubted it, and asked her whether she had ever read for a publisher.

'Well – one does in this sort of life.'

'What sort of life?'

She waved a hand round the room. 'A finger here, a finger there – a hand if you're lucky. Advertising, publicity. I live on my nerves and literary wits. It's an absolutely bloody life as you probably know, but I wouldn't change it. I like the edges of things. I hate to be involved; I *loathe* being surrounded. This coffee is going to be vile.'

It wasn't vile, but it wasn't very good. She sat down, nursing her coffee cup in cupped hands. She went on, 'Freudian, I suppose. You know father and mother were divorced – I thought they were both the absolute bottom at the time. And I suppose my sex-life is a sublimation of a brother-fixation. Or can it be a fixation if you've never had a brother? Probably some word other than fixation. Not that it matters a damn to me. I enjoy what comes my way and ignore what doesn't. Of course, as I get older it gets more difficult. Before the war I could kid myself I was a woman of my times, emancipated, tough, self-reliant.'

'And now?' I asked.

'Oh, now. I'm still a woman of my times, but the time's past. It's as mouldy as that picture up there. Have you ever seen anything so utterly pitiful? Sometimes I look at it and scream with laughter.'

'Did you do anything during the war?'

'I suppose you mean something patriotic.'

'Yes.'

'I drove an ambulance for a time. Then I served in a mobile canteen. There didn't seem much point in it, though.'

'And it meant getting involved?'

'Yes, it meant that in a way. Or rather, I thought it would. I kept putting it off because I thought it would mean that, but when I started to do my little bit the only reaction I had was an odd one.'

She drank some coffee and then drew on her cigarette. 'And it was this reaction that made me think there wasn't any point in it.'

'What was the reaction?'

'Well – whatever I was doing, you know, like driving dead bodies and what have you through the streets, I always felt there were so many other dead bodies just round the corner that I couldn't actually afford the time to look after the ones I'd got. And then when I gave that up, and went into the mobile canteen, I could never stop myself thinking of all the other gangs of people who were probably standing around somewhere else hoping for a cup of tea to turn up. So I packed it in and felt I was really back in the war. How did Alan get his M.C.?'

I told her.

'What about you?' she said.

'My military career was chequered.' I told her why.

'Yes,' she said, nodding her head. 'People like Alan have God's own luck. That boy has always *completed* things? Do you see what I mean? All the rest of us come out ragged, we feel cheated too often. Promising start, confusing middle, and bloody awful finish.'

'How has Alan completed things?'

'By setting out to do them, and damn well doing them. Doing them well.'

'But his marriage?'

'Oh, I don't mean that sort of thing. You can't make a marriage on your own resources.'

'But give me an example,' I insisted.

'Well, his soldiering career's a good one, I suppose. But as a boy – it's frightfully difficult to provide examples. He always had an air of – assurance, reliability, complete independence. But you know him too. You ought to understand what I mean.'

'What some people might call ruthlessness? Not that?'

She was looking at me hard, with her witch's eyes. 'When have you caught him out being ruthless?'

'I didn't say I had. Have you?'

She said, 'As far as I'm concerned, Alan's the only real man I've ever known. He was a man at the age of eighteen and hasn't changed. If one of the manly attributes is ruthlessness, then Alan's got his fair measure. But why the hell people try to twist a perfectly straight-forward human characteristic into something sinister, defeats me. I suppose you've been talking to that mother of his.' She paused. 'I thought so.'

'You don't like her?' I asked.

'She's a spiteful, snobbish bitch. The whole family loathed her.'

'Did they? Including Alan?'

'Alan couldn't loathe anybody.'

'What about Edward?'

She smiled. 'Oh, you've heard about Edward.'

'Only that there *was* an Edward.'

'Yes, there was an Edward all right.' She lighted a cigarette from the stub of the other which was only half smoked. 'Edward was quite clever. I got some of his poems published in one of those war-time series.'

'You must have thought well of them.'

'I thought you were a professional? I didn't think of them one way or the other, except that they were publishable, and that it lined my own pocket to get as many books in the series as possible. You could sell anything during the war as you know. The authors didn't get any royalties, but I got an editorial fee.'

I considered this. 'Mrs. Hurst said you'd done so much for Edward's poetry.'

She stared in amazement. 'She said that?'

'Yes. Is it a surprise?'

'My dear Ian! Surprise! I never heard the last of it. She could have killed me!'

'What on earth do you mean?'

Adela said, 'She *hated* the poems! She insisted they should never have been published and that I had no right whatsoever to have them published without her permission. She said they made the family a laughing stock.'

'Good Lord. But she spoke so proudly of them.'

'Wonders will never cease. Drink I suppose.'

'Were they bad?'

'I'll send you a copy if I can find one. No, they weren't bad. Derivative of course. But some of the personal poems hurt her.'

'In what way?'

'She thought they were directed against her.'

'Were they?' I asked.

Adela shrugged. 'Who knows? Edward tended to surface obscurities, but another thing she hated about the collection was the fact that there were some poems to Stella.'

'Stella? Alan's wife?'

'Yes. Stella used to be Edward's girl. She chucked him over for Alan.'

I leaned back.

She said, 'You look as though you've solved a crossword puzzle.'

I smiled. 'No. But I like things to fit in.'

'How does Stella having been Edward's girl fit in?'

I said, 'It explains why Mrs. Hurst hates her. At least I imagine it does. She hates her for having thrown over her precious Edward and married that cruel boy Alan.'

Adela stared. 'Cruel? Is that what she calls him?'

'She thinks Alan sees my likeness to Edward and brought me back especially to hurt her.'

'*Your* likeness to Edward?'

Slowly she shook her head. 'You're not really like Edward at all,' she said. But for the rest of the evening I felt her scrutiny.

'Tell me about Stella?' I prompted.

'What do you want to know?'

I said, 'Well, what was she like to look at?'

'Dark,' she said. 'Dark like a little gypsy, but wonderful blue eyes. Full of bounce and fun. Just right for Alan, I'd have said.'

'When was she Edward's girl?'

'Just before the war.'

'And became Alan's?'

'Just after the war began,' she replied.

'And they were married before or after Edward's death?'

'After.'

I considered, then asked, 'Did Edward know he'd lost her?'

'Oh, I think so. Yes, of course he did, because he had leave at the time and didn't come home. And he wrote the poems to her.' She got up from her chair. 'I've got a few inches of very bad sherry in a bottle somewhere. We might as well finish it.'

As she moved about the room I said, 'Was the general impression the family had of Edward that he was a bit of a prig?'

'I wouldn't say that. Isobel adored him.'

'What did Alan think of him?'

'They didn't have much in common.'

'No,' I answered. 'But what did he think of him?'

'Well,' she said, returning with the sherry, 'I do know he was pretty cut up when Edward was killed.'

'Not remorse for treating him badly?' I said.

'Remorse? What for? Alan never harmed Edward. Unless you count Stella. You can't blame him for that though. Edward wouldn't have been any good to her. Poor Edward wasn't much use to anyone but himself, come to think of it.'

'To himself and his mother.'

'She's the one who should feel remorse. She smothered him. Oh no. Edward was a poor fish when you come to think of it.'

'You've heard the story of his ghost, I suppose?'

'Yes, father told me. The old woman's dotty.'

I drank the sherry. We sat silently for a while.

She said, 'Did father suggest this silly biography business to you?'

'No. Did you think he had?'

She grinned. 'Well, he said it was your idea – or rather *implied* it was without saying so.'

'Actually I've never even discussed it with him. It was Mrs. Hurst's idea. She thought I ought to do it because Edward had intended to.'

She put the glass of sherry down on the floor. 'No really – this is *absurd*. It was *she* who suggested it to Edward. I remember his sitting where you are, saying, "Mother wants me to write a book about Aunt Isobel," and I said it was absolute rot and he agreed. He said the only book he'd ever write about her would be a novel with her in it as a minor character.'

'You saw quite a lot of Edward?'

'Well, yes, when he was grown up, and working in town, and I kept him in touch with things that interested him and introduced him to a few people.'

'Didn't his mother object to his wandering into the Bohemian world of letters?'

'Don't be scratchy.' She laughed. 'No, actually she encouraged it. What you've got to understand about Marion Hurst is that she's a woman who thinks she's missed her vocation. She only married old George Hurst because his sister was a popular novelist – at least that's what they all used to say. The farcical part of it is that in those days you'd think Isabella was Virginia Woolf to hear Marion talk, not that she would have the slightest idea who Virginia Woolf was – but she was quite convinced the Hurst family was the last word in literary culture. That's partly why she hated my father so much, because he automatically became more important to others, as Isobel's husband, than she was as her sister-in-law.'

'She doesn't seem to have any illusions about Isabella's worth now.'

Adela grinned, and opened her hands in a gesture of pleasure at her own grasp of situations. 'No,' she said, 'but she has the lovely excuse that father ruined Isabella's genius. I've heard her say so myself.'

'So have I.' I added, 'But we were talking about Edward coming here. You say she encouraged it.'

'She did indeed. She thought I was ever such a gal in those days. My own flat. A woman of leisure and pleasure. Oh – according to Marion I had shoals of the most important people in London pouring in and out of the flat all day.' She paused. 'I suppose I thought so myself,' she said. The grin was still there;

and the flame in her eyes. But there wasn't much more than the husk of her ambitions left. She said, 'Edward used to come on Thursdays to my "at home". It was painful, at first, he was so shy. It was here he met Stella, by the way. Did you know she painted?'

I told her I did.

'She wasn't any good as a painter – but the men liked her. At least, they did if they were normal. She had a sort of guilty looking innocence.'

'Was she ever in love with Edward?'

'Oh, yes. That's what made it so difficult for her. She was in love with Edward until she saw Alan.'

'And when was that?'

Adela reached for another cigarette.

'When Alan was eighteen his mother decided he ought to come out and get some culture.'

'So he came here?'

'That's it. Edward brought him. He loathed it.'

'And Stella and he—?' I began.

She cut in, 'Stella didn't get a chance, my dear chap. I came first.' She looked at me. 'I was quite pretty once, you know. Don't just go by that awful picture.'

'I don't. I've seen your photograph.'

She blew out smoke. 'Which one?'

'The one with you and Alan.'

'Not in swimming trunks?'

'That one.'

She drew on her cigarette again. 'Where on earth did you see that?'

'It's in the family album at Aylward.'

'Good lord.' She flicked the ash off the end of her cigarette. Her movements had become jerky. As if suddenly conscious of this she deliberately relaxed, leaned back in her chair.

'Where was it taken, by the way?' I asked.

She looked down, brushing her skirt with her free hand. 'A friend lent me a place in the country some week-ends.'

'The friend took the photograph?'

'That's right.'

I waited, because I guessed she had more to say. Eventually it came. 'I've always found it a bit obscene, Ian. Marion Hurst knew perfectly well what Alan and I were up to. And it wasn't just a question of countenancing it.'

Again I waited, but she had said as much as she intended.

She smiled at me. 'Do you find it shocking about Alan and me?'

'Why should I?'

'There was such a difference in our ages.'

'That was your business. Yours and Alan's.'

'Yes. It was, wasn't it? But what about Terry? That's worse than ever, isn't it?'

'Not unless you want it to be. Do you want me to feel shocked?'

'I don't care whether you are or not. Anyway – I expect Terry will be the last.' She grinned. 'My last fling. It's all going – that part of my life. I said I liked being on the edge of things, but that's all there's left to be on. Why do women hate growing old and men not care?'

'Oh, we care.'

'No you don't. You know you'll be wiser and more capable in your forties and fifties than you are now, and comfortably smug in your sixties. But not us. Being a woman's like watching a procession, but from what I know of men they all think they lead it.'

She looked at her watch. I had forgotten the time. 'If you're meeting Alan at eleven you'd better be moving.' I rose. 'Shall you tell him you've been with me?'

I looked at her, wondering whether she could possibly mean he might be jealous.

'Yes, why not?' I said. 'After all, if I'm going to write a biography of Isabella I've got to do my research.'

'But you're not going to write a biography of Isabella.'

She put out her hand and I took it. '*Are* you?' she said.

'No. I suppose I'm not.'

She came to the door with me and opened it. She looked at me appraisingly. 'You're only like Edward in two ways,' she said.

'And those?'

'The vaguest facial resemblance, for one.'

'And the other?'

'You have Edward's hands.'

I looked at them.

She said after a while, 'What are you thinking?'

I said, 'Whether Alan would notice such things.'

'And bring you home like a sort of Player King to frighten his mother? What rot.'

'Yes of course,' I said. It was rot. It had to be rot.

She nodded.

'Thank you for having me.'

'Any time,' she said.

When I was half-way down the first flight of stairs she called out, 'Ian!'

I halted, and waited for her to come to the banister rail. 'Why don't you ask Alan straight out?' she said.

'Ask him what?'

'Whether he thought you looked like Edward? It's quite a fascinating psychological idea.' Her interest was coldly clinical.

I said, 'Marion Hurst is a more interesting psychological specimen, I'd have thought.'

'Well, it's your case, not mine.'

I hesitated. 'Case?' I asked.

'Yes, case. That's what you're doing, isn't it? Dissecting us and laying us out on slabs. Come and see me again and tell me about yourself.' Adela grinned. 'That's what I'm interested in.'

I had to hurry to get to Victoria by eleven. It wasn't until I reached there and took up my position at the place Alan and I had chosen as a rendezvous that I consciously repeated to myself what Adela had said: 'Yes, case. That's what you're doing isn't it? Dissecting us and laying us out on slabs.'

There were others on the station, waiting as I was. Waiting puckers faces with anxiety. We must all have looked much the same.

It returned, just then, warm, penetrating; melting the ice which had formed, layer upon layer, year after year. It returned as though the image Adela's interpretation of my cross-examination had conjured was of so terrible a place – a limitless frozen plain – that you could not face it, turned your back upon it and as a reward felt the sun shine upon and colour the cheek, enter the skin, permeate flesh, invade the heart.

It had nothing to do with joy in life, or wonder at it. That would come later. It was something compounded of the air surrounding myself and those who stood close by. It came in like a warmed current and stirred the frigid roots of that desire which we express in pity.

CHAPTER TWO

WHEN Alan told his mother that he was going to Assam, she wept; but then, the tears ended, she raved, shrieked abuse at him, followed him from room to room, until, cornered, he stood undefended against the storm of her hysterical anger.

'What's to become of me?' I heard her cry and then – from another part of the flat – 'You don't care! You've never cared! You care for nothing and nobody but yourself. Go to Assam then! Go! Go! Go! Rex'll look after me. I don't need you. Go! Go!'

And then, moaning, she went to her room and locked herself in.

I did not know what to do. When he found me in Edward's room his face was still suffused, hot and shining with the effort of curbing his temper. He managed a smile.

'Sorry about that,' he said.

I asked whether there was anything I could do.

'Yes,' he said, 'come out to the George and get stinking.'

'Will she be all right, though?' I asked.

'You mean my mother?'

'Yes.'

He said, 'Let me worry about that.'

As I began to follow him out I rebelled. 'Look Alan,' I said, 'I'd better start packing.'

He stopped. 'Whatever for?'

'I think my being here upsets her,' I said.

'Don't be bloody silly. It's I who've upset her, not you.'

I said, 'I think it would be better if I went. She's got it into her head I look like Edward.'

A curious expression moved over his face, and was gone: like a swift cloud which momentarily darkens the place in which you are, chills it, and quickens your sense of environment.

'But she was drunk,' he said.

For a second or two I did not understand, but then I realized he referred to the incident on the landing, the night of my arrival. The echo of Mrs. Hurst's drunken voice came back. *'I thought it was Edward. He looked so like Edward.'* 'No,' I said. 'I don't mean that. The day you were out she said a lot of things about my being like Edward, and she wasn't drunk then.' As I said the word *drunk* I became conscious that the relationship between myself and Alan was shifting. The word *drunk* was a password. Speaking it, we entered a different phase of understanding.

'What did she say exactly?' he asked.

'Well – that physically we were alike. I can't remember everything she said, but I certainly got the impression she thought we had a lot in common.'

'You and Edward?'

'Yes.'

'I'm sorry, Ian. I didn't know she'd made you feel uncomfortable about being here.'

'She wasn't trying to make me feel uncomfortable. It's just that if she thinks I look like Edward my being here must upset her.'

He was looking at me, quite openly and frankly.

'I'm sorry,' he said.

'It isn't your fault,' I replied. 'Nobody's fault. But it makes it awkward for everyone.'

The corners of his lips went up, sketching a smile. He said, 'She's still got old Edward on the brain, you know. She thought she saw his ghost once. Did she tell you?'

'Yes. Waiting for her at the top of the stairs.'

He grinned. 'It's bloody silly.'

'Why?'

'Edward was scared of ghosts. He'd never dare be one himself. Come on, Ian. We both need a drink.'

'Do you mind if I don't? I've rather overdone the drinking recently.'

He said, 'What are you going to do, then?'

'One or two things. I might join you later. You said the George.'

'Yes. The George.'

'Well—' I began.

He raised a hand in farewell. When he had gone I returned to Edward's room.

'That's that,' I said, aloud. I understood in myself what I meant, but I could not have explained it, then, in words. The Alan of Magpyin had gone, even the Alan of Lowndes Street. The Alan I had sent off alone to the George was an amalgam of what I believed him to be, and what others believed him to be. The light of each former virtue was being darkened by my growing knowledge of his world. It seemed necessary to go, before the light had gone forever, and with it the image of a man in whom I had implicit faith.

'What are you doing?'

I swung round and she was there, holding on to the door handle with both hands. The morning sun deadened the colour of her dyed hair and etched the wrinkles and lines of her face cruelly. She was old, ugly and pitiful, her body an inadequate support for the mind's vitality. The stringy, scrawny throat was like a clutch of nerves connecting head to trunk.

'You're not going away?'

I looked down, and found that almost unconsciously I had begun to pack.

'I'm sorry, Mrs. Hurst. I thought perhaps I should.'

She lifted her hands from the door knob and, still clasped one over the other, carried them jerkily to her middle. She went out of the room and after a moment I followed her. Every step she took was an expression of her physical uncertainty. At the door of the drawing-room she rested momentarily against the jamb then moved into the passage. She opened the green-baize door by leaning forward against it. I thought she would fall. I went to her hastily, but I could do nothing for her other than put a hand reassuringly on her shoulder. I could not take her arm for she used them both to propel herself along the wall to the half-open door of her bedroom.

I stopped on the threshold, believing I should be unwelcome there, but she twisted round towards me feeling with one hand for the handle of the door, and flung it wide open, at the same time crying out, 'There! There it is! This is how he's going to leave me! This is where he's going to let me die!'

It was the most terrible room I had ever seen in my life. Terrible, because everything in it endorsed her humiliation, bore witness to her degradation. It was in wild disorder, a chaos of ill-assorted furniture crammed into every corner, the bed enormous, unmade, with the sheets and blankets tumbled over the floor. The windows were large, admitting a bleak north light which exposed the undusted surfaces, the greying over of the once white ceiling. Nothing lent it colour. It lacked even ugliness. It lay beneath the oppressive weight of light, unreflecting, cold, dead.

She was sitting on the edge of the bed, her head buried in her hands, but not a sound came from her. On the table by the bed-side was a row of empty gin bottles and a carafe of stale water, the air in it trapped in motionless bubbles.

I said, 'Is there anything I can do?'

She shook her head.

As I got to the door I felt her move. I looked round.

'There's one thing you could do,' she said.

'Yes. Anything.'

'Would you go down and ask Mrs. Voremberg to come up?'

'Mrs. Voremberg? I thought—'

'There's no one else I can turn to.'

'But if it's anything I can do—'

'I thought you were going.'

I said. 'I shan't go until Alan comes back.'

'Why are you going, Mr. Canning?'

'Well – it was only a visit.'

'Can't you stay on, at least until Alan goes to Assam?'

'But that's nearly a month.'

She looked down at her clasped hands. 'Yes. Well – if you'd ask Mrs. Voremberg.'

There was a long silence.

I said, 'What is it you want?'

She shifted her position. I looked at the empty bottles, trying not to let her see that I did so.

'Do you want me to ring Rex Coles?' I asked.

'He's in town today. He won't be back until tonight.'

Again we waited in silence. At last I managed to say, 'Shouldn't you wait until then?'

She looked away. She rubbed her left arm, slowly, pressing hard up and down. She said, 'He may not come.'

'He always comes.'

'Alan may stop him. He's afraid of Alan.'

'He'll come,' I said.

Her head came up, a skull with dry, stretched skin and a tangle of still growing hair starting up from the scalp.

'He'll come,' I repeated.

'Pray God he will.' It was a cry. I carried it with me all day.

He came that evening, as I had promised her. I opened the door to him, for Alan had gone to his room for a few moments.

'Hello, old man.' He looked at me almost humbly, his head lowered to one side, his hands kept in the pockets of the big overcoat. 'I hear you called on Adela yesterday.' He stood in the passage looking round as though this were the first visit he had ever paid.

'Yes, Alan took me round,' I said. 'Mrs. Hurst is expecting you.'

'Thanks, old man.'

He began to walk towards the green-baize door, but just short of it he hesitated.

'Is Alan out, old man?'

'No. He's in his room.'

He nodded. He pushed the door open cautiously and disappeared.

Alan joined me a few minutes later.

'Was that Rex?' he asked.

'Yes. He's gone in to your mother.'

He was filling his pipe, standing with his back to the fireplace. As he carried the filled pipe to his mouth, and put the pouch away, he looked down at me, removed the pipe and said, 'What've you decided about going?'

'Oh, I ought to go in a day or two.'

He turned to the fire, bent down to light a spill of paper. When his pipe was going he said, 'Mother told me this evening you'd probably changed your mind. I gathered you'd be staying on until I went to Assam.'

'She asked me to, but I think that's too long, don't you?'

'As far as I'm concerned I'd be grateful for the company.'

'Do you mean that?'

He said, 'Of course I mean it. But—'

'But what?'

'Well. I don't want you to feel embarrassed or under an obligation to anyone.'

'What sort of obligation?'

'Any sort of obligation.'

'To whom?'

He took the pipe out of his mouth again. 'To mother.' He grinned, a bit sheepishly. 'She has a way of imposing on people. From what she said this evening I got the impression she'd come to rely on your company.'

'In what way?'

'Over this drinking business, mainly. Have you promised to help her?'

'Promised to help? No, I haven't.'

'She seemed to think you had. Are you sure?'

'Of course I'm sure.'

'Well – *you* must know,' he said. 'She probably misunderstood.'

'What did she say?'

'Well – it doesn't matter.'

'But of course it matters. If she thinks I've promised something, I ought to know. If there's a misunderstanding it ought to be put right. You can't let a thing go like that.'

'Sometimes it's best,' he said. He was looking into the fire.

'Why?'

'She's easily upset,' he said.

I hesitated. 'I know. That's what I meant this morning.'

'This morning?' He looked at me, puzzled.

'When I said she found my likeness to Edward upsetting,' I explained.

'Oh, that. Take no notice of that.'

'Do *you* think I'm like Edward?' I asked him.

He replied without any hesitation, as though he had waited for the question, 'I suppose you are a bit. But it never struck me until mother said so that night.' He puffed at his pipe for a few moments. 'Look, Ian. Don't stay here on my account. All in all this hasn't worked out as I thought. I hoped you'd be able to sit back and take things easy. I didn't know mother would be like this.'

I suppose he saw the doubt I could not help but feel.

He said, 'The drinking, I mean. I thought she'd given it up. In fact, I know she'd given it up.'

It was in my mind to say, 'What made her begin again?' But then I realized why. She resumed drinking when she knew that Stella had left him, knew that he would be returning home, to Aylward.

Rex, coming into the drawing-room, accepted Alan's offer of a drink, but when he had finished it he stood uneasily as if gathering his courage to say something. At last he put his hand into his overcoat pocket and drew out a package similar to that I had seen him with the first time. It was a wrapped half-bottle of gin. He held it out towards me. 'Marion's asked me to give you this, old man.'

'Has she?' I asked. 'But why?'

He looked from myself to Alan and back to me. 'She just said give it to Mr. Canning because he's in charge here.'

We stood grouped in the centre of the room.

'It's a great tragedy, old man.' He was still holding out the bottle. Eventually he put it on the table. 'We thought she was cured once, too.' He shot a glance at Alan, and felt in his pockets for a cigarette. He found none, and neither of us offered him one. His empty hands hung forlornly at his sides. 'She wants to be cured, that's the devil of it. That's what makes it so pathetic, old man. It's not as though she enjoys it. Every glass is like a stab in her own back if you see what I mean.'

I said, 'What was your plan exactly?'

Rex passed a hand over his mouth, and looked sideways at Alan. 'She asked me to ration her, you see. Half a bottle at a time. The devil of it is, she can't stop herself drinking it all in one go.'

I nodded. 'How long has it been going on this time? I mean, since you thought you'd cured her?'

'Not long, old man.'

'Several months?'

'Only – what would it be, Alan – about ten days or so?'

'I don't know, Uncle. You've attended to all the details.'

'Someone has to, old man.'

In a low voice, to neither of us directly, Alan said, 'She could stop if she wanted to.'

'Or if it wasn't made easy for her?' I suggested, warily, feeling my way round the edges of their mutual antagonism. Alan looked at me almost gratefully, but Rex said, 'Easy for her? How can you say that, old man? You've seen what she goes through. What about this morning? She was desperate, wasn't she?'

I said, 'In a way,' because that seemed to be the truth.

'Exactly, old man. She said you were very kind, and promised to help.'

'All I promised was that you'd come tonight.'

'Promised I'd come? That was dangerous, Canning. I might not have.'

I said, 'I was trying to help her not to give in.'

Rex smiled. 'Well there you are. That's what she means.' He picked up the bottle and offered it to me again. 'Frankly it'd be easier for me if someone here took over the responsibility.'

Suddenly I thought I might break her of it; and that would give my stay at Aylward purpose.

I turned to Alan and said, 'I'll assume responsibility if you approve.'

He said, quietly, 'You don't have to do it, Ian, unless you want to.' He turned back to the fireplace, divorcing himself from whatever arrangements were made. Thinking he did so that I myself might feel freer to choose, I said to Rex, 'All right, I'll do it,' and took the bottle.

It was only when I had it in my hand, and saw the expression on Alan's face, that I realized the choice I had made disturbed him. There was no going back on it, though; and no escape from the knowledge that, as Edward had always done, I had pushed him into the background.

CHAPTER THREE

STELLA. This is her chapter. Dark like a little gypsy, full of bounce and fun: Adela had said. But I see her quite differently.

I see her as I did that first time, only the top of her dark head visible, and then her white, pinched face as she turned at the half-landing and climbed the few steps of Louisa's stairs, a few paces ahead of Alan as though she would appear bold and unafraid, independent of his arm. I see her with her eyes closed in idleness, her small, scarlet painted lips softer, fuller, than when first she came back to Alan. But mainly I see her as I did one day, towards the end of my stay at Aylward, her eyes open, gazing straight at me, their blueness reflecting the greyness of Helena's eyes, so that it seemed they were one: and I understood.

She came to Aylward in October. Already the first of the bitter winds that swept Europe for so many months that winter of nineteen forty-six and forty-seven blew over Pelham Common. It had been a week of hard frost. The rooms at Aylward were cold. I shivered to think of Mrs. Hurst's bedroom in such weather.

But even before Stella came home, before I knew she had come again into Alan's life, I felt her presence. She was an unheard sound, an unseen form, a sense of uncertainty, which curiously entered my head and left me suspended between the day's calm, ordered reality and its potential explosiveness. She was there in Alan's face the morning he opened her brother's letter, and in the space between the sheet of notepaper and his eye travelling it; there in the excuse he made to leave the table; in the carefully closed door as he went to the passage to phone; in the long delay between the end of his muffled conversation and the assumed indifference of his return, his voice when he said, 'I'm going to town. Would you like to travel up?'

'Something to do with the job?' I asked.

'No. Just something personal.'

I didn't go with him. It was the day after Rex had handed me the bottle of gin. I had slept badly. When he was ready to leave he went into his mother's room, but stayed only briefly. 'I'll be back after tea,' he told me. But he was not. I heard him come in, after midnight, believed him disappointed that I was not up and about, ready and willing to talk and have a nightcap. I was too exhausted. The day, alone, with his mother, had not been easy.

She had entered the drawing-room at midday, and for a split second I hadn't recognized her because of the way she had set her hair and dressed herself. She had made a gallant attempt to look smart and well turned-out. At times such as this she could express a gaiety that was difficult to share, and so more difficult to disregard. The result was akin to a charade and after a time you found yourself waiting for it to end with a cry of mock dismay that someone had guessed the word.

And the word, although I did not know it, was Stella.

There was no difficulty over lunch, for Mrs. Burrowes was 'in'. I did not have a drink or offer one to Alan's mother. When lunch was over and washed up and Mrs. Burrowes had hunched herself against the cold, and disappeared over the common for the day, we sat at ease in front of the fire.

'And what did you think of Adela?' she asked, out of the blue.

'I liked her,' I said.

'Did you discuss Isabella?'

'Well, no. She talked about herself mostly.'

Mrs. Hurst smiled. 'She set her cap at both my boys, you know.'

'Did you approve?'

'Approve? You misunderstand. I didn't mean she set her cap seriously. So approval didn't come into it in that sense. She thought Alan handsome and Edward clever and found them useful to her at her parties. Poor Adela.'

'You feel she needs sympathy?'

'She would have made someone an excellent wife.'

But I was not in the mood for this. 'Laying us out on slabs', Adela called it. I got up and stood by the fireplace and began to say 'Look—'

She had one elbow resting on her knee and now brought up the palm of her hand and rested her cheek on it. Her other arm hung loosely in her lap.

'Look,' I repeated, 'I want to talk about this drinking business. Rex says you've put me in charge.'

She continued to look into the fire, and the attitude of her arms, the way she held her head, added up to a sort of distracted misery which put her beyond mere sympathy and excited compassion: compassion, because overwhelmingly I understood her utter loneliness. That it might be the result of her own short-comings, her own simple inability to deal straightforwardly and honestly, I took into account; but that only made her isolation seem insupportable.

'You've got to tell me what you want me to do,' I insisted. She shook her head. 'Unless you tell me what I'm to do, how can I help?'

In the end, because I could not make her discuss it in any way, I went out of the room. I went to my bedroom. I found I accused myself of treating her – not cruelly – but without tact, even without good manners. Not only was this a self-accusation. It came in, as if from her, through the closed door, linking me to the image of her immobile on the chair by the fire; but when I re-entered the drawing-room she had gone. I went back into the bedroom and took the bottle of gin from its hiding place. I was pushing open the green-baize door before I remembered a previous intention, half-formed during the night. I went to the kitchen. At the bottom of the larder was a number of empty bottles. I chose the cleanest, rinsed it out under the tap, then poured half the contents of the gin bottle into it. I took the gin bottle back to my bedroom. The other bottle, holding the quota I had chosen, I took to her room.

She did not reply to my knock, but I opened the door and surprised her in the act of walking over from the dressing-table. Her hair had lost its smart, well-groomed look. She stood in the middle of the room and I thought she looked afraid of me. I put the bottle on the bedside table.

'There,' I said. 'I've poured half in here.'

She stared at the bottle, then at me, the lines of her face set in defiance; but her eyes lost and hopeless.

'Take it away,' she said. 'Take it away. I don't want it.'

Surprised, I hesitated, then I picked up the bottle, angry with myself for failing right at the start. 'Very well.' As I opened the door I said, 'I'm taking it back to my room. Please ask for it when you must. I'm willing to be of help, you know.'

She sat on the bed, looking at nothing in particular. 'Yes,' she said, 'but no one can help now.'

An hour later I heard the splintering of glass. I went to her room and opened the door without knocking. She was standing by the bed, holding a tumbler in a hand wound round with a piece of linen – a pillow-slip. She had shattered the rim of the glass so that the edge was jagged. She held this above her up-turned left hand.

Had she really meant to cut her wrists, and so – die? It was difficult to ignore the theatricality surrounding the act so far as she had taken it. In the first place, it seemed nonsensical to have protected her hand by the pillow-slip, and, in the second, I somehow got the impression that she had deliberately held the position in which I found her. Yet when I spoke to her she already seemed remote from me, as though the actual cutting of the vein were but a formality overlooked, something to which she would come back rather than go forward. I took her arm and removed the tumbler from her grasp. I picked up pieces of glass from the carpet, then I unwound the pillow-slip from her hand, half-expecting to find a cut.

'What were you doing?' I said at last.

She shook her head. She was very pale. I made her lie down on the bed; then I went to my room and brought back the bottle of gin.

'You ought to have brandy,' I said, 'but this is better than nothing.'

She had her eyes covered by the back of one hand; the other arm, supported to the elbow by the bed, stuck out with the palm of the hand uppermost. Gently I pressed her fingers round the glass.

'Please go,' she said.

'Yes. But I'm coming back in ten minutes,' I replied.

When I returned she had finished the drink, and I could see from the amount of spirit in the bottle that she had taken no more. She had put the drained glass back on the table, but her position on the bed was exactly the same, and you would not have thought she had moved.

I sat on the edge of the bed.

'Why did you say no one could be of help now?' I asked.

'Because it's true.' Her eyes were still covered by her hand.

'If you would tell me exactly what's wrong, mightn't *I* be of help?'

She shook her head.

'Then,' I said, 'it would be better if I left Aylward, wouldn't it?'

Each of her hands curled into a fist.

I said, 'But I feel you want me to stay.'

Then both hands closed over her face and she turned into the pillow and cried out into it so that the sound was muffled. 'I'm so ashamed. Please go. Please go.'

I waited for a few moments before saying, 'If I could have helped over the drinking business I'd have been glad to stay, until Alan goes to Assam.'

'Then you might have to stay forever.'

Mumbled into the pillow as the words were I was not sure whether I had heard correctly. I asked her what she had said. She moved her head into the open but kept her eyes closed.

'I said you might have to stay forever, Mr. Canning. I don't think Alan will be going to Assam.'

'Why?'

'He had a letter this morning.'

'But that wasn't about business. He said so.'

She opened her eyes, but gazed straight above her at the ceiling. 'No. It wasn't about business. The letter was from Stella's brother.'

'Oh?' I considered this. 'What about?' I asked.

'I don't know. All he would say was that he'd had a letter from Stella's brother and was going to town to see him.'

'Then, if that's all, why should you think he won't be going to Assam?'

'Because I know Stella wants him back.'

'You know?'

'I feel it.'

'It may not be so.'

'It will be so.'

I said, 'Then perhaps I may stay until Alan leaves to set up with his wife again.'

'Leave? Where for? They haven't anywhere to live now. They've only got Aylward. He'll bring her back here.'

'Well, at least you'll not be left alone. That's what you were afraid of, wasn't it?'

'I'd rather be shut alone in Aylward for a hundred years than live one day under the same roof as Stella.'

She sat up so that I had to rise. Without looking at me she reached for the bottle and poured several fingers of gin. Without adding water, she began to drink.

I said, 'Does Alan know how you feel?'

'Of course he knows.'

'Does Stella?'

'Need you ask that?'

I said, 'Then I hardly imagine they'd suggest coming here. In any case, you may be quite wrong. There are countless reasons why Stella's brother should want to see Alan. Don't cross bridges before you come to them.' I paused. 'And shouldn't you water that drink down?'

'There isn't any water.'

'There's some in the carafe.'

'It's stale.'

'Then I'll get some more.'

I took the carafe to the kitchen, filled it from the tap and returned to the bedroom. She had poured herself another drink. Gently, I took the glass and added some water.

'You're being very impertinent, Mr. Canning.'

'You told Rex I was in charge.'

'Well?'

'Then, if you'll forgive me, I'm damn' well in charge.'

'What business is it of yours?'

'You've made it my business.'

Slowly she looked up.

'Why do you bother with me?' she asked.

I said, 'I haven't anyone else to bother with, and drinking is a miserable business for everybody. For you most of all.'

'You have no need to pity me.'

'You'd be insulted if I did.'

After a while she said, 'You're not really like poor Edward. You're only like I imagine he would have been if he'd lived.'

'Do you mean physically or temperamentally?'

'Temperamentally. You can't get away from the physical likeness. But in temperament you're – I can't think of the right simile – but you're the sort of man I think Edward would like to have become. As it was, he had so much further to go, so much more to go through.'

She rose, and then, after a brief hesitation, emptied the glass of gin into the water carafe. Without looking at me she said, 'We start from now, Mr Canning. I'm in your charge from now.'

That evening we sat in not uncompanionable silence, waiting for Alan's return, but not speaking of it. Just before she went to bed she turned to me, in the kitchen where we were making cocoa, and said, 'Will you set my mind at rest, Mr. Canning?'

'If I can.'

'One of the worst things about being old is the growing consciousness of your dependence on others. People like myself can only make plans within the framework of other people's lives, we shrink from discussing those plans because we can't do so without – making those people conscious of being imposed upon.'

'What plan is it you want to discuss?'

'It's not really a plan. It's this question of your visit. I wondered whether you could promise to do your best to stay here for as long as I need you.'

'Do my best?'

'I can't ask you to stay longer than you feel is sensible. You have yourself to think of first. Besides—' she put a hand on my arm, 'you're Alan's friend. I must respect that. I want to respect it. I do try to love Alan as I should. I know that often I've been bitterly unjust to him. The terrible thing is that I know I'll be unjust again, no matter how hard I try.'

I said, 'But when have you been unjust?'

'Over his father's death, chiefly.'

She turned away and busied herself with the laying up of her cocoa-tray, and a tray for me to take back to the drawing-room.

'How were you unjust over that?'

'I blamed him for it. I've tried and tried to tell myself that it couldn't have been his fault. God knows he was as stricken as any of us. But nothing I say or think or do removes that dreadful idea that he could have saved his father if he hadn't thought of his own skin first.'

'You said it was a bus accident, I think. How did it happen?'

'Very simply. They took a chance crossing the road. Alan stepped back in time. He says he tried to pull his father back and I know he must have done. But how did he fail? Oh, if it had been Edward, poor dreaming Edward, that would have been so clear. But Alan! No, don't let me talk about it. It's such a frightful, unjust thing to think. You can help me over Alan, you know.'

'Can I? How?'

'You're his friend. He thinks very highly of you. I like to think that his being on good terms with you is a sort of compensation for him.'

'Compensation?'

'He must regret the fact that he and Edward never hit it off. It helps me if I think that if Edward had lived Alan and he would have been on the same good terms as you and Alan.'

I think she sensed that I found the idea distasteful. She said, 'Do forgive me. I don't express myself well. And that sort of thing is better left unsaid. But it exists for me. I tell you because I want you to help me get on with Alan. If he's going to Assam it might be my last chance. If he stays here and brings Stella back, I must *try* to be fair.'

I smiled. 'But how can I help you get on with Alan?'

'By telling me when I'm being unfair or unjust. I know I shall be.' She hesitated. 'When I heard from him that Stella had left him and he was coming back here I was ridiculously pleased. I thought – this is my chance to show him I do try to understand him and show him some affection. Then I knew things would be the same as ever. That's why I started drinking again. I'd given it up, you know. I'd cured myself.'

I said, 'Why did you start in the first place?'

She paused. 'No. I'd rather not say.'

'Why?'

'It concerns Alan and Stella.'

I thought: she means Edward's death: Alan's and Stella's defection in getting married. I said, 'I know about Stella and Edward.'

A most extraordinary change came over her. Her face, which had been relaxed, stiffened, and a pinched, suspicious look came into it.

'What do you know about Stella and Edward?'

'Know is the wrong word. I'm sorry. I *heard* that she was Edward's girl before she was Alan's.'

'Heard? From whom?'

'Adela Coles.'

'It isn't true! It's a most damnable lie. Edward was never such a fool.'

'But Adela seemed so sure.'

'Adela Coles is the biggest liar on God's earth. A bigger liar even than her father. She tries to make out Edward loved Stella because she tried to *get* them together. And Stella was no better. She was determined to get one of them and Alan was the fool who fell for it. Not Edward.'

I said, 'Well, you would know better than Adela, I suppose.'

'Of course I'd know better. I knew every thought of Edward's. Every hope. Every plan. Every ambition. He kept nothing back. Nothing.'

For a moment I wanted to contradict her openly, so transparent was the lie, but I saw in her eyes what it would cost her. I understood that she had twisted the truth into a pattern of her own choosing, and that to unravel it face to face, heart to heart, would be more than she could bear.

She said, still trying to persuade me, so that no breath of self-revelation might remain, 'Do you think I could have had Stella here under my roof for as long as I did if I'd thought she'd hurt Edward?'

'No, of course not.'

We avoided each other's eyes. She said, 'I always welcomed the prospect of my boys' marriages. God knows I'd seen enough of possessive mothers. When I bore two sons I made a pact with myself never to make them feel tied. I went out of my way to introduce them to suitable girls—'

'And you didn't consider Stella suitable?'

'Suitable! Alan might just as well have married a woman of the streets. Even at that age she'd lived with three men already. And gloried in it.'

'You mean she admitted it to you?'

'And gloried in it.'

'Did Alan know?'

'I can only presume so, since she made no bones about it. He should never have married her.'

'He may have loved her.'

'Then he was out of his mind.'

'Perhaps.' I smiled. 'Don't take this too seriously. But you did ask me to point out when I thought you were being unfair to him. Can't you just leave it that you dislike Stella, and will probably go on disliking her, and try not to let your feelings for her influence your feelings for him. That would stand a chance of working, wouldn't it?'

Her brows knit in concentration. She said, reluctantly, 'It might.'

'Another thing,' I said. 'Try to separate what you dislike from what you fear. Are you afraid of Stella?'

She hesitated a long time. 'I don't know. They say all dislike is rooted in fear.' We ended our conversation there. But as she went to her room she said, 'I wonder whether I'm afraid of Alan? I wonder whether that has been the trouble all along?'

I heard him go into the drawing-room that night and call my name. His tone was friendly, boisterous even, and I guessed he had been drinking. After a while I heard him in his own room. The wall of Edward's room divided us. Only the light showing beneath the door was a link; and, in time, this was extinguished.

But in the morning he knocked and entered, clothed in pyjamas and dressing gown, his hair tousled.

'Blast your bloody eyes,' he said, seating himself on the bed.

'What's wrong?'

I saw that the grim expression was only skin deep. 'You. You skedaddled off to bed before I got back.'

'I waited up until half-past eleven.'

'You know bloody well the last train doesn't get in until a quarter to twelve.'

'Sorry, I was tired.'

He hesitated. 'You weren't ill?'

I shook my head. The grim expression had gone.

'Fine bloody thing,' he said, 'I wanted to get drunk.'

'You don't look exactly sober right now.'

'Know how you look?'

'No,' I said, 'but I can guess.'

'You're right.'

'What's the time?' I asked.

'Half seven.'

'Then how d'you expect me to look?'

He tossed me a cigarette.

I said, 'Why did you want to get drunk?'

'Drown my bloody sorrows, of course.'

'What are your bloody sorrows?'

He coughed as he inhaled. Then he said, 'Can't remember 'em all.'

'Something happened about the job?'

'Indirectly.'

'What does that mean? That you won't be going to Assam?'

'Looks like it.'

'Why?' I asked.

'Didn't mother say anything?'

I recognized in his eyes that particular look of a man searching for signs of defection in another.

I said, 'Say anything about what?'

'Why I went to town.'

'Yes. She said you'd gone to see Stella's brother. I thought you might have had an appointment with a black eye.'

He snorted, relieved that I had not dissembled. 'You should see Stella's brother.'

'You mean he's got one?'

'No. I meant you wouldn't have thought that if you'd ever seen Stella's brother. Besides—' and he smiled, 'I've had one or two bloody noses but only one black eye in my life. Remember?'

We were silent. I think we were both aware how far we had come since then.

'What did Stella's brother want?' I said eventually.

'He wanted to tell me something.'

I waited, but he was determined I should ask him what Stella's brother had had to tell him. I did so.

He inhaled more smoke. He said, 'He told me that I'm going to be a father.'

His eyes were alight with pleasure.

I said, 'Congratulations.'

'Thanks.'

'What's going to happen about the job then?' I asked.

'I'll have to get a job in London.'

'Back to accountancy?'

'Back to accountancy.'

'Will Stella come here, or what?'

'Here – for the time being. No alternative.'

'Pity you gave up the Belsize Park flat.'

'The landlady'd 've kicked us out anyway.'

I said, 'Did you see Stella yesterday, too?'

He nodded.

'And everything's all right?'

'Yes,' he said. 'She's a funny girl.'

'Why?'

'She wasn't going to tell me.'

'But her brother made her?'

'Didn't make her. He took it on himself to tell me. Bossy little bastard. I never did like him. I'm glad he told me this though.' He frowned. 'The kid's due in March. She must have found out almost as soon as she'd cleared out. Yet she didn't say anything. What would she 've done, having the kid and trying to bring it up on her own?'

'Did she know you were going abroad?'

'No. I'd have been writing to her in a day or so. She'd have told me then, in any case, I suppose.'

'Are you both pleased?'

He looked at me seriously. 'Yes,' he said, 'It's brought us together again.'

'Aren't you sorry about Assam, though?'

'In a way. 'I'd 've like to 've gone East again. Still, there's lots of time. All the time in the world.' He grinned. 'I feel bloody pleased with myself, if you want to know.'

'What do you hope it'll be? Boy or a girl?'

'Lord, I couldn't care less as long as it's all right and Stella's all right.' He paused. 'She's scared stiff, I think.'

'That's because she's been facing it alone.'

His face lit up. 'Do you think so? Yes, I suppose you're right. It'll be different now.'

'I'm glad it's worked out this way, Alan.'

'Thanks. By the way, will you be godfather?'

'I don't know. I never go to church, so can I be godfather?'

'We'll keep it dark from the vicar. The kid won't mind, if he's anything like me.'

'It's to be a boy, then?' I smiled.

'*It* won't mind. That better? You're as bad as Stella. Picking me up for giving it a sex in advance. You'd better get up now, Ian. I'm meeting Stella in town for lunch. Like to come?'

'That would be most inconsiderate of me.'

'No, we'd like it.'

'She knows about me?'

'She knows you're here. She remembers your name, too, from letters I wrote in India. Seems I lied in my teeth and gave you a good character.'

'Thanks.'

'Get up then.'

As I tied my dressing gown he was talking to me through the open door of our rooms: but I did not hear what he said. The room had begun to contract and expand. I recognized the signs. I steadied myself with one arm against the wall. Alan came in.

I was only unconscious for a few seconds. When I came to, my knuckles were pressed against the cold linoleum surrounding the carpet. He had me in a grip below each armpit and I felt myself raised up. His voice came to me from the inside of my own head, distorted, clinical.

'Don't fight. Relax. Hang on now. Don't fight.'

The whiteness of porcelain hurt my eyes and was cold to the palms of my hands. There was a weight on my neck. I vomited. Then things came back into focus. I felt the sweat soaking into my eyebrows. He had led me to the basin in his room. The weight on my neck was his hand. He let me free. I saw his face behind my own in the mirror. Our eyes met. He grimaced.

'What the hell did you eat yesterday?' he asked.

I shook my head, closed my eyes.

'Well, whatever it was you've got rid of it. You'd better go and lie down a bit. I'll bring you some char.'

He let me go unaided to my own room, following just behind. I lay back, grateful for the retained warmth, the softness of the pillows.

'All right?' he asked.

'Right as rain, thanks.'

'That's the stuff.'

He went out.

Gradually I understood. Gently he was trying to teach me to ignore a condition which could not be diagnosed. When he returned with the promised cup of tea I had to say, 'I shall have to go.'

'Go where?'

I had never longed so much in my life, as then, to be able to say, 'Go home' and feel in my bones the certainty of its existence.

'Back to town,' I said.

'But you've given the flat up to David Holmes.'

'I can find a single place easily enough. I'll park up in Wendover. Use that as a base,' I added. 'I know a chap who'll put me up.'

'Isn't that what I'm doing?' he asked.

'No. It bloody well isn't. I've had a holiday. It can't go on indefinitely. Anyway, when Stella comes I'll have to clear out.'

'Damn it, Ian. That's exactly what I didn't want you to suppose. Frankly, it would suit me admirably if you'd stay on when Stella's here. I'm being quite selfish about it – Stella and mother don't get on and if they're alone here all day they'll just be at daggers drawn.'

'I don't see why I should act as a buffer state between your wife and your mother.'

I had meant it more or less as a joke, an echo of the old banter on Magpyui, but he took it seriously, saying – after a slight hesitation – 'No, of course not. I didn't really mean that. I didn't mean you could stand between them and take knocks from both sides. I meant, if you were here there wouldn't be any rows.'

I said, 'Yes, I know, but supposing this silly fever crops up.'

'We'd look after you.' Carefully, he was avoiding all mention of my self-assumed obligation to his mother. It would have been easy, now, for him to divest me of it by not resisting my plan to go.

'Who would look after me?' I smiled at him. 'Stella having a baby. You earning the daily bread. Your mother—' I stopped. 'If I go sick you'll have to pack me off to a nursing home.'

'What good's a nursing home ever done you?'

'You think I ought to go to a nut house?'

Slowly he grinned at me. 'My dear old Ian,' he said. 'You're in one.'

For a few moments neither of us moved. Then the absurdity of the situation overwhelmed me. I laughed because it seemed as though I had surfaced from a submarine world into one of wind and wave and sky. He said, taking me lightly by the arm and shaking it, 'Anyway, what's all this talk about nursing homes? There's everything in the world to live for.'

I felt that what he offered me was life and sanity. He had taken me and shoved me unceremoniously in front of a mirror. But in it, mine was not the only reflection. There was his own and that of his mother, and all the people who came and went, in and out of the rooms of Aylward: the human condition of which I was part and parcel.

I did not journey with him to town to see Stella. I felt the need for the fresh air across the common, even for the bite of the chill wind. But when I rose, for the second time, I felt very weak, unsure of the support of my legs. I shivered my way to the bathroom. There, in a medicine chest, I discovered a thermometer. I took my temperature. It was just under 100 degrees.

Quietly, I shaved and dressed. In the passage, where I put on my outdoor clothes, Mrs. Hurst came to me.

'It's happened as I said, you see,' she said.

'What has?'

'He's bringing Stella back.'

'So I gather.'

'Where are you going?'

'For a walk on the common.'

'But you'll come back?'

'Of course I'll come back.'

She came closer to me. 'You look flushed.'

'Do I?'

'Yes. Are you sure you should go out? It's very cold.'

'I'm well wrapped up.'

'I wouldn't call it that. I think you have a temperature.'

'But I haven't, Mrs. Hurst. You're quite wrong. I haven't got a temperature.'

On my return, my face burning, I went straight to the bathroom. My temperature was over 100. I looked at my reflection in the mirror.

'That's fine, Canning,' I said. *'You're down one point.'*

At lunch I did not fool her.

She said, 'I'm going to take your temperature.'

'I've taken it.'

'So you do feel ill.'

'No. I took it because you said I looked flushed.'

'And what was it?'

'Normal,' I replied, smiling, seeing the irony which she did not see.

'Has Alan been saying something to you?' she said.

'In what connection?'

'About your illness? Making light of it?'

'No.'

She said, 'Robust people can be very inconsiderate.'

I looked at her. 'You're being unfair, Mrs. Hurst. Unfair to Alan.'

She looked contrite, crumbled pellets of bread on her plate.

She said, 'I'm glad you and Alan are friends again.'

'Why do you say that?'

'I thought I detected the growth of a certain – animosity.'

'Surely not.'

She said, 'I think Alan was jealous of you.'

'Oh?'

'Because you put yourself in charge of the drinking business.'

'But you did that.'

'I suppose so. But I felt you wanted to be. You were always interested in the drinking business, right from the first evening, weren't you? And you tipped Alan off to what Rex was doing. Bringing in bottles.'

'Yes, I did that.'

'Alan was so furious I thought Rex wouldn't dare come again, even though it was explained to Alan that Rex was *helping*. He took it badly, all of it, not having known what Rex was doing, and then my putting you in charge. He was hurt about that.'

Knowing, now, that she had meant to hurt, knowing that Alan would not have shown hurt, I said, 'Was that a surprise to you?'

Her lips quivered. 'Of course it was a surprise. What interest has he ever shown? What help has he ever offered? He's never even accused me to my face of being drunk. He's just looked at me as if the very sight of me disgusted him. You might have thought the word "drunk" was entirely unknown to him.'

'Perhaps that was his way of being kind about it.'

There was a pause.

'Do you think so?' Her tone had altered.

'Yes.'

'Perhaps you're right.' She looked at me. 'And I'm glad he doesn't bear a grudge. I should never have forgiven myself if I'd unwittingly come between you and Alan. He has so few real friends.'

As we cleared away she paused, putting a pile of dishes down on the table so that I was forced to look at her.

'We'll really do our best, won't we, Mr. Canning? To make a go of everything.' She paused. 'You know about the baby?'

I said, 'Yes. It's good news.'

138

'The best news. A child gives us all a reason for living.'

I said, 'There is one thing I want to discuss.'

'What is that?'

'Well – I can't go on accepting hospitality. My stay ought to be put on a business footing.'

Her face clouded. 'Alan hasn't put that into your mind has he?'

'Good lord no.'

'I told him he mustn't.'

I had developed a special sense to deal with her tendency to hint at sharpness or greed or lack of generosity in others. It was necessary to do so if you were to keep a sense of proportion. She collected the plates and went to the kitchen. I followed with other remnants of the meal.

I said, 'Is there any reason why I shouldn't have the satisfaction of not being embarrassed?'

'Every reason in the world,' she said.

'Give me one.'

'In the first place I should never be satisfied that it wasn't due to some hint of Alan's—'

'Really, Mrs. Hurst—'

'You say "really" – but I know how tactless he can be. I told him on no account to say anything about it.'

'But he hasn't said anything. It's entirely my own idea.'

She was at the sink, piling dishes on the draining board.

'Then you must talk to Alan. Please, not with myself. And I shall always feel uneasy in spite of your assurances.'

'Right. I'll talk to Alan.'

I broached the subject that evening when he and I were alone.

He was saying, 'Mother suggested today that we give you the big room upstairs entirely to yourself, Ian. Would you like that?' He saw my hesitation. 'It'd have to be cleaned out and furnished properly, but it's a place you could do just what you liked in. Quiet for writing, too.'

'I'll go wherever you put me.'

'Not putting you anywhere. But Edward's room is pretty poky. The room upstairs could double for a bed and a sitting-room.'

Suddenly the prospect pleased me.

'Actually, I'd like it,' I said. 'But I've come to a decision today.'

'Fire away.'

'I'll only stay on here on one condition.'

'What?'

'That I pay board and lodging.'

'Don't be an ass. You give us your ration book.'

'Well, then, I'll clear out tomorrow.'

'Do you mean that?'

'Yes, I mean it.'

He began to fill his pipe. 'I'll have to discuss it with mother.'

'I've already done so. She said I had to discuss it with you. And as far as I'm concerned discussion doesn't enter into it. I'll tell you what I can afford and if you don't like it you can lump it, or rather I can.'

I told him what I could afford. I said, 'And if you don't accept it you're a damn fool. Having babies is expensive.'

He closed the flap of his pouch. He wasn't looking at me. 'I know,' he said. 'That's what I don't like about your offer. Another thing. If you're paying I can't kick you out at a moment's notice.'

'We'll include that in the deal. You can kick me out at a moment's notice. I'll pay weekly in arrears.'

'You're a bloody minded chap. You're not serious about paying?'

'I'm serious.'

He hesitated. 'Look, this is an awful thing to say, but mother hasn't hinted at anything like this, has she?'

'Of course not.'

'Well, if you must you must. But I hope it doesn't give you the right to complain about the service.' His eyes twinkled.

Two days later Stella came.

Alan had left in the morning to fetch her, and they returned in the afternoon. They came by the front door, for Stella would not climb the iron staircase. She waited downstairs whilst Alan collected the keys from his mother. It was the first time I had ever eavesdropped. I stood in the darkness on the flight of stairs leading to the attic room which was to be made over to me and which I had been pacing, considering its possibilities, its problems. And as I was descending to the main landing I heard his mother say, 'No, Alan. Not that. Not that.'

'But you must. I'm sorry. She won't come up the side stairs. They're dangerous.'

'It's not the danger she's thinking of.' Then a cry, 'She knows how I feel about the stairs. She knows.'

'If you won't give them to me, mother, I'll have to go and get 'em myself. Or force the lock. Now, which is it to be?'

'You don't know where they are.'

'I know where they are.'

'Very well. Stay there.'

I waited on the bend of the stairs. At last I heard him say, 'Thanks,' and then came the unaccustomed sound of someone running down the carpeted steps. I went softly down the last flight and stood at the bottom.

Mrs. Hurst was there, on the landing, holding the banister rail, one hand on her throat, staring down. As the door opened below she took away the hand which had lain on the rail. She turned and went into her bedroom.

And Stella returned to Aylward, her face white and pinched, her hair so dark it was like the shining wing of a bird. I went forward to meet her.

CHAPTER FOUR

THERE was nothing meek in Stella. She was a match for Mrs. Hurst. When I saw that this was so I was in no doubt about the reasons for the older woman's dislike of her.

Our introduction on the landing was brief. She hardly took in who I was. After we had shaken hands she turned to Alan.

'Where's your mother, Alan?'

'Oh, somewhere around. Do you know, Ian?'

I said, 'I think she's in her room.'

Without a word Stella moved across the landing, knocked on the door and went in.

We heard her say, 'I'm here.' She flung the words down like a challenge.

It had been agreed that for a while I should continue to occupy Edward's room, because the attic room would take some time to prepare. On that first night I excused myself from their company quite early, having arranged with Alan that whilst he and Stella sat in the drawing-room I should go to the bathroom through his – or rather – his and Stella's room. Mrs. Hurst had gone to bed after tea. When I got to the bathroom I found I had left my toothbrush behind. I went back to get it and, doing so, met Mrs. Hurst coming out of their bedroom. I thought little of it. We murmured good night to each other.

At first I lay awake in bed reading. I could hear them moving about. Someone – Alan so far as I could make out – entered the room next door and shot the bolt on the connecting door. My morning journey to the bathroom lay through the drawing-room. I could not help smiling at the elaborate arrangements which were forced upon me. There was an element of farce about the whole thing. I turned out the light and tried to sleep. Next door they had begun to unpack Stella's case. I heard them opening drawers; the unintelligible buzz of their conversation. A door opened, that on the landing, I presumed, and then I heard Alan whistling. Later, Stella came back and Alan took his turn in the bathroom. I thought of her alone in the next room. I heard the thrust and creak of more drawers; but all at once there was no sound at all. I found myself listening. When Alan returned I distinctly heard him say, 'What's wrong?'

She shouted, 'This! This is what's wrong! This disgusting thing! This filthy obscenity!'

His voice joined hers but his words were not distinguishable.

'In the drawer!' she was saying. 'In the drawer – the one she said was mine!'

Again Alan's voice.

And Stella breaking in. 'Of course she knew. She's left it here deliberately.' A pause. 'Damn Ian Canning! I don't care if he does hear.'

There was the sound of something being torn; not ordinary paper, but much thicker, almost like cardboard. Alan's voice reached me. He was comforting her, soothing her gradually. I rose, and, without putting on lights, groped my way into the drawing-room where the fire was dying. I smoked a cigarette. Eventually I turned on a reading lamp. It was then that Alan came into the room. I smiled to reassure him that I was unaware of any tension.

'Hello,' he said. 'How long've you been here?'

'Oh, I came back directly I heard you and Stella pack up. I wasn't sleepy.'

He looked relieved, but not wholly so. In his hands he carried some torn pieces of what looked like card. 'Just clearing up odds and ends,' he said, and came over to the fire to thrust the pieces into it, placing his body so that it was difficult for me to see what they were. He put them carefully on to the red parts of the fire; but one of them fell into the grate and, before he could retrieve it, I saw what it was.

Staring out at me from the jagged shred was Alan's face. On the outer edge was the face of the woman who had sat by him one summer afternoon, absorbed in the nearness of him and the knowledge which she had of him; and he of her.

The following day, I suggested to Alan that I move at once upstairs; he did not argue. Together, and with Mrs. Burrowes' reluctant help in the matter of washing the floor and windows, we made it ready. With our coats off and sleeves rolled up we took Edward's bed up the narrow stairs. Mrs. Hurst collected rugs, and brought them to us to spread on the floor. She rummaged in a trunk and found a pair of curtains. When the room was ready – fit at least for sleeping in – she asked me whether there was anything I particularly wanted from Edward's room. I said there wasn't; but, later, she climbed the stairs bearing a gift. 'I've brought you a picture,' she said. It was *L'Ennui*.

I thanked her, sought on the wall for an existing nail and, finding one, hung the Sickert. I dragged the oval walnut table over to the window while she watched me. 'We must get rid of the old spring mattress. It's unsightly.' I said, 'No, leave it. It gives the place a proper air. I shall do some work up here.'

'On Isabella?' she said. 'A book about Isabella?'

I found it difficult to tell her, to her face, that there was nothing to say about Isabella. I said, 'I don't know. I don't think I could.'

'But you must, Mr. Canning. You must do *something*, and something about Isabella would be such a pleasure for us.'

I felt almost under an obligation to her. I said, 'I'm not sure there's enough material. I know so little, anyway.'

'Isobel's life brimmed over with incident,' she said. Today she believed it. 'See Rex,' she said. 'Go to see Rex. We'll do all we can to help. I will if Rex won't.'

I said, 'Well, we'll see.' At once I thought of something, a theory I wanted to test. I said, 'Let me have another look at the photographs.'

'Of course.' She did not drop her eyes or appear in any way confused.

When she returned with the album she put it on the table. I waited until she had gone before flicking over the pages to make sure of what I already suspected. And there it was: the blank page from which the picture of Adela and Alan had been carefully removed in order that it might be put where Stella would come upon it, without warning.

It was the living who interested me, not the dead.

That afternoon I went to see Rex. I got his address from the index pad which hung on the wall near the telephone: 2A, Pelham Parade. It was a flat above a greengrocer's shop and I had to ring the bell at the street door. The door was opened by a woman whom I took at once to be Trixie. She was short, middle-aged, with dark-red hair and a lot of white, frilly decorations on the blouse which she wore beneath a black coat and skirt. She was very plain.

'Is Mr. Coles in?' I asked.

'Oh, I'm not sure. Who is calling?' (as though I were a voice only).

'My name is Canning. I'm staying at—'

'Oh, Mr. Canning. Do come in. You're up at Aylward, aren't you? I've heard such a lot about you. Rex *will* be glad you've called. He was only saying just now he'd have to go along this evening. He likes the walk you know, but I tell him he ought to be careful with the wind in the east like it is. He's a terror for catching colds is Rex and I always say better to be safe than sorry, but you know what men are—'

We had climbed the stairs and had arrived on a narrow landing.

'Will you come into the lounge?' she said. 'Make yourself comfortable and I'll tell Rex.'

I went into the lounge. The walls were bare, the sofa and two easy chairs square and forbidding, patterned with green zig-zags against a beige background. The carpet was green, set all over with brown rectangles and semi-circles which transfixed each other, flushing mauve at the points of intersection. A lamp standard had a chromium pole. The fireplace was a low-built structure of glazed tiles, a light oatmeal colour. In it stood a portable oil-stove which gave off a heat incapable of penetration beyond a short radius. But the paraffin-smell was strong.

It was obviously Trixie's room, furnished to Trixie's taste. When Rex entered, one saw that through habit he had become accustomed to them both.

'Hello, old man,' he said, looking very melancholy. 'I thought it must be a creditor at this time of day.'

He forgot to ask me to sit down and so, for a few moments, we stood. The door had closed behind him, apparently of its own accord, but, no doubt, it was actually pulled to by Trixie. She was the sort of woman who effaced herself from the world of masculine affairs. I felt obliged, in the event, to talk business, although I should have preferred to feel my way with greater care.

'Isabella,' I began.

'Yes, old man.' He paused. 'Won't you sit down? I'm sorry about the oil stove, but we've overrun our coal ration. Lord knows what'll happen to the country if this cold snap lasts. They're already talking about electricity cuts. Poor Trixie can't stand the cold.' He hesitated, looking round the room as though, when he consciously took it in, it never ceased to sadden him. 'She's a good woman is young Trixie,' he said. 'You were saying about Isabella' he went on.

'I was talking to Brian Selby about it,' I said.

'I wrote him about some letters but never got a reply.' He looked at me rather accusingly. I sat in one armchair, he in it's twin, each on one side of the fireplace. He sat leaning forward, elbows on knees, hands loose between his opened legs.

'Oh, didn't you?' I said. 'I thought he was going to let you know he'd arrange for me to see the letters if we went further with the project.'

'No. He told me nothing.'

I said, 'He's very forgetful.'

'A useful trait, old man.'

I offered him a cigarette, which he accepted. The end of his sleeve was frayed. I said, 'I've come to discuss what our financial arrangements might be if this biography goes forward.'

'It won't go forward, old man. It won't go forward.' He sounded in very low spirits.

'You're probably right.'

'There's nothing to write about,' he went on. 'Poor Isobel never did anything. You realize that when you think about it. She wrote books. But she wasn't a woman of the world. Poor Isobel. She was a saint, old man. Too good for any of us. We ought to leave her in peace.'

'Selby seemed to think there was something in an idea I had.'

'What was that, old chap?'

I told him what I had told Selby. I added, 'He would commission it if we agreed on the broad outline.'

For some time he was silent, looking at the tiny mica window of the oil stove behind which the flames burned steadily.

He said, 'But what you've described isn't a biography of Isabella. It's a book about us.' He looked up at me. 'There's nothing special about us, old man.'

He was so determined not to be helped that I was puzzled. I said, 'The other day you told me Isabella oughtn't to be forgotten.'

'Did I?'

'Yes. Why have you changed your mind?'

Again he stared at the oil stove. At last he said, 'She's already forgotten, you see. We're all forgotten, Canning. We're all back numbers. We live in the past, old chap, and it's nice to think of the past as something comfortable and pleasant which it wasn't, of course, but still—'

I said, 'Then you'd be afraid of the book? Is that it?'

He looked up at me. He said simply, 'Yes, old man.'

I said, 'But why? It goes without saying I shouldn't be such a fool as to put anything in which would offend living people.'

He put one pudgy hand down, close to the oil stove. The yellow line of bone down the centre of his nose was more accentuated than ever, his cheeks flabbier, heavier, pulling harder at his lower lids. The little silver wings of hair above his ears showed sparser in the uncompromising light.

'Old man,' he said, 'I don't see how you could avoid it. Besides—' He looked around the room but not at me. 'Besides, you writing people have a way of putting things it's difficult to cotton on to at first glance.'

He was thinking of 'Opal'.

'Much better forget it, old man,' he said.

'You make it sound as though you were a family of monsters,' I said, smiling. 'I'm beginning to think there may be some dramatic twist that would make the whole thing a definite commercial proposition.'

'No,' he said. 'No,' then, 'I wish there had been. I'm in great financial stress.'

We sat for a while without saying anything, smoking our cigarettes.

'You're not really serious about it are you, Canning?'

'Mrs. Hurst seems to want it.'

'Adela said you weren't serious.' He frowned at the oil stove. 'I oughtn't to say it but she seems to think you are just using it as an excuse, old man.'

'Excuse?'

'For living easy at Aylward.'

For a moment I hardly knew what to say. I tried to picture Adela, tried to hear her, saying what he said she had said. I replied eventually, 'Adela lives in the sort of world where people are always living easy off each other – as you call it.'

'You mustn't abuse Adela, old chap. She's had a bloody awful life.'

'For which you're partly to blame.'

He said, 'I know. I admit that.'

At any moment, I thought, he's going to cry, and then I understood what had happened. My presence at Aylward had put his nose out of joint. I said, 'You oughtn't to get in your own digs at me by passing them off as Adela's.'

'I don't follow,' he said, knowing perfectly well what I meant.

'It's *you* who think I'm just looking for ways of living easy at Aylward, isn't it?'

'Well, if it comes to it, aren't you, old man?'

'Forgive me again, but would it be any business of yours if I were?'

He hesitated. In a tricky situation he had long since learned the value of weighing every word.

'Yes, I think it would be my business, Canning old chap. It was always understood between George Hurst and me that I'd look after Marion if anything happened to him.'

'Frankly I don't see what that has got to do with my staying at Aylward.'

'No, old man?'

'I'm Alan's guest.'

'Yes, I know.' Again he looked round the room. 'But it isn't Alan's home. It's Marion's.'

'Mrs. Hurst has asked me to stay as long as possible.'

He said, 'I'm not disputing *that,* old man.' He looked at me, smiling slightly, as though he had gained a point. It was impossible for me to ignore the implication. 'Do you mean,' I asked, 'that Mrs. Hurst is easily imposed upon?'

He made no answer, but let the smile disappear, and looked grave instead.

'It does rather look like that, doesn't it, Canning? I don't say you've really done it deliberately.'

'Well, thank you. In what way have I imposed on her?'

'Old man,' he said, 'she seems to have come to the conclusion you're indispensable.'

I thought for a moment. 'Is it that which rankles? My supposed indispensability?'

He folded his hands. 'I'm not sure I like your tone, Canning old chap.'

There seemed no point in staying longer. I rose to go. As I did so Trixie knocked and came in with a tray of tea. She had only laid it for two.

'Oh, you're not going are you, Mr. Canning?'

I looked at her, and at the tray. It was arranged carefully.

'I'm afraid I must.'

She was dumb with disappointment.

'I do apologize,' I said. 'You've gone to so much trouble.'

'Oh, no. No special trouble.'

She put the tray down carefully and turned her back on it. 'I'll see you to the door.'

'Please don't bother.'

'Oh, it's no bother. The catch is a bit awkward.' She went out of the room, leaving the door open. I turned to Rex, and said, 'I apologize for any rudeness on my part. But there you are. Let's leave it like that shall we?'

He got up. He had not risen when Trixie entered.

'Righto, old man. I'm afraid you've taken things too personally.

I suppose I oughtn't to blame you if Marion's taken a shine to you.' He looked at the tray. 'Trixie's done the same, old chap. You must have a way with women.'

He winked and put out his pudgy hand.

I did not take it.

I said, 'It won't work, Coles. You're not going to *shame* me into leaving Aylward.'

He was very angry. His face flushed.

'You oughtn't to speak to me like that, Canning. I'm old enough to be your father. I guessed you'd be a rotter when I saw that letter of yours to Selby about poor Isobel.'

'My letter was written for Selby's eyes alone.'

He flushed deeper. 'Are you implying I saw it without Selby's approval, old man?'

'Selby implied that was the case,' I said.

His mouth opened, and shut. The flush went, leaving him pale. He was speaking the truth. 'I shouldn't think I need to tell you Brian Selby's not a man to be trusted,' he said. 'I hope you don't imagine he's any friend of yours, old man.'

'He employs me. I'm not interested beyond that,' I told him.

'I don't think he'd employ you if it weren't for his father.'

I was genuinely puzzled. I had been Brian Selby's protégé, not his father's. Rex added, with a touch of malice, 'He told me that if it weren't for hurting his father he'd get another reader—'

'He has a number of readers—'

'Another reader in your place. He thought your illness had impaired your judgment.'

'He stood by my judgment.'

'He was influenced by that so-called figures expert Barnstaple. If it hadn't been for Barnstaple he'd have republished poor Isobel's books, or one or two of them. He said so. He told me to my face.'

'Then no blame attached to me.' But I was sorry for him, because I could see how Selby had misled him.

'Yes it does, old man. Selby said Barnstaple used your report as the final argument *against* republishing. If you'd recommended republishing Selby says he could have swayed Barnstaple.'

'I'm afraid you've been subjected to Brian Selby's spineless charm. He finds it impossible to say "No" to your face. And I ought to add, it was *he* who took me into the firm, not his father. His father has no views about me one way or the other.'

Rex looked at me, sadly. 'I'm afraid one of you is lying, old man.'

'Yes. One of us is lying.'

'It makes me very angry, old man. To be lied to. Why should anyone lie to me? I can't do them any harm. I'm past the age when I can be looked upon as a potential source of embarrassment to be pushed off with this tale or that tale. All I know is, old man, that Brian Selby told me Barnstaple refused to agree to republish Isabella, and when I asked why he shoved your letter across the desk and said, "Because he's seen that".'

I said, 'Very well. I take your word for it. I know Selby.'

He said, 'So you'll understand, in the circumstances, that I didn't view your sudden arrival at Aylward with any great joy. I gave you the benefit of the doubt at first, though. Now – well, as you'll have gathered, I find it difficult to do so. You see, old man, I appreciate that when you wrote that letter to Selby you probably had no idea Isobel was related to your old friend Alan. When you found out I thought you were going to see what you could do to alter Selby's decision – but there aren't any signs of that. The only sign there is is of your tucking your feet under Marion's table and making some pennies for yourself out of this bloody silly idea about a biography.'

'Yes. Well, we've got back to where we began. The question of the biography and the financial arrangements.'

'There can't be any financial arrangements, Canning. I definitely refuse to authorize you to write up Isobel's life.'

It was this side of him I disliked so much. My hackles rose again. We were getting nowhere.

'You realize I could do it without your authorization?'

'Yes, old man, but there's a thing called libel. Not of the dead, I know, but it'd make it awkward.'

'Wouldn't it be possible for me to write a biography of Isabella without libelling you, defaming your character or holding you up to ridicule?'

'I don't think so. Some one else could, but not you, old man.' He moistened his lips. 'You don't like me. Marion's seen to that. I've moved heaven and earth to help poor Marion but she always looks on me as an enemy. And you're too much under her thumb not to do likewise.'

'I thought she was supposed to be under mine.'

'It comes to the same thing when a woman's involved.' He put his hands in the pockets of his jacket as though their weight had become too much for his arms to carry unsupported. 'That's something life'll teach you, old man. Anything a woman finds she can't control undergoes a funny sort of change in her mind so that it becomes part of her. Then she can kid herself she controls it after all.' He paused. 'The bloody part is that nine times out of ten she'll be able to. After a while you begin to see what's happening. All the things you used to do to show her you were entitled to go your own way, or whatever it was, you find yourself doing because *she* makes you. You do them through her, old man. Women are all the same. You can't possess them without them possessing you. It's this way they're made, old man. All this bloody womb business—' He put a hand on my arm. 'Think of it, old man. If you had a place inside you that was capable of growing something. It would be all right if you could fertilize yourself. As it is you're born with this sort of inescapable burden of dependence upon others. Wouldn't that make you bitter, old man? And that's it, of course. Women can't help being bitter. They need people but hate them because of it.' He put the hand back in his pocket.

'They need men, do you mean?'

'That's only the biological part of it. It goes wider than that, Canning old chap. They need to be possessed and in return they want to possess. They want to possess anything, everything, people, places, things—' He looked round the room, as if to orientate himself. 'And men, old man. Oh, we can do our stuff and satisfy them for a time. But that isn't enough, you see. It's a tragedy really, old man. They have us for ten minutes or so every so often, and then perhaps what we've left behind for nine months. But after that the thing that really matters is over and all the rest is in their imagination. That's what they can't stomach, Canning, having to let go and start all over again.'

Beyond the room, somewhere, a door shut. I remembered Trixie. I wondered whether she had been listening. Rex cocked an ear and then looked back at me.

'Take Trixie for instance. This is her flat, if you must know. That stuff on the tray is her best china. It all means something to her, old man. She hates it when I go up to Aylward because it destroys her illusion that everything in the flat, including myself, belongs to her.' He paused. 'She wouldn't change any of it for the world, you know, but she can't help despising me. That's irony for you, old man. She can't help despising me in her heart for *being* dependent on her. I suppose it's more rewarding to a woman to possess a chap who supports her the way a man thinks he should.' He laughed. 'That's an illusion too, old man. We only think we ought to support women, and defend them, because that's what they want us to think. A chap who lives the way God made him couldn't care less. I often look back now and regret that I never took my courage in both hands and went out into the world. That's really what a chap should do, Canning. Get out and look. Otherwise,' again he paused, 'Otherwise you never really see yourself, old man. And it's all so small and petty. A man isn't a man any longer.'

For a while I was silent. Then I said, 'Generalizations are dangerous, Coles.' I turned to go. We were no longer angry with each other but there was no point in pretending there was any feeling of friendship on either side.

He showed me to the door. 'Look at Alan,' he said. 'There's a boy I thought would make his way. But what's happening? At the first waggle of his wife's little finger he goes running to her, old man.'

'There's a child on the way.'

'And when it's born, Alan's sunk, old man. Properly sunk. The only reason my first wife and I stayed together was because Adela was coming. We lived a cat and dog life, and Adela ended up hating us both.'

'She doesn't hate you now.'

'Am I supposed to be grateful for that? I gave up every opportunity life had to offer for Adela's sake. Oh, I can't blame her, Canning. I can only blame myself. But I'm just showing you. And Alan will find out. You'll find out too, old man. All human relationships are meaningless. Sometimes I wonder whether it's worth going on, old man. What have we got to look forward to, when all's said and done? Hardly enough food to keep us healthy. All the old gang still playing politics. Everyone being levelled out so that no one man'll be able to raise himself up and say he's what God intended. And at the end of it all a bloody big explosion. The silly part is, Canning, that when we die in it we'll all have expressions of surprise on our faces, as if we didn't know it was coming.'

On the landing he said, in conclusion. 'The trouble is, you know, we're all of us bloody fools and humbugs.'

He came down the stairs behind me and helped when I had trouble with the latch. The shop fronts were lighted and there was a short queue outside the greengrocers. The cold struck at my face.

'Look at them, old man.'

I looked at the people in the queue, hunched against the winter, patient, silent.

'That's us, old man.'

'Yes,' I said.

'It'd be a jolly good thing if they dropped the bomb now, wouldn't it, old man? Dropped it now and ended everything.'

I looked about me, and then back at him.

'No,' I said. 'That would be a bad thing, Coles.'

I turned my collar up and stepped out into the street, leaning against the wind, half-blinded by it, but glad of it, and the feeling it gave me of being alive.

CHAPTER FIVE

STELLA

It was difficult to grasp the idea of Stella; easy, before she came, to do so, to feel tenderness for her, to evolve in your imagination a set of problems you could believe were hers, so that you could consider the solutions to them against the day when she might be in need of them, grateful for them. Dark, like a little gypsy, Adela said; and I had conjured a picture. How wrong it was.

Stella.

I used to say her name like that, aloud, punctuating my thoughts of other things as I sat in the attic room, or climbed the dark stairs; braved the cold wind of the common. I used to say her name to convince myself of her reality, of the fact that the fiercely self-contained creature who sat such long hours alone in the drawing-room was actually she who bore it.

One morning, before I had risen, Alan came up to see me.

'Lord, it's cold here isn't it, Ian? Are you all right?'

'I'm fine.'

I leaned up on one elbow. He stood at the foot of the bed. 'I'm going up to town,' he said.

I looked at the frost-encrusted windows. 'I don't envy you exactly. For my part I'm going to stay in bed a bit.' I paused. 'Stella going with you?'

He shook his head. 'I wish she would really. But she's got to go down to the clinic and she's not keen on town. Anyway – I'm going looking for a job so she's best at home.'

'She ought to get out more.'

He grinned. 'Now don't you start.'

And I recalled, too late, his mother using the same words only the night before. You ought to get out more, Stella. Stella had raised her eyebrows: Get out more? she had repeated. The words must have been in my head.

Stella had been with us for a week. This would be Alan's third trip to town in search of a job.

I leaned back on the pillow, smiling. 'Anything I can do?'

'Yes. Be a good chap and go with her to the clinic. She says it's all right by her if you want to.'

'Are the roads frozen again?'

'Yes. There's been a bit more snow in the night, too.'

'Righto, Alan. Tell her we'll break our necks together.'

The clinic was run by the County Council. It lay, as such places so often do, in a relatively inaccessible spot at the top of the steepest hill in Pelham Green. Stella had to go there for pre-natal treatment. She took my arm half-way up the hill, although I had offered it before. I waited for her on a bench in the hall of the old house where the clinic was conducted. The place was very quiet. It looked as though, in the war, it had been a temporary barracks for soldiers: uncarpeted floor, uncarpeted stairs; scars on the paintwork; and cold; a suitable place for the head-quarters of a rifle company.

Stella came through a door, clutching a bottle of orange juice. I nodded my head at it. 'The Welfare State?'

'Yes,' she said. 'The Welfare State.'

She was apt to kill jokes like that, by taking them neither jokingly nor quite seriously enough for you to believe she re-buked you. Question: answer. A conversation was difficult to sustain.

She wore no hat. You felt she was proud of her hair. Her face was an almost perfect oval, but the flesh below the cheekbones was a little sunken. She seldom had any colour: what there was looked natural. Her eyebrows were beautiful. I suppose she plucked them with infinite care; perhaps she darkened them. Only her lips were obviously aided artificially. She favoured scarlets and bright reds and, so far as I could see, contented her-self with painting them in their natural shape. Her eyes were bright blue. When you saw them in a particular light – as now I did, facing her in the cold, empty hall of the clinic – the colour was quite startling. You forgot, for a moment, that they expressed nothing.

She was short, coming up no higher than my shoulder. Alan always towered above her. She put the bottle of orange juice in the pocket of the cheap fur coat she wore. She did not take my arm until we began the descent of the hill.

I said, 'Are you having the baby at home?'

'At Aylward.'

'That's what you prefer, I take it?'

We had walked several paces before she answered. 'Nursing homes are expensive.' We went a little further and then she added – and I was sure this was the first remark she had ever volunteered to me – 'I left it too late to get a hospital bed.'

'I suppose they get filled up pretty quickly,' I said.

'Apparently.'

'What sort of notice do they need, then?'

There was a faint smile on her lips. She said, 'I rang two and they said they were booked in the maternity wards for the next eight months and that everywhere was the same.'

'Good Lord. People must book on the off-chance, almost.'

At the bottom of the hill we had to turn right and enter Pelham High Street. I remembered having seen a tea-shop.

'Would you like some tea, Stella?'

She gave me a fleeting glance. She had already let go of my arm and was walking with shoulders hunched, hands in pockets. I was quite sure she would refuse. She stood still. The wind was making her eyes water.

'I would,' she said. 'Thank you.'

'There's a place a few doors—' but I stopped, realizing she would know better than I.

It was called Polly Anne. A plywood lady in sunbonnet and crinoline stood in the sheltered entrance holding a cellophane-covered board in which there was a menu card. There was a faint smell of cats as we entered, but you didn't notice it for long. The waitress had yellow hair and wore a smock. It was early for the regular trade. I enjoyed the sense of leisure our being the only customers gave me. We could watch the shoppers go by. Later, I noticed that the paint was peeling from the walls. We had to say which of us took sugar.

When the waitress had gone I said, 'What do you have to do at the clinic?'

'Oh, they check you up.'

'Do they look after you later, I mean, at the time?'

'Yes. It's all laid on with the District Nursing people. I met the midwife today.'

'Did you like her?'

'I think so.'

I said, 'When is it actually to be?'

'About the beginning of March.'

She looked away, conscious that, as people usually do, I was counting. The beginning of June. She must have conceived a few days after Alan's return from abroad. She must have been over two months pregnant when she left Alan. She must have known.

She turned back and looked at me.

'That's right,' she said. 'I left Alan knowing I was pregnant.'

I smiled slightly, hoping it was a kind smile as it was meant to be. 'He realizes that now, I suppose.'

'I'm not sure that he does.'

I said, 'Well, it doesn't matter.'

'No.'

The waitress brought tea. We all three agreed that it was a cold day; that it would be colder yet; that we could stand almost anything but the cold; but that it was to be expected we supposed. There was a ritualistic quality in this exchange. It went with the place, with the tea. It gave an additional edge to my sense of time and place. It helped me somehow to see Stella – not as Alan's wife, but as herself.

I said, 'You can still smell your oilpaints in the chest of drawers upstairs.' I did not look at her as I said it, but at her hand, stirring the contents of the teapot. I looked up. Expression had come into her eyes, but I could not give it a name; it was a flicker only, of something which moved, asleep.

'Do you ever paint now?' I asked bluntly.

'No, I don't, I'm afraid.'

'Alan said you were quite good.'

'Did he?'

'Quite good, from Alan, is praise isn't it?'

'I suppose it is.'

'He said you did portraits.' I waited, I said, on the spur of the moment, 'I wonder whether you'd have a crack at mine?'

'At your portrait?' She seemed to study my face, but nothing was registering. 'No,' she said, 'I couldn't.'

'Not as a relaxation? I wasn't implying I was worth painting.'

'A relaxation for me?'

'Yes, for you.'

She looked out of the window. A woman in the street was looking at the home-made cakes.

'It wouldn't be a relaxation,' Stella said. She sipped her tea, still watching the woman outside. Her left hand rested on the table. It was clenched into a tight fist.

'Did your painting displease you that much?'

Slowly she turned her head in my direction.

'I'm afraid it did.'

In the kitchen they had turned on the wireless. Someone was giving a talk. It filled in the ever-lengthening gaps in my conversation with Stella. There was no getting through to her. Hers was an armed withdrawal into herself.

A pattern began to emerge. On most mornings I walked, sometimes probing beyond the town, southwards, to commonlands which fringed an arterial road. After lunch I stayed upstairs in my room without explanation, but aware that this action helped to establish in Marion Hurst's mind the belief that I was working on writing of some nature. Oddly, I felt I owed her that much. In the evenings the four of us sat and read or listened to the wireless. At nine Mrs. Hurst retired.

I would rise from my chair fifteen minutes later and go to my room. From there I would take the bottle of gin down to her. I poured out her ration. Sometimes she did not speak. On other occasions she would begin a conversation with no other object than to emphasize, by omission of any reference to what I was doing, her wish to ignore it, to treat it as though it were not happening. Sometimes I had the uneasy feeling that she had no need of it, maintained the illusion only because, within it, I moved and acted according to her will.

But on the night Alan had returned with the news that he had got a job, was starting directly – indeed, the following morning – I found her seated on the edge of her bed, with her head buried in her hands.

She was making no sound, no movement. I poured the agreed measure of gin into the tumbler. Alan's news had forewarned me of difficulties. I had gone to her resolved not to be put upon, to remain deaf to any entreaties to increase her ration. So keyed up had I been with this determination, that when I found her silent, dumbly accepting that she and Stella would henceforth virtually be alone for the greater part of the day, all my prepared resistance went. Without pausing to think out the consequences, conscious only of her taut body, her hidden face, I made my gesture, my offering, as a parent would to a child who had done wrong but was so sick with the misery of its sinning that the misery filled the room and hammered at the heart.

She did not even look up when I set the bottle down with an unmistakable impact on the surface of the table. The bottle contained the following nights' ration. When I got back to my own room I understood the folly of what I had done. I returned to her door. It was locked. She took no notice of my knocking, my quiet calling.

In the middle of the night I heard her screaming. When I reached the landing Alan was already with her, holding her where she stood at the head of the stairs, crying out, 'He's back! He's back!'

When it was all over, and Alan came back across the landing, I confessed to him. He was about to reply, but thought better of it. Eventually he said, 'For Pete's sake don't do it again, Ian.'

'I'm sorry.'

'It's all right. But don't be soft with her.'

'Has it upset Stella?' I asked.

He looked over my shoulder and, turning, I saw that she had come to the door of their room.

'Stella's all right,' he said. 'She's tough.'

I stood aside to let him pass. His back was to me. She looked from his face to mine. She said, 'What was that she was shouting? It sounded like "He's back." Who's back?'

Alan said, 'She meant Edward, I suppose.'

'It must have been Ian,' she said, still looking at me. 'She must have seen Ian. Have you been sleepwalking or something?'

I dreamed that night that Stella had the power to extinguish things and people merely by looking at them.

CHAPTER SIX

THE roads remained treacherous. We were in for a hard winter. Everybody said so. The Russians were to blame, they said, sending their stinking Siberian weather to us on lease-lend. The woman in Polly Anne got to know Stella and myself. Twice a week I climbed the hill with her to the clinic, waited in the frozen hall for her to come out of the sacrosanct inner room, and gave her my arm down the hill again. We talked only of life outside Aylward, and because of this Aylward became the point of fusion for our unspoken thoughts; and these thoughts would smoulder, threaten to burst into bright flame and burn the reality out of our mild and innocent meetings.

As we drew nearer the house on the return journey we had a habit of falling silent as though Aylward were the centre of a walled, defensive area within which it was dangerous to speak openly.

Only Stella had a key to the front door. Only on these occasions did I use the main staircase, coming up behind her, armed briefly with her authority. I never came to the half-landing without feeling that from somewhere we were watched, our footsteps counted.

I had almost forgotten about Mrs. Voremberg.

She was there, one day, at her own front door as we entered Aylward, waiting, it seemed, to speak to us or to be spoken to. I had never been close to her before, never seen her other than from the height of an upstairs window as she bent to her tasks in the garden which now lay rigid and frozen, unyielding to the vicious little thrusts of her spade. It was a surprise to find her so tall. Her bulk was accentuated by the shabby overcoat she had on. She looked gross, unhealthy, forbidding. She spoke to Stella.

'Ah so, Mrs. Hurst. You are come back.' She ended her sentence with a nod.

'Yes, Mrs. Voremberg.'

The hall had been partitioned so that now you passed through the old front door into a lobby. The staircase lay behind a wall in which there were two doors: the one on the left for ourselves and that on the right for the tenant below.

'Come in,' she said, 'and let the gentleman come too,'

I looked sideways at Stella, trying to assess her reaction, ready with an excuse should I see signs of reluctance to accept the invitation.

Stella said, 'Thank you.'

Mrs. Voremberg stood aside to let Stella go in.

'How long must it be since we met, Mrs. Hurst? I ask myself this the other day. Time is quick. Life is short.'

'Over three years,' Stella said.

Mrs. Voremberg exclaimed, not in surprise but to show pleasure at this proof of her view of time's habit: a harsh, Teutonic 'Ach'.

Then, because Stella had gone in and I had not automatically followed, Mrs. Voremberg looked at me.

'And the gentleman who I do not know?'

Murmuring something polite, I followed Stella. I felt weight and darkness close upon me. The door shut. Stella had gone forward, knowing her way about, it seemed. There were no windows in the passage, only closed doors and one, half-open, through which Stella was going.

A hand gripped my arm.

'You are not used to my dark house, Mr. Edward?'

I stared at her.

'What did you call me?'

'I? Call you?'

She was grinning. My eyes were getting used to the lack of light.

'You called me Mr. Edward.'

'I? I? No, you are mistaken.'

'My name is Canning. Ian Canning,' I said firmly.

'Ee-un Kan-ning. Ah.'

Then we went in.

The room was big. Light could have flooded into it, but at the tall bay window the heavy velvet curtains were closed to within a few inches of each other. The place was like a furniture depository, and at once I thought of the bedroom upstairs. There was a disturbing similarity. But Mrs. Hurst's room was all cold, naked light. This was a subterranean echo of it.

'Come to the fire, children. You will have tea. This is a British habit I have become a slave to.'

A kettle whispered on an old-fashioned hob. The fire gave off no flame but there was heat from it; welcome heat after the bitterness outside. Stella stood in front of it, holding her bare hands out to it.

'Thank you, Mrs. Voremberg, but we've had tea,' she said.

'You call that tea, at Polly Anne?' Mrs. Voremberg asked.

I said, 'How did you know we'd been to Polly Anne?'

'But where else should people of your class have tea but at this Polly Anne? In the war always Polly Anne was full. Officers only. And officers' wives. In Polly Anne the British could forget the war for democracy.'

'Did you disapprove of that?' Stella asked.

'Disapprove? No, I did not disapprove. We are not born equal in this world.'

She made tea there in the room, rummaging in dark corners for the caddy, the bottle of milk, the sugar. She carried the tray to a little oval table which stood near the fireplace, and sat beside it, upright, her knees thrust outward by the weight of her belly. She had not taken off her overcoat. On her legs were thick woollen stockings knitted in intricate patterns. She cupped each knee with a hand. Her fingers were swollen and the wide gold band of her wedding ring looked as if it was counter-sunk into her flesh. Her nails were wide and blunt, unhealthily white.

She said to Stella, 'So, tell me why you have come back.'

'Why shouldn't I?' Stella replied. She was sipping tea, her coat opened, the edges folding over on the carpet. I turned my attention to the older woman, who said, 'Why? Only that three years ago I heard you say to your mother-in-law that never you would live here again.' She raised her hand suddenly, palm towards us, in a gesture suggestive of pushing us away. Her lips formed roundly as though she were about to say Oh! but she said, 'Please! Please!' and added, chuckling, 'You were shouting in those days. Oh, so much shouting and quarrelling.'

Stella laughed. 'I expect we were,' she said, 'and I expect I said I'd never come back, but I have, you see.'

'But why? Why?'

'Because I'm going to have a baby.'

Mrs. Voremberg pushed her closed lips outwards and stared unashamedly at Stella, moving her glance with deliberation from Stella's face to her waist.

'So. So.' Her head gave a series of short, jerky nods. 'And the little home you had made, this was not suitable for having babies in?'

'No, it wasn't at all suitable.'

Again the German woman nodded. She said, 'When a place is not suitable, when a place is not a good place, then turn your back on it, children. Turn your back on it and do not return. Stand up.'

'I beg your pardon?'

'Stand up,' she repeated. 'Stand up and turn to the light.'

Stella hesitated, then she obeyed, rising almost aggressively, putting her tea cup down, suffering herself to be turned towards the light by Mrs. Voremberg, who had now left her chair.

'Pull the edges of your coat away. There, like that, hold them there.'

For a moment the two women faced each other without moving and then Mrs. Voremberg slowly brought her hands up, pressed them into Stella's abdomen, spanning its roundness with them. She began to smooth her hands over the swelling, muttering to herself. I watched, fascinated at the outrage Stella suffered in silence. Momentarily I expected her to dash the probing fingers away in disgust, but she did not. Instead, she said in a tone of indifference, 'Well, what is it to be? That's what you're doing isn't it? Deciding what it's to be?'

Mrs. Voremberg straightened up, took Stella's face between her hands and said, 'A boy. A boy. Look, you carry him all to the front and low down. That's how a boy shapes in the womb. All to the front, and low down, impatient to escape. Wait ...'

She went to a large mahogany bureau. Even from where I sat I could see the indescribable chaos disclosed by the opened lid. She was opening and shutting the many little drawers. At last she said, 'Ah! Ah!'

She came back to Stella, holding something small and flat on the palm of her hand. Picking it up with the fingers of her free hand she held it out in front of Stella's eyes. I could not see what it was, but imagined it to be a charm of sorts, a lucky coin, a tiny silver cross.

'Are you offering that to me?'

I looked at Stella quickly. Her face was tight, angry.

'I am giving it to you,' Mrs. Voremberg said, her eyes intent on the object she held up. But she must have realized that Stella was angry, for suddenly she stared at her.

Stella said, 'A swastika? You think I want a bloody swastika?'

Mrs. Voremberg looked from Stella to the swastika and back again. She said, 'You do not understand.'

'No. I don't. I don't understand what a Jew is doing with a swastika in her house. Especially a German Jew.'

'A Jew?'

'Yes,' said Stella. 'That's what you are, isn't it?'

Mrs. Voremberg took Stella's wrist. 'That was my husband only, Frau Hurst.'

'I see. Then you're a Nazi. Is that it?' She freed her wrist.

'You think this cross was not known before *them*? You think *they* invented it?'

She turned to me. 'You, Ian Canning, you know what it is, this cross?'

'It's a symbol, isn't it – of good luck, really. Good Fortune.'

Stella looked at me. Her anger was ebbing. For an instant, before the armour of indifference was reassumed, I caught in her face the look of a lost child. 'I see,' she said. 'I'm sorry. But I don't want it, thank you very much.'

'No. I was for a moment foolish. I it is who must be sorry.' She threw the swastika on the table and we all looked at it. I heard Mrs. Voremberg say, 'For you it means things *I* have forgotten, is that not it? I meant that you should have it to bring you fortune. A fine boy. A fine son.'

'Fine sons have to be soldiers, Mrs. Voremberg.'

I looked up at Stella. She was no longer looking at the swastika. She added, 'I'm sorry again. That's a trite thing to say.'

'Trite?'

'Silly.'

'This is silly, you think, that a boy must be a soldier?'

'No, it was silly of me to imply it was unfortunate. It no longer matters these days, does it? War is strictly non-selective of its victims.' Stella drew her coat around her and I stood up.

'It is we who suffer most in war,' the older woman said. 'Women. Mothers. Oh, and in peace.' She looked at me. 'It is a man's world, this world, and men are never content with it. So restless they are, so restless they make even a room which no longer holds them restless.' She paused, but almost at once, because from the corner of her eyes she caught a movement from Stella which was a preparation for leave-taking, she went on, 'This room. Oh, this room is such a restless room. All the weight of my husband's many pieces cannot make it still. Over here, over here by the window is most restless of all.'

I moved forward a few paces, until I stood close to Stella's shoulder. Mrs. Voremberg had gone to the window and now stood with her back towards us. She turned. We could not see her face or any detail of her body other than its outline. It was growing dark outside.

She said, 'This I could never understand, why here at the window was most restless of all. It is less so now, because I know why it should be so. Shall I tell you Herr Canning? Frau Hurst, shall I tell Herr Canning what I found out about this room?'

I felt Stella shiver.

I said, 'It's getting late. Some other time perhaps.'

But Stella said, 'You may as well know. She wants to tell you.'

I hesitated. 'All right,' I said, 'what did you find out about this room?'

Mrs. Voremberg moved. She began to walk round the room. She moved as a shadow amongst the dark shapes of the furniture, her voice coming to us from different corners, sometimes clear, sometimes muffled as though she had turned her head towards a wall, to listen. I took Stella's cold hand in mine.

'When my husband lived it was not noticeable, this restlessness, and when he died I thought it was that he had come back. But after a time I knew that this was not so. It was not the restlessness of the dead but of the living.

'I thought also it is those who once lived here. One day, Herr Canning, one day it will be possible, they say, to turn a dial on an instrument and listen to the voices of all the people who have ever spoken in a room, all together, all speaking at once with no – what is it? – barrier of time. Perhaps if they are clever enough, these people, with their dials and their scientific instruments, they will isolate one voice at one moment of time. Otherwise it will be Babel. Like Babel. The restlessness of all these voices. The words of them will be indistinguishable.

'And some of us are like these instruments. We do not hear, but we feel. And we do not feel only what has been said, but what has been left unsaid. Also we have this power to select. We are sensitive to what is most powerful, what most audible, what most restless.'

She ceased her wandering and stood quite still just beyond the reach of the glow of the fire.

'When the old Frau Hurst came here to live I was anxious to learn about the house in those days when all her family were gathered under the roof. Also, the restlessness in this room seemed to increase. Many times I tried to speak with her but she was too proud, too aloof to be friendly. Only when Herr Edward came home on leave was there peace in this room. He came home twice. When he had gone back for the last time I called on the old Frau Hurst. She was lonely. For the first time she accepted my invitation to visit me. She told me then that this had been the big dining-room where all the members of the family had sat down to eat, at separate tables.'

Mrs. Voremberg laughed. ' "Just like an hotel," she said. Never did I believe the British would take their insularity so far. She and her husband had a table *here*—', she must have pointed but we caught only the shadow of a gesture, '—this Isobel and her husband were *there*. Sometimes the other sister, the Louisa, she also would eat at the table of Isobel, but mostly in her room. Sick. Ailing. A strong, ailing woman. When the family entertained, all the tables were placed together and covered with a big cloth. In those days there were servants. Oh, yes, lots of servants, the old Frau Hurst said, a butler, and a maid and a cook and a woman for the rough work. All those servants to wait on these tables, the table of the old Frau Hurst, the table of Frau Coles and the table of the little boys – that was the table in the window. The table of the little boys. When she told me this I knew that it was the spirit of one of the little boys that brought such restlessness. Also I knew it was the young Edward, for when he came home to the old Frau Hurst the restlessness lessened. And it was because I knew this restlessness that also I knew the moment when the young Herr Edward died.'

Stella was holding herself quite rigid. Gently, I tightened my grip on her hand. She might not have felt it for all the response she made.

'His aeroplane was shot down over the Channel,' Mrs. Voremberg was saying. 'Is this not so, Frau Hurst? Is this not what you found out and once told me? In a little raft the crew drifted all night. In the morning, a German fighter flew over and machine-gunned them to death. So they were found a few moments later by the rescue boat. The old Frau Hurst knew none of these things. Nor I, at the time. Only I felt him come back just after dawn, come back searching, wondering. I waited all day for the telegram. The next day I went up to her to offer her comfort. As soon as I got into the sitting-room up there I knew he was with her. I did not tell her then. But later when she came down to see me and would not be comforted I told her that he was home, that she should not be afraid. She seemed a brave woman. She said she did not believe me but that she was not afraid. I went with her to her own little front door and when she opened it I knew he was on the stairs looking down at us. I meant to warn her, but when she saw I was going to say something she told me to be quiet. She said, "You think I believe your silly stories? For what would he come back?" Silly stories! For what would he come back indeed? What do we know of death to say, Why should he come back? She locked the door on me and I heard her climbing the stairs and then, Ach! Screaming! Screaming, screaming!'

She spat out the word as though in disgust.

'She would not answer my knocking. I was afraid for the sanity, you will understand. For two days I tried to get her to answer, but she remained upstairs. I knew she had done nothing foolish, because I could hear her moving about. Then, when I had recovered myself from the shock, I considered all that had happened. I thought that if I was aware of *him,* he must be aware of me. I was not afraid, you will understand, Herr Canning. Powers like mine do not remain if you are afraid of them. You know what I have done? I robbed the old woman of him. I sat down here and willed Herr Edward to leave his mother. I willed him down into this room. He knew that I was not afraid, and he came. Only twice since have I lost power over him.

'Once, when the young Frau Hurst came here to live. Then it was that I told her this story. She did not believe me. She does not believe me now. But I told her, to warn her. You, Herr Canning, you need no warning. When you came, also he left this room. Not yet has he come back. Where has he gone? You understand? Not yet has he come back. And a few nights ago the old Frau Hurst saw him. Is this not so? Is this not so, Herr Canning?'

'No,' I said. 'She saw me. She thought it was him, that's all.'

Stella removed her hand from mine. I said, 'You made the same mistake once, Mrs. Voremberg. You saw me looking out of the window of Edward's room and thought it was him.'

I went over to the door, striking my foot on the leg of a chair because it was dark and I could not see. At the door I found what I searched for: the light switch. I turned on the light. The bulb was unshaded. The room lay naked under its illumination. The only shadows were those cast directly by the clear cut shapes of tables, chairs and the other pieces of furniture which filled the room. There was something theatrical about it all, but in a behind-the-scenes, unmiraculous, work-a-day sense. Mrs. Voremberg was stripped of her mask, her assumed mystery. In the light she blinked her eyes and her face looked taken unawares, surprised into stupidity.

'You ought to be careful,' I said to her. 'People who pretend to play about with the supernatural sometimes find they've bitten off more than they can chew.'

'What do you know of the supernatural?' she said; but she was more frightened than angry.

'No more than you.' I looked at Stella. 'We ought to go,' I said.

Mrs. Voremberg made no attempt to rise. We stood, Stella and I, by the table, looking down at her.

'Thank you very much for the tea,' Stella was saying. 'Please don't come to the door. We can let ourselves out.' Suddenly she put out her hand and picked up the tiny silver swastika. 'May I change my mind and have this, Mrs. Voremberg?'

'Why? You refused it before.'

'Just that I've changed my mind.'

'Take it. Take it or leave it. Do as you will. It is nothing, nothing.'

'I know,' Stella said, 'that's why I'd like to have it.'

It was dark in the lobby, but a light from the flat upstairs shone through the frosted window of the door. I closed the door of Mrs. Voremberg's flat and joined Stella as she searched in her handbag for the key.

'Why did you take the swastika?' I said.

'As a symbol,' she said.

'Of what?'

'Not being afraid. It's like getting a medal. It's what I came back to Aylward for.'

IT began from then: whatever it was which grew between Stella and myself; a drawing apart which made us aware of the other's nearness, something unspoken which each of us heard, something in darkness which we saw. That night her eyes were alive whenever she looked at me.

I awoke restless, eager to achieve something in a world miraculously transformed by sunshine. At breakfast I spoke to Alan of going to town with him, but he said, 'Take Stell. She oughtn't to be cooped up.'

'How's the job?' I said, having so often forgotten to ask.

'Seems all right. I'll soon get into it again.'

'Any prospects of a partnership?'

'Yes, if I qualify.'

'That means study.'

'Study,' he repeated, adding, 'At night.'

'Will you do it?'

'Yes. But not for the partnership. Ordinary practice is no good these days. All the plum accountancy jobs are going in industry.'

He looked at his watch. 'Better be off,' he said. 'Shall I just have a word with Stella?'

He meant about the trip to town. He was so eager for her not to brood, for her to have a change of scene, of air. When he came back he said, pleased, 'Nothing she'd like more, Ian.'

'Shall we all meet coming home tonight?'

'She ought to be home before the rush,' he said at once.

'Of course. We'll start home about three.'

'Good.' As he was going he said, smiling, 'I'll just tell mother.'

Stella and I reached town about eleven o'clock. I had an absurd desire to show her London as though she had been a stranger to it. We took the tube to St. James's Park. There was only a partial thaw. On the lake, water had begun to cover the patches of ice. The ducks looked incongruous, seeming to stand on the lake's surface. We halted on the bridge and looked down.

'We should have brought some bread,' she said.

In Pall Mall I hailed a taxi. Already it was time for lunch. I gave the driver the name of a restaurant in Greek Street.

Repeating the name, which he had not heard clearly, I thought: No, not there. Cancel that.

But I let things take their course.

The waiters were different, but the proprietor remembered me, not as an individual with a name but as a face. I saw him looking at Stella. Not recognizing her, he was uncertain about me.

She said, as I helped her loosen her coat over her shoulders, 'Your usual place?'

'No. It's some time since I was here.'

We were the first patrons. I found it impossible not to watch the door.

She said, after I had ordered drinks, 'Look, don't think me rude, but would you rather change your mind and go somewhere else? This was a mistake, wasn't it?'

'How did you know?'

'From your manner, I suppose.'

'I'm sorry.'

'I'm thinking of you, not myself. A sandwich in a pub would be just as much of a treat.'

'It was a mistake, but it isn't now.'

She looked at me seriously. 'Why?'

'You've laid the ghost by mentioning it.'

She nodded.

At the end of the meal she did a wonderful thing. She had drunk no wine but had agreed to join me in drinking brandy. In the brief moment of expansiveness that the ordering of the brandy created, she took the silver swastika out of her handbag and put it on the table between us. It was a theatrical gesture, which she regretted perhaps; but it was done, it was made.

The brandy came. When the waiter had gone I said, 'You'd better put that swastika away. They might poison us.'

She laughed, toyed with it and then pushed it further in my direction.

'Who was the ghost?' she asked. I put my fingers on the symbol as though it were a relic and would impose truth on me.

'A woman.'

'Your wife?'

'You know about that?'

'Alan told me a little.'

'How little?'

'Just that. That you were married and separated.'

I said, 'Her name was Helena.'

'Yes.'

'And you're getting a divorce.'

'Yes.'

'When?'

'When the lawyer's come off the sick list.'

'Your lawyer or hers?'

'Mine. Someone I've been recommended to.'

She was revolving the brandy glass in small, tight circles on the table cloth.

'One of you has grounds for divorce, I take it.'

'God knows. That's for the lawyers to sort out.'

I pushed the swastika away. She picked it up, looked at it, closed her fingers round it, holding it tightly in her fist. 'I want to tell you something,' she said.

'Go on.'

'Just a confession. I know about the abortion.'

'From Alan?'

'I was inquisitive.'

'That's all right. Why shouldn't you be? What else?'

She wasn't looking at me but, I suspected, at my reflection in the mirror on the opposite wall. She said, 'I tried to abort too. Gin, hot baths. It didn't work. I was too scared to try anything more.'

I said, 'Why try at all?'

'Because I'm scared of having the baby. My mother died because of me, and I had a friend who died as well. I associate childbirth with death, I suppose. A man can't see it the same. It's something remote. Not to be thought of. He comforts any twinge of fear or guilt by thinking of hospitals with polished floors and lots of chromium equipment all clean and aseptic, all handled by sterilized, rubber-gloved hands.'

I waited, but she had finished. I said, 'Helena was afraid of nothing. She just found the whole thing an enormous bore.'

'Did she?'

'And you aren't really afraid, Stella. If you were—'

It was her turn to wait. She looked round at me. 'If I were?' she prompted.

I had been going to say: If you were afraid, you wouldn't have come back to Aylward to have the baby. But I knew that she had come to Aylward as though to the root of her fear, to face it.

She was big with child. She carried the burden of fear within her, and I watched her, as the days went by, move ever more awkwardly, ever more conscious of the shifting centre of her gravity. Sometimes I would enter the drawing-room and find her there alone, sitting by the window, staring out at the snowscape.

I would say, tentatively, 'Stella?' in a low voice, so as not to startle her, for she seldom seemed aware that I had come in. But she would say, without surprise, 'Yes, Ian? What is it?'

Once I said, 'You always look as if you're waiting for someone out there.'

'How odd,' she said. 'I feel it the other way. It looks as if it's waiting for me.'

Later, she added, 'Everything is. Waiting for me.'

It was true. Her pregnancy was like the weight of the snow beneath which the house lay mute; still. Marion seldom appeared. Mrs. Burrowes came in every day to clean, to make a meal – a task with which Stella often helped. Marion fed in her own bedroom, rose in the afternoon. Each night I knocked on her door, poured out the ration of gin. She never drank it in my presence. She never mentioned Stella.

I had given up all pretence of work.

Stella.

Early in December it was her birthday. Two days before, I had gone to Pelham Green and there, in a stationer's shop which carried a line of artists' materials, I bought some tubes of primary colours, flake white, turpentine, oil, brushes, a palette, one canvas.

When Alan saw them he said, 'I say, Stell!' He looked at me, gratefully.

In the afternoon, I heard her calling to me. I left my attic room, found her and followed her into Edward's bedroom. At the window she had set up a table piled with books to make a rest for the canvas. All the paints lay in readiness. A chair had been set, facing the window.

'Please sit,' she said.

Then, 'Yes, like that. A little more to the left.'

At first I thought things were going well. I could see her movements from the corners of my eyes: they were brisk, assured, professional. But then, as time went on, I detected a note of panic in all that she did. I felt my heart beating.

She gave a little laugh and said, 'Come and see.'

It was paint applied to canvas, correctly. The planes of flesh were there, the feeling for the skull beneath. The beginning and the end of a talent. She knew too much about painting to produce a canvas which would get by on its integration of wrong values. She had too little art to finish what she had started in the way she had begun. She had reached the limit of her understanding.

'Well?' she inquired.

'It's good. If you painted every day for a year you'd master it.'

'Once I painted every day for two years. Anyway, you're wrong. I shall never paint. It's this—' she said, and picked up the tube of yellow paint, squeezed an inch of it on to her fingers. 'This – see it? A plastic substance with three dimensions. It defeats me physically.'

She looked full at me. 'Defeats me. You see what I mean? Defeats me. It's the same with you and writing, isn't it?'

'But I've mastered them,' I said, after a moment's thought.

'Them?'

'Defeat and fear.'

'I only said defeat.'

'Aren't they inseparable?' I asked.

'Perhaps. How. How have you mastered them?'

I shrugged. 'Mastered is wrong. Left them behind. Turned my back on them.'

'A man can do that. A man can always start again.'

'Not a woman?' I asked.

'At a cost,' she said. 'Helena tried, didn't she?'

My eyes lowered, involuntarily almost, taking in the heavy breasts which already sagged, towards the thrusting belly.

'What did it cost her?' I asked.

'God knows,' she said. 'Something surely. Irreparable loss. How do you assess the cost of that?'

'She invited it. She was glad of it.'

She shook her head.

I repeated, 'Yes. She was glad of it.'

Stella said, 'How do you know?'

I laughed. 'Don't tell me about Helena and how she felt. I know how she felt.'

'Did she know how you felt?'

'Of course. That's why she laughed,' I replied.

'I can understand that. But that's all she achieved, hurting you.'

'You know a lot about it, Stella.'

'I know now how I'd have felt if I'd done successfully what she did.'

'You aren't like her.'

We looked at each other.

'Nor you like Alan,' she said, 'But in some things you are. Fundamental things.'

'Such as?'

'You can turn your back.'

'Has Alan done that?'

'He was ready to. Assam, wasn't it? A clean sheet.'

'It was you who wiped it clean for him, by leaving him.'

'I know,' she said. 'In its way that is what was unfair. It was my own slate I wanted clean.'

'May I ask why, Stella?'

She still had the paint on her fingers. Now she began to remove it with a rag.

'Yes, it's quite simple really. I knew that marriage with Alan was a mistake.'

'I can't believe that.'

'It was a mistake. It is a mistake. Nothing will ever alter it.'

'But why?'

She stared at the paint rag in faint surprise and said, 'Because when the mutual physical attraction has gone there'll be nothing to take its place.'

'What should take its place?'

She crumpled the rag. 'That's what I don't know. I don't know what, but I know something should. I feel something should. But we draw further apart. I don't know him. He doesn't know me. When we no longer want each other what shall we do, Ian?'

I said, lamely, 'There'll be the child.'

She cried, 'But it's Alan I want. What use is the child without Alan?'

'The child *is* Alan,' I said.

'Is that the sort of thing you said to Helena? That the child was you?'

'I don't remember.'

But I did, now. Stella watched me. I felt her lay a finger to the pulse of my memory, my memory of Helena's face close to mine, her teeth white and even. 'Why shouldn't I?' she had shouted. 'Why shouldn't I?' My reply came, 'Kill it you mean? That's what you've done. Killed it.'

It wasn't that I said it to her, in the end, but the words had raced through my mind: It's part of me, part of me you've killed. Part of me. Part of you. And that night, as the nasal echo of the anti-aircraft guns had begun to sound, she had wept in my arms.

But no physical act of union could ever join us again. I had known it. She had known it. Perhaps she wept because of it.

The walk to the clinic grew longer, laborious. Now Stella took my arm as soon as we stepped outside the front door of Aylward on to the packed, rutted snow. Once I looked back at the house and saw Marion Hurst watching us; saw her move quickly away to escape detection.

'Are you writing about Isabella?' Stella asked me.

'No.'

'Did you ever intend to?'

'No. But I pay for my board. I'm not a parasite.'

She smiled. 'Masculine freedom,' she said. 'What a wonderful thing it is. We even need you to stay.'

'Need me? How?'

'Since you started to pay your board we can afford Mrs. Burrowes every day. Didn't you notice?'

'I hadn't connected it.'

'What should we do without Mrs. Burrowes? In other words, without you?'

'Do I detect bitterness?'

She stopped abruptly. 'No. Oh, no, Ian. That's not what I meant.'

On the bleak common we stood looking at each other.

'What did you mean?'

'That I'm – beholden to you.' She laughed, 'For benefits.'

In Polly Anne, after the clinic visit, I said, 'Tell me about Edward.'

'What sort of thing and why?'

'I gathered there was, what? An engagement between you?'

'He thought so,' she said.

'And you?'

Her brows contracted. 'I wasn't sure.'

'Did you never speak of it to each other?'

'In vague terms. Edward was vague. He didn't know where he was going or what he was doing. The war dumbfounded him, when it came. I remember him saying, "I can't believe it. It's all so damned futile." Futile was his favourite word. Futile.'

She seemed to test it on her tongue as if it might conjure a thought of Edward that would put him into perspective, here, in Polly Anne, seven years after the war had begun.

'I think,' she said, and then, repeating herself, 'I think if he'd said *then*: Let's get married Stell—' She stopped.

175

Stell was what Alan called her.

'Yes?' I prompted. 'If Edward had said—'

'Let's get married – Stella – I think we would have.'

'But he didn't.'

'No.'

Later, she said, 'I've given you the wrong impression. I wasn't ready to fall into the arms of whichever one said it. Not in that way. Not in that way at all. But I needed direction.' She smiled. 'A strong arm. You see, I agreed with Edward. It was all so futile. But it was there. It existed. It had to be faced. War, futility. What looked like the end.'

'And Alan was facing it.'

'Without knowing it. To him it wasn't futile. He almost welcomed it.'

We walked home in silence until we got to that part of the road where once we had entered a zone of silence.

'It was like being shipwrecked,' she said. 'Like being in a shipwreck with the two of them. One of them watching the sea closing in and the other fighting it, striking out for a raft. I suppose—' and she hesitated. 'I suppose it was my own life I loved best.'

I said, 'When did Alan ask you to marry him?'

'I think – when he knew Edward wasn't going to. Perhaps he asked him. That would be like Alan. To make sure he wasn't hurting Edward.'

'And you accepted at once.'

'No. No, he asked me several times. We only married after Edward was killed.'

'So Edward never really knew how you and Alan were?'

'Oh yes, he knew. He knew better than I did, I suppose.' She paused. 'He had a miserable bloody life.'

'I've always understood otherwise.'

'Have you?'

'From all I've heard I've got the impression he was treated as if the sun rose and sank in him.'

'Yes, that was true. But you see, he was treated like that, as if the sun rose and sank in him, but he knew it didn't. He knew he was a deceitful, lying little prig when he was a child. He told me so. He told me how badly he'd treated Alan, splitting on him, getting him into trouble. He also told me what stuck in his throat.'

'And what was that?'

'The way, once they were grown up, Alan never showed

resentment. Edward once said it was as if Alan was apologizing to him for treating *him* badly. As though all the talk about what a sensitive, intelligent and clever fellow Edward had been and would be had fooled Alan, and as though Alan was treating him like someone living on a higher plane. And he said, "That's what sticks in my throat. I can't decide whether it makes me despise him or myself".'

We were approaching the house and, on a mutual impulse, slowed our pace.

'And you,' I said. 'What view of Alan did you take?'

'I didn't take a view, Ian. I couldn't be near him without feeling – physical infatuation. When we weren't together I dismissed him from my mind. But he only had to walk into a room—'

We were, I knew, in our thoughts, both in Adela's room: she remembering it as it had been, with Alan coming into it for the first time: I remembering it as it now was, a shabby room which housed only the ghosts of Adela's friends.

As we walked towards the house I looked up at it. The daylight was going and the snow, giving off light, distorted perspective. There it was, the façade of Aylward, with the steps leading up to the front door. Behind the façade you had the impression the house was vanishing with the day.

A letter from Commander Owen awaited me.

Dear Old Ian,

Nearly Christmas time. Was wondering if you could join me for a few days over the holiday. What rotten weather it is; but do come if you can. There won't be anyone else here, so you can rest up.

I showed it to Alan.

'Will you go?' he said.

'I'd better, hadn't I? He's getting on.'

Part Three

PARTURITION

CHAPTER ONE

AT the end of January, when it was all over, I came back to town. I called to see Thurlow. I sat in the padded velvet chair.

'Did you have difficulty getting back after the funeral?' I asked him.

'We were on half-power, I think, if that's possible. Anyway the train crawled.' He added, 'I rang you in Wendover the next day but you'd come up to town apparently.'

'Yes, just for the day,' I told him.

On the desk, without pretence that things were any different than they were, was a folded red file. I saw it upside down, but could read the abbreviation for 'deceased' after the Commander's name. Commander Owen, Decd.

'He's left you everything,' Thurlow said.

There was no answer to this: but there was a question.

'What about the woman who used to come in. Mrs. Baines?'

'He suggested in his will that you make provision for her if she outlived him, Ian. I told her at the funeral, because she was rather expecting a will to be read. Unprofessional, I'm afraid, but she's a decent old soul. I didn't want her to think she'd been forgotten.'

'No, of course. What sort of provision would you suggest?'

'That's entirely up to you,' he said.

'No, I have no experience. An annuity, I suppose.'

'Or a lump sum.'

We stared at each other, as if across all that remained of a man's wordly goods. 'Please help me,' I said. 'Tell me what is fair.'

'Well.' He opened the file and began to talk. There was not a great deal. The house. Some investments. Some cash at bank and on deposit. After he had finished speaking I considered all that he had told me.

I said, 'I'm a pretty fortunate chap, aren't I?'

He turned to me, smiling slowly.

'It gives you added security.'

I said, 'Yes.'

'And Mrs. Baines?' he asked.

'A lump sum, I think. Do you agree?'

'You can't really afford a decent annuity out of it.'

'How long did she work for him?' I asked.

'About fifteen years.'

'Five hundred pounds?' I asked.

'I think that's too much. Much too much.'

'Then what?'

'Two hundred pounds would be adequate. She'd never have known such riches. And if you keep her on as housekeeper—'

'No,' I said. 'I shall sell the house.'

'I see.' He closed the file and moved it to the far side of his desk. Once more he was looking out of the window. 'He hoped you'd live in it, you know. That's what he said when he drew up the will.'

'When did he draw it up?'

'Just after you married Helena.'

I said, 'How odd. I always thought he disapproved of Helena.'

Thurlow turned towards me. 'I think he did. But he'd promised your parents he'd look after you, you know.'

'He'd done that. He'd fulfilled his promise.'

'Well he had no one else to leave it to. Let's put it that way.'

'Would he have left me the house if he'd known I wouldn't live in it?'

Thurlow said at once, 'Of course. He wasn't a possessive sort of man.'

I said, 'Was he in love with my mother?'

Thurlow smiled. 'Yes. I rather think he was.' He pulled the file toward him again. 'Two Hundred Pounds?'

'What?'

'For Mrs. Baines.'

'If you think it enough.'

Thurlow made a move. I rose. 'I'll let you know what I decide about the house.' I said, 'Thank you for all you've done.'

'What about Rossiter, by the way?'

I said, 'Is he better?'

'Oh yes. Weeks ago.'

'I'd better see him some time.'

Thurlow took my hand. I felt the thrust of his shoulder and in a moment or so I was outside in the passage.

In the streets the snow had been churned into yellowy-brown, translucent mud, brittle in parts, the same texture as the flavoured and coloured tubes of ice which children bought in summer. From where I stood in High Holborn I could see the pink towers of the Prudential building, flat, lacking third dimension against a smoky sky. The wind was bitter again. More snow was in the air. I walked to Bloomsbury and booked a room at the hotel where I had stayed for one night, the day after the funeral.

In the lobby there was a telephone booth. I rang David Holmes at his ministry.

'Holmes here.'

'Ian Canning.'

A pause: then, 'Hello, old chap.'

'You never sent my things to Wendover, David.'

Another pause. 'I know. Look, are you in town?'

'At the moment.'

'Come round tonight. I've got something rather pressing on at the moment.'

'Come round where?'

'The flat. Lowndes Street.'

'What time?'

'Seven? We'll pop round to the club after.'

'All right. At seven.' I rang off. It was time for my appointment. Outside the hotel I hailed a taxi and gave him an address in Harley Street.

'This is Peterson,' said the man I had seen on the previous occasion, the day after the Commander's funeral. Peterson, a large, fleshy man, smiled at me encouragingly. He said, 'We won't waste time, Canning. But a few questions first.'

I was invited to sit. The consulting-room was overheated.

'The temperatures began in nineteen forty-two, I see.' He was looking through a file, flicking the pages quickly, summarizing verbally the whole history. He came to the last page and looked up. 'And now there's the tummy trouble. When did it begin?'

'About three weeks ago.'

'Not earlier?'

I said, 'I was sick one morning a couple of months ago. I thought it was something I'd eaten.'

'Where were you three weeks ago?'

181

'In Wendover.'

'You consulted the local man?'

I hesitated. 'No. Someone in the house was very ill.'

'I see. How is it now?'

'Better, I think.'

'You were in India for how long, now?'

'From nineteen forty-two until nineteen forty-five.'

Peterson turned to his colleague. 'And the X-rays show nothing?'

'Nothing at all.'

Peterson leaned back. 'I'd like you to see a chap who's up in Edinburgh. Would you like me to arrange it?'

'Of course.'

'I'll get in touch with him, then. I take it you could spend a few days up there in, say, two or three weeks?'

I said, 'Yes, I could do that.' I paused. 'Is there anything you can tell me yourself?'

Peterson got up, his hands in his pockets. 'Well, Canning, these tropical things are difficult to pin down.'

'Could you hazard a guess at one in particular?'

He looked at me. 'I would hazard a guess at two. The internal disorder, coming at this stage, gets us nearer to it.'

'Would one be better to have than the other?'

I saw him glance across at the other man.

Peterson's colleague said, 'Not really, old man.'

As I was going, Peterson held my arm in a professionally friendly grip, 'We're experimenting all the time, Canning. I don't want to say more. Wait until you've been to Edinburgh. Meanwhile, just carry on as usual.'

What had I expected? Not this sense of separateness, of having become detached from, of having grown out of Lowndes Street: its front door, to which I found I still had a key, the flight of stairs, the flat itself.

'I heard your step,' David said. 'Have you still got a key, then?'

'Yes, it never struck me I had. I just fished for it on the ring automatically.'

He stood on the top landing, thinner, his nose and cheeks blue.

'Come in,' he said. 'The pressure's almost non-existent.' He pointed at the feeble flame of the gas-fire. 'God, what a winter. They say it's the Russians. They've discovered a way of lowering the temperature.'

He rubbed his hands vigorously, expunging doubt, seeking warmth.

'Where's Pegs?' I asked.

'She's gone away for a bit. The flat was getting her down.'

'The stairs,' I said.

'Oh yes. That.'

'You got married?'

He nodded.

I said, 'And the baby?'

It was the question he had expected and had not looked forward to. 'False alarm,' he said, briefly.

He was afraid I would think there had never been a baby and that it had been a trick to force my hand. But it had only been a trick to force his. His whole face bore the imprint of Peggy's deception: that, and the tightness of his own determination not to admit it.

'She hasn't left you?' I asked.

'Good God. Left me? Of course not. No,' he went on, tidying something on the mantelpiece. 'No, old Pegs wouldn't leave me.' He faced me. 'But, to be frank, we had a bit of a tiff. She'll be back in a couple of days. She——'

His face slackened. I think he had been about to say: She always is.

'Women,' he said, and paused, seeking plain words from the jumble of his cliché-ridden life, 'women are the devil.' He looked straight at me. 'The silly thing is I still bloody well worship her. It'll be all right. Come on. Let's have that drink.'

'It's the war,' he said, as he clutched at my arm outside, to stop himself slipping on a patch of slush. 'It was worse for women. They didn't get the excitement of it. Not that I did, stuck in the ministry. But then, yes, being a man I got the excitement of it.'

I thought, obliquely, of Commander Owen, the picture of the Spitfire. Feeling his death, anew, I felt for David because he was there with me, walking companionably through the sludge.

The club had changed. Already you could tell that its members were going elsewhere. I said so to David. 'I know,' he replied. 'What is it? A month or so ago everyone came here. Now they go somewhere else. It'll close down soon.'

'It was used as a rehabilitation centre,' I suggested. 'Every month a batch of customers passed the test and went.'

'That's a thought,' he said. 'Just us left.' He raised his glass, was momentarily lost in thought, then drank half the pint of beer it contained. 'That's about the size of it.' He turned to me.

'Ian, I am sorry about your stuff, the books and things.'

'What happened?'

'Nothing. We just kept putting it off. You know' – and he settled himself comfortably – 'Pegs and I used to sit there and once in a while one of us would say: Hell, we ought to pack Ian's things and send 'em to him. But, Lord – well, what is it, do you feel the same? – at the end of a day we both came home whacked. Whacked to the wide. And some of those books looked bloody heavy.' He drained his glass. 'My round, now,' he said, and went to the bar. His heavy shoulders were rounded. He looked shabby and down at heel. It took him rather a long time to find the right amount of small change to pay for the beer. In the end he had to open his wallet. It was a ten shilling note he handed over. I wondered whether it was his last until pay day.

'But I'll really get them packed up now,' he said, sitting down again. 'Wendover, you said. I'd better make a note of the address again.'

'No,' I told him. 'I'm selling the house.'

'Selling? *You're* selling? Is it yours then?'

'The Commander died ten days ago. He left it to me.'

'I say. Lord, I'm sorry. You thought a lot of him, didn't you? What happened?'

'He caught cold and developed pneumonia.'

'Were you there at the time?'

'Yes. I went up to stay over Christmas.'

'Lord, that was rotten for you.'

'It was all right. I think we entertained each other while he was well. That was the main thing. I'm glad I went. At least—'

And I hesitated. I had said this to nobody. David was sufficiently distant to make it possible. 'At least,' I said, 'in one way I'm glad. But in another way I can't help wondering.'

'Wondering what?'

'If I hadn't gone he'd have stuck indoors huddled over the fire like old men do. I think he wanted to what? Express his fitness? Walks, not long walks. But the weather was treacherous.'

I could see him now, turning in at the gate, just behind me, his lips suddenly blue, stretched over his teeth in a grin, and above, in his eyes, a look of disbelief.

'You're shivering,' I had told him.

'Am I?'

I had taken his arm. In the dark hall, the butterfly net stood in a corner awaiting the sun-filled days of summer.

'He's overdone it, sir. He's overdone it,' Mrs. Baines had said, coming down from his room with an empty coal-scuttle.

The fire in his room had drawn me. Long hours I had sat with him, knowing in myself that he would die. Sometimes I could not bear to look at him: not when his eyes were full of panic, but when they looked upon me alight with gratitude. The last words he ever said were, 'Ian, your mother and I—'

He was already approaching a state of coma.

David said, 'But he was pretty active always, wasn't he? Better to go like that, quickly, before he really had time to face it.' He added, 'What will you do?'

'He's left me some money. And the house of course. It makes a difference.'

'You'll sell the house?'

I nodded.

'I wish I could buy it, Ian. God, I wish I had enough to buy it. Pegs has always hankered after the country. That's why things aren't going well. I mean, as well as they might. How much do you want for it?'

'You could always look at it and then make me an offer.'

He said, 'No, whatever you asked I couldn't pay. I haven't a bean and I can't saddle myself with a mortgage. I'm trying to get into the Control Commission, Ian. It was Pegs' idea, but the more I think of it the better I like it. We'll be in Germany for years, and serve 'em right, and while we're there there'll be the best of everything, quarters, servants, all of it. What a young man used to be able to get by going East in the old days.'

He put his beer down on the table. 'That's what beats me, Ian. There's no scope for a man any more. We've won the war and lost the Empire in the process.'

'You used to favour its disbandment.'

'Hell, we all did. I mean, us. Chaps like you and me. We were as far Left as we could be.'

'We had to make some sort of gesture.'

'I know, I know.' He relapsed into a silence in which his hopes scattered like mice into holes.

'Spain,' he said, after a while. 'That was so bloody wonderful once. Like what? Like the Holy Grail.' He grinned. 'Poets with rifles. Civil servants with a conscience.'

'Some died,' I said.

'The lucky ones,' he rejoined. 'The lucky ones died. The rest of us stayed on to face the futility.'

'You don't really feel like that, David.'

'Don't I? I damn' well do. The whole damn' thing is futile.

Hopelessly bloody well futile.' His eyes narrowed, as though he were suddenly determined I should admit it. 'Look at you, old chap. You're like me. Just too young to have eased yourself into a rut, just too old to believe you can escape one. What the hell can we look forward to? By the time we get where we think we're going we'll find that's where all the youngsters have started from. They'll be way ahead of us and the old gang will be way ahead of us, fighting the new gang. Every so often there's a generation like us, Ian. Our only *raison d'être* to be blown to pieces in a war we imagine we believe in ideologically. And at this moment the new gang is cooking up ideologies for their sons to believe in and fight for and die over.'

He was getting drunk, easily, as emotionally disturbed men are inclined to.

'And who is the new gang?' I asked.

'If you lived in town you'd know. You'd know if you worked in the Ministry. Young bastards, cynical as they come. But – and this is the point Ian – cynical, what? Academically? – not cynical like you and me because we've been through the mill of our own bloody delusions and come out on the other side, some of us, come out on the other side and seen what it was all for. If they start like that where are they going to lead us?'

'They're only expressing what they find. Perhaps most of what they find is us.'

'What do you know about it? Stuck away in – in Wendover or in where is it? Pelham Green.'

I was silent. Almost irrelevantly a thought came of Terry, the boy Adela kept.

'You see?' David said, triumphantly. 'You don't know. But I know. They're in the Ministry, everywhere, working their way in everywhere while we try and catch our breath. And with luck they'll just be too old for the next war.'

'Will age matter?'

'Eh?'

I said, 'Will age matter, in the next war?'

David snorted. 'You've got the push-button complex. One big bang and *kaput*. But it won't be like that. Won't be like that at all.'

I said, 'Perhaps it won't even be at all.'

'Don't put your head in the sand. Don't go pious on me. Even *they* see through that sort of old-maidish piety. I give 'em that. What are you trying to do, old man? Fool yourself you've a future?'

I said, 'Is there any point in going on, if you can't fool your-self?'

He began to laugh. He was perilously close to maudlin tears. 'Of course not. That's where we're got by the short and curlies. We cling on. I'm clinging on. You're clinging on. Perhaps that's all the future is, only there because you cling on.'

Without warning he stood up, his face sweating, white. He was going to be sick. He lurched towards the stairs and a group of drinkers stood back, quickly.

I followed him, stood by him at the wash basin and listened to him say, over and over again, 'God! God!'

I could not bring myself to help him, for his sickness disturbed me. But I could not leave him alone; the narrow cell was so squalid, a place for suicide.

When we went back into the club room the few drinkers stared at us. I remember noticing the letters stuck in the rack and wondering whether they were the same I had seen before. I helped him down the stairs. The cold air struck us, breathed new life into us.

'I'm so bloody ashamed,' he said. 'I can't ever go there again.'

At the door of the flat we stopped.

'Will you come up?' he asked.

'Thanks, but not this time.'

'You've had no dinner.'

'There's plenty of time.'

He said, 'Forget all that nonsense I talked.' The light from the streetlamp fell on his face. Mine, I knew was in shadow, as Alan's had been that night, months ago: not so many months ago.

'You'll be all right?' I asked.

He nodded and said, 'You guessed, didn't you?'

'Guessed what?'

'That Pegs had tricked me about the kid. She wasn't in the pudding club at all.'

'She could have thought so.'

'No.' He shook his head. 'It was just a trick. I don't mind really. I always wanted us to get married, but it's made a difference somehow. I suppose I deserved it.'

'How?'

'You know how it is. You get lazy, everything's all right as it is. Getting married – you put if off – like we put off sending your stuff. Well – I suppose she got fed up. Frightened even. Best years of her life and all that. She got to the point where she had to pin me down, make sure of me.'

I waited.

He said, 'But it's made it — I don't know — it's like having something invisible in the flat, something that comes between us. Look, do come up.'

'Not now, David.'

'No, well. That's how it is. Something there coming between us. Every so often she gets out for a few days. But she always comes back.'

'It'll be all right, David.'

'I know. I wish we would have a child though. That's what I'd like.'

'Would she?'

'Don't know. Haven't thought really. Lord, I was as pleased as punch that time she said there was one on the way.'

'Another one to face futility?' But I was smiling, and the words carried no sting.

'Lord, I don't know. What is it, Ian?'

'What's what?'

'What suddenly makes having a child important? I'd never given it a thought before. Been bloody bored at the idea, truth to tell. But when she said that time that there was one, I was like, well, a cat with two tails. It was something, you know, substantial, something definite to look forward to. I suppose I used to talk about it too much. Must have got on her nerves, knowing she'd lied about it and, well, it probably made her feel she'd been a bloody bitch about it.'

'Forget it, David. It'll happen soon enough. The real thing.'

'She says we can't afford it. Women's logic.'

'Good night, David.'

'Good night, Ian. Thanks. Oh, I say—'

I turned back to him.

'Where are you now?'

'Moving around. The Pelham Green address would find me. Good night.'

I walked towards Sloane Street and thought of a child; something substantial, something definite to look forward to: a male child, a projection of yourself in flesh into a future you would not otherwise know.

Adela got back into bed. She had a bad cold. The morning light scoured the bedroom, stressed its untidiness and her unhappy independence. On the walls were portraits of her lovers, young men of varying good looks, mostly displaying their physiques in athletic poses. One, of Terry, in boxer's shorts and with bandaged fists, squaring up to the camera, was on the bedside table.

'You're a sweet,' she said to me, 'no one came near me yesterday.'

I jerked my head at the portrait. 'Not even him?'

'He's in the Army. Gone for good. Or bad.'

'He'll get leave.'

'And come back to me?' She laughed.

'Can I get you some medicine or something?'

'No thanks, Ian.'

She wasn't looking at all well.

She said, 'I nearly didn't answer the 'phone when you rang. I'm glad I did. I wanted to talk to you anyway.'

'Oh?'

'Have you left Wendover?' she asked.

'Yes, I've left.'

'I was sorry to hear about your godfather. Alan told me.'

I said, 'What did you want to talk to me about?'

She hesitated. 'About the situation at Aylward,' she said.

Her face was so disarranged by the effects of her cold that I could not detect any particular expression.

'Oh,' I said. 'Is there a situation at Aylward?'

'Are you going back there?'

I nodded.

'Do they know?'

I said, 'I rang Alan last night. He seemed to take it for granted.'

'But why are you staying in London, right now?'

'Only to sort out a few business matters. I've inherited some stuff from the godfather. Did you think there might be some other reason?'

'I don't know. I suppose I wondered whether you'd been aware of – well, let's keep on calling it the situation at Aylward.'

'Go on,' I said, 'explain what the situation is.'

'I don't know what it is. I've only gathered—'

'From whom?'

'Father.'

'I see. They've all decided I'm finding an excuse to live easy – I think that's what the expression was. Is that it?'

'No.'

'Well then.'

'It's about Stella,' Adela said.

'Stella?' I suppose my puzzlement showed.

'About Stella and you.'

I waited a little before saying, 'What is that supposed to mean?'

She said, 'I thought you'd be able to tell me.'

I laughed. 'For God's sake, Adela, let's stop sparring for openings. Tell me what has happened.'

She said, warily, 'I take it nothing has actually happened. If it had I imagine Alan wouldn't let you go back.'

'Do you mean there's a suggestion Stella and I—' I stopped, then said so vehemently I even surprised myself, 'What in heaven's name could there be between myself and Stella?'

'You'd better ask Marion,' she said.

'Have *you* asked Marion?'

'No,' she said, 'but she's been talking to father.'

'Saying what?'

'She says you shouldn't be allowed back in the house because Stella's fallen in love with you.'

'It's absolutely monstrous.'

'It's not true?'

'Of course it isn't true.'

Adela said, 'How do you know? Supposing she has fallen in love with you?'

'I should have said it's psychologically impossible while she's bearing Alan's child.'

'In ordinary circumstances I'd agree with you.'

I said, 'What's not ordinary about this case?'

'Your likeness to Edward.'

I stood up. 'Damn Edward! Damn, blast and perdition to bloody Edward.'

But suddenly I was disturbed.

'Which reminds me,' Adela said, 'I promised to give you something. It's in that drawer.'

'What is?'

'Open it and you'll see.'

I went to the drawer she had pointed out, and opened it.

'It's crammed with all sorts of things,' I said.

'Isn't there a book with a yellow jacket?'

There was: a slim, demy octavo volume with a typographical dust cover. *Bitter Spring and other poems, by Edward Hurst.* As I picked it up I saw what lay underneath: a duplicate of the photograph of Alan and Adela, framed in *passe-partout.*

'This as well?' I asked, holding it up.

She stared at it. 'Put it back,' she said, 'I'd forgotten it was there.'

But I brought it to her bedside, with the book.

'Please put it back, Ian.'

'It should go on the wall with the others,' I said.

'Well it used to. But after Terry met Alan he was jealous.'

'Terry's gone now.'

'Don't rub it in. Please put it back.'

'No. I'm going to tell you something.'

'I know about it.'

I said, 'What do you know?'

'That Marion left a copy in Stella's drawer. Alan told me.'

'You've seen him recently.'

'Now that he works in town he sometimes looks in.'

'Adela,' I began, and she saw that I was serious; 'you said, that first evening I came, that Marion knew about you and Alan, that you found something obscene in it because it wasn't just a question of condoning what went on.'

'Yes. That's all true.'

'If it wasn't just a question of condoning it, what was it?'

'It's a complicated story.'

I shook my head. 'Don't put me off. It must have a simple basic line.'

'I suppose you're right,' she said. 'Put that way you could say Marion asked me to seduce Alan so that he wouldn't cut Edward out of the running for Stella.' She paused, smiled ironically. 'The fact that I'd already made up my mind to seduce Alan is neither here nor there.'

'Did Stella know about it?'

'Of course. As soon as it became obvious to everyone what Alan and I were doing Marion lost no time in telling her.'

'Telling? Really telling?'

'Well, hinting. I expect she used to shake her head and tell Stella she was worried because Alan was seeing so much of me and he was so much younger.'

'And all the time she'd *asked* you to seduce him?'

'Not in words of one syllable. She told me she was worried because Stella was hurting Edward. She didn't like Stella, and never cared what happened to Alan, but to stop Edward being hurt was her first consideration. She encouraged Alan to see me. She raised no objection when he took to spending week-ends away from home on the most flimsy pretexts. I used to get him to tell me what excuses he made. He was very young and they were laughable.'

I said, 'But does Stella actually *know*?'

Adela paused. 'Only in the way a woman thinks she knows. She's usually right.'

'Alan's never admitted it to her?'

'No. Of course not. But it wasn't necessary for him to do so, was it. It's a knowledge they share without ever having mentioned it.'

'Was Alan shaken by what his mother did recently?'

'The photograph in the drawer?' Adela grinned. 'He was shaken all right. Even he had to admit it had been put there deliberately. But you know Alan. Things don't stay with him. He comes out unscarred.'

'Does he?' And to myself I repeated: Does he?

'Oh, yes,' Adela said. 'He was laughing about it. That's what I like about him.'

I nodded.

'As he grows older and I grow older, Ian, it's starting to come back.'

'Your feeling for him?'

'Yes,' she said. 'But like what I imagine love becomes after ten years of married life.'

'Are you asking me to free him of Stella for you?'

'Don't be a damn' fool.'

We were both laughing, but something unspoken lay between us. 'I'm too old,' she said. 'An older sister. A woman though. He can't *not* be gallant to a woman. He's a bastard really. It's in his eye all the time. That calculating, physical look that only a woman understands.' She laughed, and nodded at the pictures on the wall. 'He smirked at all that lot, but he was awfully annoyed really. Tell me, Ian, why is it that once a man's had a particular woman he likes her to stay had, even if he doesn't want her himself ever again.'

I took out a cigarette while I thought about this.

'It isn't really true, Adela.'

She said, 'It *is* true, it's possessiveness. Just like women. Men are no better.'

'A different sort of possessiveness, then.'

'Yes,' she said. 'A damned cold possessiveness. There's always warmth in a woman's.'

'Cold, warm,' I repeated. 'It's the difference between a man's world and a woman's.'

'What *is* a man's world, Ian?' she asked, laughing.

'Outside him. Drawing him towards it. But he has to stay outside it so that he can see it.'

'Give me one of those cigarettes.'

'Will you be able to taste it?'

I handed her the packet: lit the cigarette she withdrew from it with her stained fingers.

'So these are Edward's poems,' I said. I flicked the book open. ' "My eyes are not the eyes of a man" ' I read.

And Adela went on from memory: ' "Light does not enter them, they do not endure." How does it go on?'

> ' "They are like the eyes of mountains,
> calm,
> like the eyes of a deep sea.
> My brain is a sun
> my limbs, planets.
> O! I am over the universe like a god
> moved, blind to a creation".'

I turned back to the title page. Opposite, in the copyright lines, was a note giving the year of publication. Nineteen forty-three.

'But he was dead then,' I said.

'I know. A posthumous publication.'

'Was the collection chosen by him?'

'No, I chose it.'

'I see.'

'What do you mean, you see?' she asked.

I flicked more pages. 'I'm looking for the poems his mother objected to.' I looked up at her. Slowly a flush of embarrassment came on to her cheeks. 'Is it this one?' I said, 'Poem to Stella?'

Adela said, 'I don't remember which ones. All the sonnets are derivative of course. He had a Rupert Brooke period.'

I read a few lines, but could not take them in, put the book down on the bed.

'Aren't you going to take it with you?' she said.

'No,' I replied.

'Are you cross about something?'

'No. I was thinking Edward might have been as annoyed with the collection as his mother was.'

'He wrote the bloody poems, didn't he?'

'He wrote them all right, but he didn't have a say about which of them should be published, Adela.'

'I chose the best,' she said.

I grinned at her. 'That's the correct criterion.'

'Correct? You're being stuffy with me. Or is it—' and she hesitated.

'Is it what?'

'That you didn't like the poem to Stella? That you didn't like the idea of Edward writing it?'

I gave Alan's name, and my own name, and sat down to wait for him in the lobby. Opposite me, on the wall, was a board, mahogany stained, with the names, blocked in gold paint, of all the companies whose registered offices were here in the building where Alan had found his job. Behind the reception counter a girl was typing a fair copy of someone's Balance Sheet, on a machine with a long carriage.

Alan came through a door which was paned with frosted glass. I stood up.

'Hello, Ian,' he said, and stuck out his hand. I searched his face for any sign that my visit was an interruption, my presence unwelcome to him personally. I found none.

'I wondered whether you could lunch.'

He jerked his head round to look at the old-fashioned clock high on the wall above the door.

'That'd suit me fine,' he said. 'Hang on here a tick and I'll just get something laid on.'

'I'm not putting you out? Not upsetting—'

He broke in, 'Good Lord, no. Just hold on.'

In five minutes he was back, wearing his overcoat and a check scarf.

'No bowler or umbrella?' I asked.

He smiled, took my arm, and guided me through several sets of swing doors to the lift, a shoddy, old-fashioned affair, so narrow, so confined, it was like a vertical coffin.

'Breathe in,' he instructed.

We stood chest to chest, our heads drawn back so as not to breathe in the other's face.

Freed, we went out into the bitter cold.

He had found a pub where it was possible to get a decent meal quickly, quietly. He took me there.

'You've got yourself organized,' I observed.

'It's quite good, isn't it?'

'How's the job?'

But the waitress was at his side. He did not answer. He asked me, 'What'll you have?'

'There's Irish stew today,' the girl said.

'Is it any good?' he asked. They smiled at each other. 'What d'you say, Ian. Irish stew?'

'Fine.'

'And a couple of pints of bitter.'

I said again, 'How's the job?'

'All right, but how are you?'

'I'm fine.'

'Have you cleared up all the legal paraphernalia?'

'As far as one can ever do that.'

He said, 'You must have had a rotten time.'

'How's Stella?' I asked.

'She's a bit under the weather, but everything's going along to pattern. We'll both be glad when it's over now. The last weeks drag on.'

'Next month, isn't it?'

'Beginning of March, yes.'

Our beer came. 'Well, all the best, Alan.'

'Cheers.'

I said, 'I saw Adela this morning. She's in bed with a cold.'

'How was she otherwise?'

'A bit down in the mouth, I thought.'

He looked at his beer, then at me again, smiling. 'She's lost her young bruiser,' he said.

'So I gathered. She still keeps his picture by the bed.'

'In her portrait gallery.' He laughed. 'Lord, she's a queer cuss is Adela.'

'In what way?'

'Well, all those pictures of her conquests. I told her I thought it was bad psychology. Damn it all, Ian, think of a chap just getting down to the job, full of his own onions, and suddenly feeling all those other chaps' eyes boring into the back of his head.'

'Did you say that to her?'

'Yes.'

'What was her reaction?'

'She said it mostly had the opposite effect. That the latest chap felt in honour bound to prove he was better than any of 'em, or all of them put together.'

'She's been lucky then.'

'Well, she's always gone for the damn-you-jack-I'm-all-right type. She's just about at the end of her innings though. I'm sorry for her.'

'She wouldn't like that. Being felt sorry for.'

'Oh, I don't know. She's not as tough as she pretends.'

When our meal was finished, he said, 'Have you made any definite plans, you know, for the future?'

'Yes, I think I have,' I began, then drew back as the waitress put two coffee cups down on the table.

Alan said, 'Good, let's hear what they are.'

'The first is to get really fit again.'

'And then?'

'To get a job. Abroad perhaps.'

'Do you need to have a job?'

'I could get by financially without. A bit more than get by.'

'But all the same you want one?'

'Want and need one.'

He said, 'Any particular line?'

'No. So long as it's congenial.' I smiled. 'Not with Brian Selby. Not that sort of thing at all.' I paused. 'I may be going up to Edinburgh for a few days quite soon to see a man someone thought might help.'

He was stirring his coffee. Suddenly he looked up at me. 'You're a lucky bastard,' he said. At first I wondered what he meant, but then I saw for the first time the marks of a prisoner stamped on his brow. That they were self-inflicted through his own sense of duty made them no less moving to look upon.

I said, 'There's just one point.'

'What's that Ian?'

'May I come back to Aylward for a few weeks?'

'Of course. We'd already arranged you should.'

As he spoke he turned his head away, and stretched out for two of the four lumps of sugar which lay on a miniature dish. I knew then that he was not unaware of the rumour which linked my name with Stella's.

CHAPTER TWO

SINCE leaving it I had thought of the house as dark, melancholy, full of ghosts, unbidden memories. It seemed so no longer. It was as if the windows had been widened, heightened. Perhaps it was the effect of the snow reflecting light. I noticed the shabbiness of everything; threadbare patches on the carpet in the drawing-room; an uncleaned, uncared for look which might once have depressed me. It was too matter of fact to do so now. You saw it, registered it. It had no special effect.

It was Stella who had let me in. Her face was pale, but rounder, calm, the eyes steady, sharp almost, as if they could cut. The round hump of the child thrust forward, stretching the blue-patterned smock whose colour matched her eyes.

'Hello,' I said. 'How are you, Stella?'

'I'm fine,' she answered, and stood aside to let me in. 'I thought you might come down with Alan tonight, actually.'

'We decided not. The rush hour's the sort of thing a chap copes best with alone. I'll leave the bag here if it's all right.' I put it down.

'You've changed,' she said.

'Have I? In what way?'

'I've no idea.'

She went down the passage and opened the kitchen door. 'Mr. Canning's arrived, Mrs. Burrowes, so he'll be an extra one for tea.' She shut the door, opened the drawing-room door. 'Come in,' she said.

I followed her. When I was in the room I saw that Marion was there. The first thing I noticed about her was that she had stopped dying her hair. The grey was beginning to show through. She looked smaller, much older. I went to her, put out my hand which she touched, briefly.

'Are you quite recovered?' she asked. Her voice held no friendliness.

'Recovered?'

'From the shock of your godfather's death?'

'Thank you, yes. It wasn't really a shock.'

Stella said, 'Will you be all right for a bit? I'm supposed to rest now.'

I said, 'Of course,' and she went, leaving me with Mrs. Hurst.

'I didn't expect to see you again, Mr. Canning. So soon, that is.'

'No?'

'We all thought you'd stay at Wendover. He's left you the house, I understand.'

'Yes, he has.'

'I want Alan and Stella to have a house. But they're so expensive. He can't manage it yet.' She warmed her hand by the fire. 'You're a very fortunate young man. But then I suppose you know that.'

'Yes. I expect I shall sell the house.'

'You should get a good price. It's disgraceful the prices which are being asked.'

'Yes, isn't it? Of course you don't get so much as far out as Wendover.'

'I suppose not. Wendover's all right if you don't have to rely on public transport. But none of our family has ever lived far out of town. We've always liked to be in the centre of things – or at least near enough to the centre to get there without difficulty. Wendover's a place to retire to. A sort of invalid's place, I suppose you'd call it.'

'Well, it's a bit noisy for that.'

'Noisy?'

'Aeroplanes.'

'Oh, yes. But then we all have to suffer that. When Alan buys a house I hope he'll go even closer into London. St. John's Wood, somewhere like that. Of course they'll have to have quite a big place now that the children are beginning to come. I was talking to Alan about it only the other day. What a pity it is that Aylward's been spoiled. It would have been perfect for them. Rex knows a man who says he could re-convert it quite cheaply, but of course there are all sorts of regulations. You'd have to get permission from some Ministry or other.'

'How is Rex?' I put in.

'Well, thank you. He was looking at some property the other day down at Worthing. A frightful place with a most dreadful smell of seaweed. Do you know it? He said the prices for the most poky little places were fantastically high.'

'Is he moving then?'

She paused, deliberately, I felt. 'Well, yes he is. The flat he has is quite unsuitable. It's a great problem, Mr. Canning, this business of accommodation. You can hardly get a flat for love or money.'

She leaned back, fingering her brooch. 'Well, tell me what plans you have made.'

'Yes,' I said. 'I ought to tell you first that I shan't be writing that biography of Isabella.'

She smiled. 'I'm so glad. You've taken Rex's advice. He's quite right, you know. It was a stupid suggestion. I suppose I was mainly concerned to give you something to turn your mind to.'

'Rex's advice?' I asked.

Her smile was still there: a level, social smile. 'He said he'd advised you not to go ahead.' She smoothed the skirt of her dress. 'Rex can be quite astute sometimes. Of course, he's always been a man of the world. If he hadn't had this dreadful weakness for unsuitable women he might have made a great deal more of his life. Fortunately his affairs never last long.'

I thought of Trixie.

'He has tremendous energies,' she was saying, 'even now – and he's getting on like all of us. He was here the other night with an awfully nice man who runs the cricket club. His name escapes me for the moment. Alan's going to play next year – I mean, this year. It doesn't seem like a new year with all this snow around. An awfully good thing for Alan you know. He's not getting nearly enough exercise for a man of his weight. And of course this sedentary job he's taken doesn't help. He's doing it for the best, of course, but when he qualifies I hope he'll go into something with more – well, outdoor opportunities. Stella agrees with me, too, and I'm sure Alan would jump at anything of that kind which offered.'

'You were saying about Rex and his energies.'

'Yes. I'm sorry. This man who runs the cricket is quite a figure in Pelham Green. Not an old inhabitant, but he fits in awfully well. He and Rex have a number of schemes.'

'Do you approve?'

'Approve?'

'Of Rex having more schemes?'

Her face was quite blank.

'But why shouldn't I?' she said. 'A man has to have some occupation.'

I nodded slowly. 'What sort of schemes does Rex have?' I asked.

'Oh—' she waved a hand. 'There are several things. One of them which struck me as very go-ahead is for a – what would you call it? A Help Yourself Laundry? You require very little capital. The lease of a shop, half a dozen or a dozen washing-machines. People bring their laundry to the shop and take it

199

away dry to iron. You see, Mr. Canning, people can't afford laundry charges these days. As Rex says, it's a question of considering what irks *you* most and then doing something about it for the community.'

'Very business-like.'

'I thought so. Another scheme is for a high-class errand and house-work service. There are hundreds of young fellows out of the Army who don't want to settle down to the sort of humdrum occupations usually open to them. Rex thought that if you took on, say, six such fellows and started a central service office, you could make a great success of it. Supposing I hadn't got Mrs. Burrowes and was ill, or handicapped in some way? You can't depend on neighbours, and it's wrong if you do. But if you could ring up somewhere and pay someone to do your shopping or whatever it is, well – you'd be delighted.'

'And Rex is going to start this kind of thing?'

'It's not as definite as that. Everything needs capital.'

'Yes, of course.'

'But your own plans, Mr. Canning? You've only told me about *not* doing something, not writing a book about poor Isobel. Oh, and selling the house in Wendover. I'd forgotten that.' She crossed one leg over the other. My eye went to her foot. I expected her to begin the monotonous swinging up and down. But she did not. The room was very still. She was very composed.

I said, 'I may go abroad.'

'Just to travel? Not many people are in a position to do that these days.'

'No. I was thinking of taking a job which would send me abroad.'

She looked down at her foot. 'Poor Alan used to have high hopes of that. Of course he's *made* for that sort of thing. He took to India like a duck to water, you know. I was only saying to him the other day what a pity it was he hadn't seriously considered remaining in the Army. None of the family has ever been Army, but I think Alan was cut out for it, don't you?'

'He had other responsibilities,' I said.

'Yes,' she said, 'and he's bearing them splendidly. He studies hard nearly every evening. Too hard, I think. He hopes to take his finals next year, perhaps he told you? That's why we encouraged him to take up his cricket again. The poor boy'll need some relaxation in the summer.'

'Well, yes,' I said, 'and it won't be easy to study with a baby in the house.'

'Oh, we've made arrangements for that,' she said. The foot began to swing. 'We'll have the upstairs room as a nursery and Alan will have the little room next door as a den.'

It took me several seconds to realize which room she meant. It was no longer called Edward's room.

'Ah, here's tea,' she said. 'Bring it over here will you, Mrs. Burrowes? And you won't forget a cup for Mrs. Alan, will you?'

She turned towards me. 'I'm afraid my memory isn't as good as it was. I can't recall whether you take sugar or not, Mr. Canning?'

'Two lumps please.'

'They're not lumps, I'm afraid. I don't think they make loaf sugar any more—'

Her hands were deft, the nails well-cared for. Graciously she handed me my tea. It was then that I understood what had happened. She had rolled the years back and had begun all over again.

'She's cured, old man. She doesn't touch a drop.'

At six o'clock I had gone to The George in Pelham Green. There I had come across Rex Coles.

'Not a drop,' he repeated.

'I'm glad,' I said. 'When did she stop?'

'It was the baby coming that gave her the will-power, old man. She just stopped. Now when would it be? You left us before Christmas. She'd eased up a lot then, hadn't she? I took over from where you left off. Then about three weeks ago she told me not to bring any more for her. Just like that, old man.'

'I'm glad,' I said again. 'Can I get you another?'

'Thanks, Canning.'

When I returned to our table, bearing the new drinks, I saw that his air of well-being was matched by his clothes. They looked new, or almost new, best clothes brought into daily use; perhaps to make an impression.

'You look well,' I said, and we raised glasses to each other.

I said, 'I saw Adela yesterday. She was down with a cold.'

'Was she, old man? I'll have to ring her.'

'How's Trixie?' I asked, after a pause.

He looked into the bottom of his glass. 'I don't know how she is, old man, to be perfectly frank. She's gone off to her sister in Clacton.'

'You've parted?'

'Yes, we've parted.'

'She's left you with the flat?'

Rex looked at me, then away again, quickly. 'I shan't be staying on.' He sank back in his chair, as if lost in thought. 'You know, old man, women – I mean some women – are awful fools.'

'Why, particularly?'

'Well, look at Trixie. The only assets that woman's got are her flat, her furniture and a bit of money in the bank. You wouldn't think she'd just go off and leave me in possession of two-thirds of her capital, would you?'

'She could hardly throw you out.'

'No, old man. That's right.'

'What was the trouble?'

He drank some of his beer. 'Poor old Trixie was a dreadful bore, old man. Used to get on my nerves, you know. Made me bad-tempered, I suppose. She couldn't stand that. Whenever I lost my temper she used to look at me with that awful hurt look women can put on. That only made it worse. I say, Canning, I don't need to tell you all this. Nothing new in it. Happens every day.'

'When will you leave the flat?'

He drank again, turned to me, smiling. 'Can't stay after quarter day, old man. She knows that. Knows I know.'

'Have you decided where you'll go?'

'That rather depends on you, old man.'

'On me, why?'

'Because I planned to go back to Aylward.'

'I didn't know that. Mrs. Hurst said nothing.'

'Well,' he said, 'we haven't actually got down to discussing it. It's the obvious thing for me to do, though, Canning. Alan and Stella won't be there for long. Young Stella'll see to that. What happens to poor Marion then? She's getting on, you know. She needs looking after. Hell, I need looking after too, Canning.'

'Of course,' I said, 'but why d'you say your going to Aylward depends on me?'

'But doesn't it? While you're there there isn't any room for me.'

'I only need to be told to shove off.'

'Shove off, old man? I wouldn't dream of telling you to shove off. You're there by Alan's invitation. You're Alan's guest. Alan's a good boy. A damned good boy.'

I said, 'You had no qualms about telling me to shove off before.'

A sad expression softened his face. 'Don't hold that against me

Canning. I was under great stress then. Great stress. You wouldn't understand and I shan't burden you with my difficulties. Only don't hold any of that against me, there's a good chap. Drink up and have the next one on me.'

He brought double whiskies. I had seen from the furtive look on the barmaid's face that something special was being arranged.

'Drink up and say nothing, Canning,' he said when he returned, and winked. It was like, yet unlike, another evening months ago when Alan had brought brandy and watched me drink it, thinking, 'Good Lord, the chap's done for.' But I wasn't done for yet. How much did I owe to Alan? I was not conscious of a debt. The things which he had helped me to did not seem measurable in such terms.

I raised my glass and said, 'Your good health.' I drank. Here was warmth to dispel cold, cleanliness to dispel grime.

I felt him watching me, like a cat a mouse. The warmth, the cleanliness went.

I said, 'Whisky is an honour in nineteen forty-seven. You must have influence here.'

'I suppose I have. But then I've contributed not inconsiderably to their profits over the past years, old man.'

We both laughed.

'Talking about profits, old man, have you heard about a little scheme I have on hand?'

'Marion told me,' I said.

'Did she? About the washing-machine centre?' He seemed surprised.

'Yes, indeed. She spoke highly of your plans.'

He twisted the whisky glass by its stem, holding it out of sight just below the level of the table. 'I'll never understand women, Canning. When I told her about it she just sneered, like she always has done. But then Alan said the same thing as you, that she'd been full of it. How silly can women be, old man? When will they learn that it doesn't spur a man on?'

'What doesn't spur a man on?'

'Their sneering and saying things won't work, to your face; plans you have?'

I did not feel he expected a reply. I was right. He went on. 'One thing I liked about Trixie, Canning. Never sneered. Always backed me up. Urged me on to follow my instincts. Of course that can get wearing too. That urging. They end by trying to think for you, that type.'

'You can't have it both ways.'

'I've been a damn' fool in my life, old man. I've let opportunities slip by, seen them too late, seen them long after a woman's seen them. Refused to see them because *she* has. Not that only though. I've let myself be held back; old man. Held back by women.'

'Has there always been a woman to blame?'

In his eye came the wounded look which I supposed he had learned from Trixie. 'I know, Canning. It's not right to blame anyone but yourself for what goes wrong. It's a human thing to do though, isn't it?'

'Yes, it's human.'

'You've had your troubles, old man. Wasn't it difficult not to blame other people for them? Oh, not that I mean other people mayn't have been to blame. But isn't it the first thing a man does, or a woman, I suppose, look for a reason and find the reason in what someone else has done or hasn't done? Don't you agree, old man?'

Once again his questions were rhetorical. As he spoke he let his gaze roam round the room as if seeking the attention of anyone who cared to listen. 'It's loneliness really,' he said. 'What's it they say about man being lonely? When you're in a fix, having only yourself to blame and knowing it, I mean, knowing all the time it's only you, what does it do old man? Just emphasizes how bloody alone you are.'

He took a drink of whisky and lowered the glass again, quickly, to its hiding place.

'The worse thing is, old man, and you're too young to have experienced it—' He paused, as if wondering whether he would later regret his confidence, then continued – 'much too young. But the worse thing is to see the end of the road getting nearer and to know that when it comes you'll be by yourself.' He turned his head to look at me now. 'We're lucky in a way. It usually takes a lifetime to see that'll be so.'

He drained his glass, then said, 'Sorry old man. I'm being depressing. Let's talk about something else.'

'Of washing-machines?' I heard myself say. He looked at me sharply. 'Not washing machines,' he said. 'Not at this time of day.'

He fell silent, speculative, trying to work out, I suppose, whether he had been a fool not to accept the opportunity I had given him.

'About Aylward,' I began.

'Yes, old man?'

'When are you going to talk to Marion about your moving in?'

'That would hardly be possible. I honestly don't want to put you in a difficult position. Or Marion. If I talked to her about it she'd feel embarrassed on your behalf, wouldn't she? And there's Alan and Stella. No, old man, if you'll just tell me how long you plan to stay I'll act accordingly. In any case, these business schemes have to mature a bit before I can really make plans myself. Who knows, old man? I might make so much money I could buy Aylward and bribe the Ministry of what-not to turn the other tenants out.' He nudged me good-humouredly.

'That's what Marion would like, isn't it?' I said.

He became serious. 'Wouldn't we both? It's sad how little we appreciated those days at the time. Good days they were, old man. Dear old Isobel. Poor Marion and stuffy old George. Lord, Canning, it was only Louisa I couldn't stick. Not at any price. But I suppose she wasn't so bad as bloody-minded old maids go. We had some jolly decent times, old man, parties, friends in, and the two boys you know. Children are a pest, but they're a tonic too. Young Alan was always full of go. Not Edward so much, but Alan got up to some pranks, I can tell you. Kept us in fits sometimes.'

'The years have forgiven,' I said.

'What, old man?'

'Nothing,' I said, seeing that he had not heard, seeing that the years had not only forgiven but had transmuted the present into the precious substance of memory alive; false, but vital because it could warm and strengthen and support.

He said, 'We all have a place in life, Canning. At least we like to think so. Takes years to find it sometimes. But I think Aylward is ours. Mine. Marion's. Alan and Stella will make their own.' He frowned. 'That's all of us that are left.'

He looked at his watch. 'I must go, old man.'

'One for the road?'

'Not for me, old man.' He put out his hand. 'I've enjoyed our talk. Have lunch one day. They do a good lunch here. I'll give you a ring. I'll tell you all my schemes if you're interested.'

'Thank you.'

'Give my love to them all at the house. I'll be up one day soon.'

'I will. I'll tell them.'

'Good night, old man.'

'Good night.'

When he had gone, I opened the little box of pills which I had

205

brought from London and swallowed two. I ordered half a pint of beer, returned to my seat and watched the business men calling in for the evening drink which warmed them after the cold journey from town. Cheerful, red-faced; quiet, pale-faced; they came, seeking the sanctuary of habit.

And one of them was Alan.

'Well,' he said, putting down his pint. 'How's things?'

'I've been talking to Rex.'

'Was he here?'

'Just now.'

Alan grinned. 'Did he tell you about Trixie?'

'The bare outline.'

'That's all we'll ever know, Ian. And when Rex is sensitive about the end of an affair you can bet your bottom dollar he's been a bastard about it.'

'Maybe.' I offered cigarettes. 'I was sorry for him in the end.'

'We're always sorry for Rex. Damn his eyes.'

'He reminded me of something.'

'Who? Rex?'

'Yes. Of the night you stuck a brandy in my hand.'

'Stuck a brandy in your hand?'

I watched the memory come back to him slowly, painfully almost, crossing the hurdles of forgetfulness erected between an altruistic action and consciousness of it.

I said, 'I thought of it first because he scrounged whisky for me in the way you scrounged a brandy for me.'

'Rex scrounged a whisky for you? Here?'

'Yes. It struck me what a difference there was in motive. You gave me brandy because I needed it. He gave me whisky because *he* needed it. The whisky was to prepare the ground.'

Alan said, 'But prepare the ground for what?'

'For me to help him in some way, I think.'

Alan hesitated. 'You haven't done so have you, Ian?'

'No.'

'Or agreed to?'

'No. He never came to the point.'

'Well don't let him, or if he does, kick him in the pants.'

'You didn't kick me in the pants.'

Again he hesitated, then he found the right level, the level on which he came to understanding a problem through its solution. 'If you let Rex soak you for anything I'd bloody well kick you in the pants then. Drink up.'

He returned with two fresh pints.

'You're right,' I said.

'Right about what?'

'That I'd deserve a kick in the pants if I helped Rex. It's odd.'

'Why should it be odd?'

'Well, he's obviously in a spot of some sort. So was I. Why does it seem spineless to think of helping Rex when he may need it?'

'Because he doesn't need it. The devil looks after his own. Come to that, Rex can look after himself.' Alan swallowed beer, then said, 'Rex can look after himself, Ian, even if it costs him a double here and there.'

As we walked across the common, home, he said, 'You're not still worrying about Rex?'

'No. I've stopped worrying about it.'

'But not thinking about it?'

'If I helped Rex I'd be helping myself, wouldn't I? Getting a kick out of appearing good-natured.'

'I suppose so.'

I looked at his shadowy figure beside me, aware of a sudden lessening of warmth. I wondered about it, then realized what I had said.

'I didn't mean—' I began, but stopped. It was not really possible to say: I didn't mean you were getting a kick out of helping me.

I said, 'You know what I didn't mean.'

He stopped, put a hand briefly on my shoulder. 'Look,' but the warmth was back again. 'can't you ever see things just simply as facts, Ian? If Rex really deserved a leg up you wouldn't be beating your brains out as you are. You'd know—'

'Know a deserving case?' I began.

'That's right. You'd know a deserving case.'

'What was so bloody deserving about my case?'

It had to be said.

'Your case?' he repeated, as if to gain time.

'My case.'

He said, 'I don't know. Does it matter?'

'You were taking a risk, weren't you?'

'What sort of risk?'

'Putting a roof over my head. Making me one of the family. I might have made myself indispensable. It might have ended up with your never getting rid of me, with my sponging off you, turning your family against you, alienating the affections of your wife—' I stopped, relieved to have said it, to have brought it into the open as he would never do, to have given shape and substance to the dark shadows he surely could not in himself ignore.

'You might,' he said. Suddenly there was no burden any longer for either of us, because now that we shared it each of us found it nothing. He went on, 'But you've done none of those things, Ian.' He said it with certainty and simple, uncomplicated belief. Perhaps, in all the years he had responded to life according to his code of upright dealing, it was the first time another man had shown he recognized the charitable understanding the code demanded; the dark abyss it bridged; the doubts it overcame.

It took us much longer now to reach the clinic. The hill had begun to tell on her.

'Why on earth do they have it up here?' I asked her.

And Stella said, 'I suppose there was nowhere else.'

Unlike Aylward, the waiting room in the clinic had undergone no change. Perhaps the echo of soldiers' voices, the sound of boots on bare floors, had lessened; but that was all.

Stella appeared. Even the fur coat could not disguise her pregnancy. You love a woman, I thought, and make her ugly. But was she ugly to Alan? I remembered his words of the night before as we sat alone, having a nightcap of beer mulled by a red-hot poker.

'You can feel him moving,' he had said, his face relaxed in sleepy pleasure. 'Even see him sometimes, like a chap under a collapsed tent waving his legs and arms about.' And I had an impression of the gentle affection he felt for Stella: the restraint of passion for the outward body; its growth into something more deeply rooted.

I said to Stella, 'All right?'

'Yes,' she said, 'everything goes according to plan.'

'You sound—'

'What?'

'As if you resented that it should.'

We had reached the gate before she said, 'The inevitable is always unnerving.'

Back in the town we entered Polly Anne. I had half-expected her to resist this part of the routine. When she did not, but turned towards the door almost before I did, it came to me that perhaps this was the last time of all, and that she had known it, and saw no reason to resist.

As we waited for tea I said, 'Have you gone to the clinic alone while I was away?'

'Marion came once or twice.'

'Did you come to Polly Anne?'

'No,' she said. 'Why?'

'I just wondered.'

Conversation was not easy. It was like the enforced prolonging of a railway station farewell, when a train has been delayed.

But at last she said, 'I didn't expect to see you again.'

'Didn't you? Any particular reason?'

'When someone goes away they become legendary.'

'I don't understand.'

'You became a legend, Ian.'

'Is legend what you mean? It seems the wrong word to me.' She said, 'I think it's the right word.'

'Fantasy with its roots in fact.'

'Yes.'

I said, 'What was the fantasy?'

'You know what it was.'

I said, 'I suppose I do.'

'They were wrong, of course. I didn't fall in love with you.'

'Of course not.'

'Then you did hear what they were saying. Who told you?'

'Adela, as it happens.'

'Adela.' And she looked out of the window. Her spirit seemed to have diminished until it was only a pin-point of flickering light which had somehow to warm and illuminate the disproportionate body.

'Don't be afraid of Adela,' I told her.

'It's part of the legend,' she said.

'Long ago, forgotten.'

She was still looking out of the window. She said, 'It's not a question of remembering. It happened. I saw it happening. I thought I was in love with Edward because when I was with him he was none of the things people said about him. Not weak. Not tied to Marion. Not ungenerous or hurtful to Alan. But when I saw Alan I knew Edward could never mean anything to me. Then he became all those things.'

She went on, because I made no reply, 'How can you understand? I wanted Edward to need me but I needed Alan. He hardly looked at me. Not after the first time. Adela had him. He must only have looked at me when I didn't notice.'

'Is that what rankled? Your not knowing he wanted you too?'

She did not answer at once.

'What was I to think?' she asked, eventually. 'When he was finished with Adela there were other women. There were other women because he thought I belonged to Edward. But' – and now she looked at me – 'but I only wanted to belong to myself. I didn't know that a woman could ever do so.'

I stirred my tea, thoughtfully.

'Since when have you told yourself that?' I asked.

She turned back to the window. 'Since this afternoon, at the clinic.'

'Why?'

'Because it's going to happen. You could see from the way they acted, taking it all for granted, there wasn't any getting out of it. There's no stopping it. No stopping it at all.'

'But you haven't hoped there would be?'

'I don't know,' she said. 'I thought – I'd accepted it. I thought it was all all right after all. The right thing. The natural thing. They call if fulfilment, don't they?'

'Isn't it?'

Slowly she sat back in her chair. The fur coat, unbuttoned, fell away from her full breasts. She was smiling, a peculiar twisted smile.

She said, 'Fulfilment? I wake up at night sometimes, and think about what's going to happen. Alan goes to sleep with his hand here, on the child, and it's as though an act of intimacy were lasting for nine months. I feel I'm caught in a web. A web of flesh. I think of what I shall be like when it's over. Shall I be like Marion? Like Marion and Alan? Like that with *my* child? Hating him? Feeling love for him? Physical love? Being fulfilled all over again when he gets his child? In me, through his wife? Accepting him then? Loving him too late? And if it's a girl? What then? Be possessed by the man she marries, by him through her?' – and she stopped as if afraid of what she had revealed; not only to me but to herself. I looked into her eyes and it was then that behind their blueness I saw the grey of Helena's. It was then that I really understood. She opened her handbag and began to collect items of make-up. She said, her head bent over her bag, 'We learn so much about ourselves these days, don't we? It makes it difficult. Does Alan know how fortunate he is, I wonder?'

'In what way is he fortunate?'

'To see life as he does. Simple, direct, almost motiveless.'

'How can you tell in what way he sees life?'

She said, smearing powder on her chin. 'I interpret his actions.'

'They can't tell the whole story.'

She twisted a lipstick up from a gold tube.

'Alan has no inhibitions, Ian, he feels himself utterly free. Free to cut loose at any moment he wants to—'

'The way a man should feel.'

'The way he should! Why should he?'

'So that he can assume his bonds voluntarily, as Alan does.'

She clicked her handbag shut. 'And what bonds has Alan got?'

'He has you. He has the child. A home to hold, mouths to feed. The ghosts of Aylward to live with. A longing for sun and sky in place of electric light and dust and ledgers.'

Her head was bent as she buttoned up her coat.

'It sounds fine,' she said. 'There's only one thing you haven't explained to yourself.'

'And that?'

'Why should he go voluntarily into prison?'

I held her eyes for a few moments before I answered: not to impress her with my own certainty, but to try to detect, behind the curtain of fear which was blinding her, an answering certainty, an understanding of the point at which she was bound to Alan, and he to her, in a way which transcended everything else. And then I was face to face with it, feeling it sharply in Stella, through Stella and because of Stella, and I believed that in time she would feel it too.

I said, 'He goes voluntarily into prison, Stella, because that is where love is.'

Two weeks later the call came and I went up to Edinburgh.

CHAPTER THREE

It was March. Helena had changed. I pitied her for the lines of age which had begun to close in around her eyes, until I saw that she watched me with the same expression I felt on my own face. Then we both smiled and she said, 'Yes, we neither of us look up to much, do we?'

I had forgotten how adept she was at knowing what I was thinking.

The waiter brought sherry.

'Have you been here since we used to come?' she asked.

'Once,' I said. 'What about you?'

'I don't think I have. I don't remember.'

We ordered food. I clearly recalled her favourite dishes. They were still on the menu for the restaurant changed little – but it seemed ungallant to offer them, now. I let her choose without suggestions. She did not choose any of her one-time favourites.

'Well, Ian. What did you want to talk about?'

I found it difficult. 'It's this divorce business.'

'I see. What do you want? The name of the man I'm having an affair with now?'

'No, Helena. If there's to be a divorce you'd better divorce me.'

We looked at our own sections of the table. She said, 'Have you given me grounds, Ian?'

'Not sufficient for the court. But these things can be arranged.'

'Then do I get alimony?'

'I imagine so.'

She said, 'I don't think I need alimony. If we divorce I shall probably get married again, and he's well off.'

I felt that she wanted me to ask his name I said, 'Anyway, those are all details. The main thing is, do we end it legally or—'

'Or what?'

'Try again?'

I turned towards her. She was in profile to me, not even looking at my reflection in the mirror opposite.

She said, 'Are you going to die?'

'Die?'

'Yes. Have the doctors said you're going to die?' She turned her head slowly, looking full at me. 'You look as if you're going to die. Not long for this world. That's the expression isn't it? When I saw you as I came in I thought: Oh, he's for it. He's done for. He wants me back to look after him and nurse him. After all Ian, you never really had any guts. Asking me to come and hold your hand while you breathed your last is just about what I would have expected.'

'I'm sorry. I haven't been told I'm going to die.' Very slightly I emphasized the word 'told', but not enough for her to notice.

She laughed. 'You haven't changed a bit. You never could stand criticism or leg-pulling. That's why you bored me, Ian. That was the trouble with your generation of so-called intellectual young men. All of you unmitigated, bloody bores with sloppy ideas and no remotest idea how to come to terms with life. When you found life coming to terms with you, you all wondered what the hell had hit you.'

I said, 'You haven't changed either, Helena.'

'Let's stop it,' she said. 'Let's just pretend we're having dinner and you're hoping to get me on my back like that first time.'

'How is the new novel?' I asked.

'Nearly finished. Brian – Brian Selby, that is, of course, likes what he's seen.' She cocked an eye at me. 'Did you ever read the first?'

'No, I didn't want to.'

'You were afraid of reading a few home-truths?'

'I didn't need to read them,' I said.

She paused, with the sherry glass half-way to her lips. 'You're not by any chance trying a sort of manly I-was-to-blame-for-it-all, please forgive-me-dear act, are you?'

I smiled, shook my head, not trusting myself to speak for a moment.

She said, 'Well, I'm thankful for that. A new facet to your character at this stage of things would be more than I could cope with.'

'May I ask you a question, Helena?'

'Don't be utterly inane, Ian. All this polite chit-chat. Since when did you ask my leave to ask questions. It used to be all questions, I went question-crazy.'

'All I wanted to ask is why you agreed to lunch with me, if all the time you couldn't really care less?'

'I thought you always prided yourself on knowing women? It was one of my crosses, surely, that frightful, pseudo-masculine self-deception that you knew women.'

'All right, I was quite unbearable, Helena. I didn't know

women. I don't know women. So I want you to tell me why you came.'

'That's rather funny, because actually I expect you've guessed right this time. I was curious. Curious to see you and make quite sure I didn't want you back for a bit.'

'Obviously you've decided.'

'Obviously,' she said. She waited. 'Well—?'

'Well what?'

'Aren't you going to get up and walk out like you once did?'

'No.'

'Aren't you temperamental any more?'

'Just hungry.' I glanced at the door from which the waiter would come.

'If you've lost your temperament, what the hell is left? It was the only thing I thought anything of.'

'Nonsense. If I had walked out you'd have said that was my one trait you really detested.'

The waiter brought our food. She ignored the fact that he was there; or rather, took advantage of it. She had done it before, many times.

'If there is one trait of yours I dislike more than another it's your infernal habit of saying, "Now, Helena, this is what you think, this is what you would have done or said if—" '

When the waiter had gone I said, 'Who's the chap you're living with now?'

'Why?'

I had wanted to say, 'Because I'm bloody sorry for him'. I began to eat while Helena sat by, watching me. At the end of the room I saw the waiter hesitate in the act of talking to a colleague who tried to disguise the fact he was looking in our direction.

'You haven't answered my question. Why?' she repeated.

I heard the quaver in her voice as I went through the motions of eating unconcernedly – not for public effect – but because I saw there was nothing I could say or do to counteract the acid of Helena's venom, and, in this, recognized in myself what she had once called my cloak of assumed indifference, and knew the reason why I wore it. There was not one single act or speech the sincerity of which would not be questioned, which would not be ridiculed. Even the pity which existed beneath my anger would be scorned if shown, sharpened into a weapon she could use against me.

'You asked me the name of the man I'm living with. I want to know why.'

'I thought I might know him.'

'Did you? So that you could tell him about me?'

And the answer to that hung on my tongue. Years before I would have said, pat, 'No, Helena, there wouldn't be any need. He must already know.'

'Your food is getting cold,' I said, not looking at her, but at her plate.

And then it began: the silent, dreadful weeping that had broken me on its rack so often in the past. With one hand half covering her eyes, her elbow supported on the table, she gave way to the bitterness as to something, the punishment of which, while she had the strength, she had to ward off by loosing on others.

When it was all over, when – somehow – the meal had been got through, when Helena's tears were dry and I had seen on the waiters' faces something akin to respect because, between us, we had kept the scene within the bounds of propriety, I took her outside and, together, in the slushy street, we waited for a taxi. Light snow was falling again, blowing lightly on the wind.

We had, eventually, to walk to the end of the road and there a cruising taxi found us.

'Where to?' I asked her.

'I want to go to Selby's.'

I gave the publisher's name and address to the driver.

'Will you come with me as far as there?' she asked.

I hesitated. Then I climbed in beside her. It would, I supposed, be the last time I should see her. I said, 'In a way you were right.'

'Right about what?'

I braced myself for it; expecting her triumphant laughter, clenched my teeth. Then I turned to her so that I could say it to her face.

'I've been seeing a specialist in tropical diseases.'

'Oh?'

'A chap in Edinburgh.'

'What did he say?'

'He's been able to pin-point what it is.'

She looked away. 'What is it then?'

'It has an unpronounceable name.'

'Can they cure it?'

I said, repeating the words I had heard so often, 'They're researching all the time.'

Her left hand was on her lap. She still wore her wedding ring.

She said, looking out of the window, 'Are they likely to be in time for you?'

'That's what I'm going to find out.'

'Where?'

'A place they have. On the Continent.'

She said, 'I see. So you didn't have much to offer did you, Ian?'

'No, nothing to offer really.'

'What does it feel like to be – to have your time limited?'

'It always is. Mine is only rather more restricted perhaps.'

She looked round at me. 'Perhaps?' Again she turned to the window. 'You believe in their research, then, their power to cure?'

'It's something we'll work towards. And yes. I believe in it.'

I wished there were a way of explaining to her that I had come to her neither for comfort nor support. I tried to find the right words, and could not find them. Perhaps I had never interpreted in the form of a communicable idea whatever it was that drew me back, that once, to Helena. Sometimes I think of it now, and then it is on the tip of my tongue. It was the offering of a chance to her, but not that, a chance to me, to both of us, and yet not. Perhaps it was an attempt to uncover again, like something long buried, the love which once we bore, one for the other.

I said, 'Will you treat what I've told you as confidential?'

'Does nobody know, then? Not even the people you're staying with?'

'They least of all.'

As we drew up outside Selby's office she turned to me with a white face, offering her confession in return for mine, and said, 'It's Brian.'

'What's Brian?'

'I'm having an affair with Brian Selby.'

And as she said it I saw the whole horror of her tortured, beaten life come like amazement into her eyes before, like a light extinguished, it went, and left her staring at me as though she were blind and knew me only through the hand which I suddenly placed on hers in order to forgive, and be forgiven.

It was midnight before I reached Aylward. The snow had fallen thick and deep in my absence. The marooned hulk of the house was muffled under its white roof. I climbed the iron stairway, and let myself in. No light showed from under any door and I went up to my room.

It was time to pack. For a moment, I toyed with the idea of going before morning, but then sense prevailed, brought well-being with it, strength, resolution.

I packed my few things and stood the bag by the chest of drawers in which there still clung the smell of oil-paints; fainter now, but still unmistakable. Then I undressed.

A chapter was ended. A new one would begin in the morning. I slept.

It was about three when I woke, disturbed, not knowing what had disturbed me. But as my senses returned to me I knew very clearly where I was, understood sharply the thing which had come about. For an instant, as I sat up in bed, felt the chill air freeze my skin, strike at the bone, and saw with the clarity of eyes opening to the night the odd, luminous quality of the darkness beyond the window, I shivered with the apprehension of a child coming from the safety of sleep to the strange, adult world of wakefulness. I put on slippers and dressing gown and went to the door, aware, without there being any sound, that the silence was temporary, that it had been disturbed, would be disturbed again. And as I opened the door, saw the confirmation of the lights from the landing below, Stella moaned.

I went down quietly. The door of Alan's and Stella's room was half-open. I stood on the bottom step and then, realizing the open door could mean only one thing, I went past it quickly, not heeding Stella's sudden call, 'Alan?' but going towards the green-baize door. Pushing through it, I found Alan at the phone.

'No,' he was saying, 'only ten minutes ago.' He paused. 'No, but shouldn't you come now?' Again he paused. 'All right, I'll do that. I'll ring in an hour.' He put the phone down.

'Can I do anything, Alan?'

He wasn't quite awake. He ran a hand through his tousled hair. He hadn't put on a dressing gown and he was shivering.

'I don't know, Ian. They say it can't be for hours yet.'

'But the midwife's coming, isn't she?'

'That was her I rang. She said ring back in an hour.'

I said, 'Well, she must know what she's talking about.'

'I suppose so.'

'Put on a coat or something. You'll catch cold.'

'I'd better dress, I think.' He went to the baize door, turned. 'Ought I to wake mother, Ian?'

'It might be as well. I'll make some tea.'

He nodded. As he opened the door we heard Stella calling.

'Coming Stella!' he shouted. I followed, feeling that this was all wrong, that a confinement should not begin on this note of urgency.

The sound she was making came to me clearly; an odd, haunted sound, not of pain, more like that of someone sustaining a heavy weight, and then, quickly, letting it go.

Her voice was already edged with weariness. 'What did she say, Alan?'

'It's all right, Stell. She said if the first pain was only ten minutes ago it won't be for hours yet. I'm to ring in an hour to report.'

I went to the kitchen. Whilst I was there, making tea, I heard Alan's voice and that of his mother – the sounds of her stirring in the room next door. Making the tea brought me fully awake. My eyes, robbed of sleep, hurt in the harsh brilliance from the naked bulb. As the kettle boiled I lighted a cigarette. I took the tray of tea into the drawing-room, encountering the stale warmth, noticing the fire change from a dull red to an unwelcoming dead brown as I turned the light on.

It was as I placed the tray on the gate-legged table that Stella cried out. I stood quite still for a moment, and then, hearing Alan call for his mother, I went back to the passage, pushed through the green-baize door just as Marion came past. I heard all that was said.

'Ring the midwife will you, mother?' His voice was held steady in the way a man determined not to show panic might hold it.

'I'll stay with Stella, Alan. Go and phone now. I know what has to be done.'

But Stella said, 'Don't leave me, Alan.'

I went back to the passage. On the pad, Alan had previously written in block capitals the telephone number of the midwife. I dialled.

'Yes?'

'Nurse Brownlow?'

'Yes.' A tired, professional, infinitely patient voice.

'I'm speaking for Mr. Alan Hurst.'

'Yes?'

'Would you please come? Mrs. Hurst is in labour.'

'Yes, I know. But he was going to ring back in an hour.'

'I'm ringing for him.'

A pause, and then the voice changed a bit, as if the speaker had risen higher in bed, the better to take in what was said.

'How often are the pains?'

'I don't think they've been timed.'

'Mr. Hurst said he would. Ask him how often the pains are coming. There's no point in my coming hours before it's necessary. There may be an urgent case, you see.'

'Hold on.'

As I left the phone, Mrs. Hurst opened the door. She looked shaken.

'They want to know how often the pains are coming.'

She didn't answer, but took up the phone.

'This is Mrs. Hurst Senior speaking. Will you please come, nurse? It's happening much too quickly.' A pause. 'No. Yes. I know what to do. But if you will. Thank you.'

She put down the phone and went into the kitchen. I heard water running from the tap.

And then Stella cried out again.

The door was still open. I had gone to it to offer a service I could not myself define.

Alan was on his knees by the bedside, holding one of her hands, and she clung to this as though to life, her back arched. I turned away, ashamed to have witnessed it.

'Don't go.'

I stopped, but it was to Alan she had spoken. 'Don't go. That's all. Don't go. I won't do it again. I won't—' But a gasp concluded the sentence for her. Her voice was lost in the giant exhalation of her breath which culminated in a groan of pain seemingly too great to be borne; pain pushed to the extremity, then lifted as though a wind had come and blown it away. All this was a sound which beat down like wings through the well of the stairs and back again to the room in which she laboured, and I was caught beneath it, smothered by it.

I faced Marion Hurst, and for a split second it seemed to me that the cry had come from her own lips, dragged out by its roots from her own withered body, and that the cry had clothed her bones firmly in flesh, brought colour to the cheeks, pigment to the now almost grey hair.

'Don't stand about, Mr. Canning,' she said. 'There's nothing you can do.' She hesitated. 'But you might listen for the bell.'

And that is my last memory of Aylward: sitting hunched against the cold at the bottom of the stairs, awaiting the stranger who would come to tend to Stella. As I sat there I was not alone.

They were all there: dim figures passing up and down: Louisa: Isabella, Rex, Adela and George – the shadowy, scarcely remembered husband of the old woman who moved to and fro above, conscious that time had come and gone and left reality unchanged: and Edward. I think he sat with me, waiting for a hand that would touch him, a heart that would understand, an eye that would see as his mother's once had done.

And the Commander passed by, it seemed, with a nod of recognition, and Thurlow, the tang of the sea to which he had once turned for adventure still freshening the dust the shadows hid but which his heart could not: David and Peggy, Brian Selby, Helena.

They moved and had their being in the darkness and the sound of Stella's loneliness; in the sudden ring at the door, its opening, the nod from the uniformed woman and the young girl who came with her to watch and learn and help: all the past gathered into the thud of footsteps which hurried up the stairs because Stella had called harshly at the climax of parturition. I understood their obstinacy as Alan would not be removed from the room in which Stella lay; understood their fear as I sat alone; their patience as I waited; their desperation as the child first cried its hunger to the world; their love as the cry was stilled.

Stella Hurst was delivered of a son at half-past four in the morning of March fifth, nineteen forty-seven. Her husband had stayed with her throughout the confinement.

It was nearly five when he came into the drawing-room where I had kept solitary watch, and as he came in I remembered him once taking me by the arm and saying, 'There's everything in the world to live for.'

I said, 'Congratulations, Alan. Everything all right?'

He tried to grin at me and managed to say, 'Everything's fine.'

Then he suddenly covered his face with both hands and sobbed as if his heart would break, as if the joy he felt, the physical proof of his convictions were more than he could bear.

ALSO BY PAUL SCOTT IN GRANADA PAPERBACKS

STAYING ON

Philip Larkin, the chairman of the judges, said of the winning novel:

'Of all the books I read, *Staying On* was, simply, the most moving . . . Paul Scott brings his two main themes to triumphant resolution: the end of an empire, and the end of a long, inarticulate love that is as poignant as it is convincing. *Staying On* covers only a few months, but it carries the emotional impact of a lifetime, even a civilization'

'From the absurd ironies of the human condition Paul Scott wrings the unresisting acknowledgement of laughter. He sets up, for us to love, a superb gallery of larger than life caricatures who, by some alchemy of art, grow into characters to whom one can relate as personally as Forster would have wished . . . This is a rich and joyful book written by a man who has known and loved another country well enough to be brilliantly disrespectful of it'
Jeremy Brooks, *The Sunday Times*

'Mr Scott's new novel is certainly his funniest to date and, I think, his best . . . It is a first-class book and deserves to be remembered for a long time'
Auberon Waugh, *Evening Standard*

Price £1.50

THE RAJ QUARTET

THE JEWEL IN THE CROWN
THE DAY OF THE SCORPION
THE TOWERS OF SILENCE
A DIVISION OF THE SPOILS

The Raj Quartet: -
'One of the most important landmarks of post-war fiction . . .
a mighty literary experience'
Susan Hill, *The Times*

'A saga whose slowly gathering force has immense power . . .
The Raj Quartet . . . defies further fictional excursions into
the last years of British India'
Max Egremont, *Books & Bookmen*

'He shows all the skill of an accomplished historian in laying
bare the complex and often conflicting inter-relationships of
the era; and the ramshackle grandeur of the Raj is
brilliantly realized'
Sunday Telegraph

1st Volume £1.50   2nd Volume £1.95

3rd Volume £1.95   4th Volume £1.95